Irish Intelligence

– PETER HAMMOND –

www.fast-print.net/store.php

IRISH INTELLIGENCE

A catalogue record for this book is available from the British Library

ePub ISBN 978-178456-966-2
Mobi ISBN 978-178456-967-9

Also available as a paperback: ISBN 978-178456-349-3

First published 2016 by Fastprint Publishing,
Peterborough, England.

Dedicated to my wife Anne who has had to live with this type of thing for 35 years.

Chapter 1

P eggy was on her knees in front of me. She was breathing heavily. Her eyes narrowed in the low light so that she could see my face. I stayed perfectly still. My heart was pounding like it was trying to escape from my chest. I tried to think of something to say to suit the moment, but nothing came to me. Even if I had found the words, my jaw had locked my tongue inside for its own safety. Eventually it was Peggy who broke the silence.

'Come out from under tha' bed, ya little shite!' she said.

I was irritated that my dear wife had found me in such an awkward position. What was she doing rooting around under strangers' beds anyway? Maybe people as a general rule when they come into a bedroom, check under the bed to see if anyone is there. It may be the done thing, but I never do it. You could be under my bed for years and I wouldn't be any the wiser. Other than shoving an occasional slipper in at you I would leave you in peace. The two of us could live happy, independent lives and remain complete strangers to one another forever.

'There y'are!' I eventually said by way of a greeting. My motto is that there's never any harm in being polite, even if you've just been insulted up to the eyeballs. Civility is rarely wasted, but it looked like it would be on this occasion. My bag for life didn't look like she was in the mood for light conversation.

I hadn't encountered Peggy since that lunchtime when we had chatted amiably of this and that, just like normal people. I can't remember what exactly was on the agenda. It might have been domestic arrangements or news updates on the lives of our daughters, Angela and Marian. It won't have been hold-the-front-page stuff. When a couple are married as long as we have been, most of what was ever worth saying was said a long timeago. What remains is mostly Peggy talking and me grunting agreements at what seem like appropriate intervals. I don't argue or offer contrary opinions as Peggy doesn't think much of free speech. I remember Iggie Farrell coming into Magowan's one night with a black eye. When I asked him how he got it, he said: 'I was talkin' when I shoulda bin listenin'.' 'There but for the grace of God go I,' I thought.

By following such simple rules happiness and contentment normally reign in the Flynn household. Even from my awkward position under the bed I could tell that something had been lost in the amicable relationship since we'd last met. I felt that it would be in my interests to rekindle the companionable tone. From the way Peggy was grinding her teeth and clenching her fists I was not confident of success.

'Have ya bin here long?' I asked, trying to sound apologetic that I might have been keeping her waiting.

'Come out!' she ordered again, like Jesus calling Lazarus from the tomb.

I gave her proposal due consideration, and after weighing the pros and cons for it against the pros and cons against it, I decided to stay where I was. Although Peggy was now well past her prime, she had spent her youth on a farm in County Carlow, lassoing and branding cattle. I knew that much of the old skill was still there, and that she could have me roped and ready for the hot iron before I could even begin to enter a plea for the defence. She was looking at me in the way that John Wayne eyed livestock just before he burned a hole in their arses and deleted their prospects of procreation.

If you are a student of the Western genre, you will know that what a cowboy needs to do his best work is space, and plenty of it. Give him the wide open prairies and he is all business; he is happy and in his element. He can bend the herd to his will with little more than a rope, a horse and an occasional 'yee-haa'. But shove the herd under a bed and the cowboy is stymied. He takes his hat off, scratches his ear and says: 'Aw shucks.' He packs it in for the day, retires to his campfire and sings about sick dogs and purty little girls called Ellie Sue. So holed up under the bed was where I resolved to stay.

Peggy was now back on her feet and pacing to and fro like a lioness whose prey had given her the slip. I also noted that there were now four female ankles before me. I deduced that, unless Peggy was auditioning for the pantomime, Teresa Horgan had joined the scene.

'Is he under the bed?' Teresa asked, confirming my suspicion.

'He is,' Peggy replied. 'But don't you worry. He won't be there for long. I'll soon have him out of it. Have ya got a sweepin' brush?'

'I have bu' listen to me, Peggy Flynn,' Teresa said. 'Ya needn't start a domestic in here. I've me ornaments ...'

'Feck you an' yer ornaments,' was Peggy's uncharitable response.

Teresa would have been rightly concerned that her little nest might undergo the kind of re-arrangement that John Wayne sometimes inflicted on saloons. Peggy was a house-proud woman herself and normally would have sympathised with Teresa at a deep sisterly level. But in order to achieve the objective of me in her custody she would have been willing to countenance an element of collateral damage. She would have subscribed to the principle that the making omelettes requires the breaking of eggs. She issued a final demand for my total and unconditional surrender.

'FRANK! Get yer arse out from under tha' bed!'

I didn't answer as I feared that any response would only hasten her assault on my position, and I didn't much like the sound of the sweeping brush tactic. Horizontal and choking on decades of Horgan dust and fluff, I was in no position to fend off energetic pokes from brushes - especially if those pokes were administered by a fired-up and enthusiastic Peggy. Thankfully Teresa did not feel that the last word had been spoken on the matter of her bedroom becoming a scene of violence and destruction. Like most Dubliners her general motto was 'mi casa es su casa', but there are limits. And guests engaging in combat in the master bedroom would definitely be placed in the 'taking the piss' category.

'Who do ya think y'are anyway, Peggy Flynn?' Teresa wanted to know. 'Bargin' into this house, an' diggin' aroun' under me bed. It's not Liberty Hall y'know. This is private property. If me husband was here ...'

'Well yer husband isn't here, is he?' Peggy said. 'An' he wouldn't a gone off gallivantin' with tha' young wan if ya were any good.'

Even as a statement of the facts as they were then known, Peggy's statement was contentious. Joe was indeed guilty of the charge of gallivanting as set out by Peggy. But whether Teresa was in some way culpable was another thing. Such judgements are always difficult for the uninvolved, and generally it is better not to make them. This is where Peggy went wrong. Even if her view was balanced and reasonable, it wasn't likely that Teresa was going to accept it as fair comment and leave it at that. The inference that it was her poor wifely performance which had caused Joe to seek his comforts elsewhere was serious. It was unlikely that Teresa would allow it to go on the record without challenge.

Teresa clearly agreed with my analysis. Rather than settling for a barbed response – what I believe the French call 'mots justes' - she decided on action. Her war-cry was followed by the unmistakable sound of hand striking kisser at speed. Peggy – the obvious owner of the kisser – emitted a howl which sounded like a moose being impaled on something blunt.

Although the noise of battle made my blood turn to iced piss I took a moment to reflect on the novelty of the situation. When it comes to smiting Peggy is normally cast in the role of smiter rather than smitee, so this will have been a novel experience for her. In a split second her brain will have dealt with a parade - led by pain and followed by surprise, confusion and anger. Her impromptu reaction was impressive.

'Jaysus! Teresa Horgan ya feckin' bitch,' she said. 'I'll be dug outa ya!'

If Peggy has a particular hallmark it is that she is a decisive woman. She quickly weighs up situations and she acts. Smack her in the mouth and she will not indulge in a period of reflection before she gets back to you. And it was so on this occasion. After briefly sketching out her intention of being dug out of Teresa, she went onto the offensive.

Unfortunately I didn't have a good view of the ensuing combat from my position in the cheap seats, so I can't give you a blow by blow account. The changing disposition of feet, with the accompanying sound effects, suggested a rapid exchange of fire, with Peggy making a steady advance on a retreating Teresa.

As a keen fight fan I would have liked to see the contest through to its conclusion but it struck me that this was a good opportunity for Frankie to take his leave. Anyway it was never going to be an even match and the result was a foregone conclusion. Peggy was in the super middleweight class while Teresa would struggle to make bantam level. Even with home advantage and speed on her side, Teresa was unlikely to get past round one. If she had a trainer he would have been looking for his towel and the bookies would have been ready to pay out on the favourite.

I slithered over to the far side of the bed away from the scene of battle and crawled out into the open. A good and merciful Saviour had put the door on this side of the room. Without bothering to get myself fully to the vertical I scampered away on all fours, like a chimp getting off the forest floor away from two demented lionesses. In a flash I was through the door and, without pausing, swung, rolled and fell down the stairs. Snatching my coat from a hook on my way I crashed through the front door. I suspected that it was the coat - the treacherous bastard - that had given me away. Peggy would have recognised it and like a bloodhound given the scent, came sniffing after me.

As I emerged onto the doorstep, thinking 'free at last, thank God I am free at last', one of Teresa's ornaments exploded on the concrete beside me. I think it was a small china elephant or a large china mouse. It was definitely grey, china, and an animal of some sort. I could see its sad little face looking up at me, seeming to accuse me for its misfortune.

'Wait 'til I get ya, ya sleveen,' Peggy shouted from the bedroom window. 'Ya'll be pickin' yer teeth up with a broken arm when I lay me hands on ya.'

Hardly the words you would expect from a loving wife but I report the facts as they occurred. She was taking aim again with what looked like a perfume bottle and I feared the worst. The words 'sitting' and 'duck' came immediately to mind.

Thankfully Teresa still had some fight left in her. Like in that scene in Fatal Attraction when you think that Glenn Close has breathed her last, Teresa came lunging up at Peggy. Her timing was perfect and the attack was enough to put Peggy off the complicated maths required to hit a moving target while allowing for direction of travel, speed and distance. Without Teresa's help I would definitely have had her eau-de-canal mingling with my pure Celtic blood. Peggy was forced to postpone the bombardment and give attention to defensive manoeuvres. I heard Teresa yelp as Peggy hit her – hopefully not with the perfume bottle. Even as I focused on the preservation of my life and limb I felt a small swelling of pride. We Flynns are a sporting people and we can't help being partisan in any competition that involves our own. In the circumstances it was only the smallest of swellings and it would have suited me if Teresa had a tad more fight in her.

I processed these thoughts in a nano-second. If you have a picture of me leaning against the doorpost musing on Peggy's fighting skills, delete it now. I was a blur. If you had been observing the action from across the street, and you glanced down to flick a speck of dust off your trousers, you would have missed me altogether. My exact speed is not recorded but I definitely established a new personal best for getting beyond the range of perfume bottles.

Once around the corner and out of the line of fire I turned off the turbo boosters. At a brisk nervous walk I glanced over my shoulder every few seconds. Peggy doesn't give up easily and is capable of giving chase. I knew though that brute force and cunning are more her strengths than speed.

The sanctuary of Magowan's Bar beckoned to me like a cow crying for its lost calf. My nervous system had been subjected to severe trauma and adrenalin was buzzing around inside me like a swarm of angry wasps. I badly needed Magowan's afternoon library ambiance, Betty's soothing tones and a few pints of the draught that cures all ills.

★★★

You may have heard me speak of Magowan's before. It is a public house of the old style, copied the world over - never successfully. It is impossible to match authentic features like our genial proprietress Betty Magowan and the hand-written notices proscribing everything from drug-dealing to children to messing with the television settings. There are tin ashtrays screwed to the tables even though smokers have long since been banished. It's traditional and that's a good enough reason to keep them. Most importantly Magowan's consistently provides the perfect pint. No shamrocks, harps or other cod art – just lovely creamy heads that never fail to delight.

Generations of Daymo citizens have regarded Magowan's as a home from home – a place of refuge and support away from families, police and the revenue commissioners. Men come through the door with the cares of the world weighing on them. After two good swallows they're standing six inches taller and grinning like a priest after the second collection.

That day I badly needed to drown my sorrows before the buggers learned to swim. I was only halfway through the door and Betty had already diagnosed my condition, assessed my symptoms and prescribed the necessary medication. Without me even asking, she was pouring a pint of the black nectar that is a settler of the stomach, a balm to the nerves and a comfort to the spirit.

'Are ya alrigh', Frank?' she asked. 'Ya look a bit shook.' She didn't say: 'Give me your tired, your poor, your huddled masses yearning to breathe free.' But that was what she meant.

Nothing would have suited me better than to unburden myself and to seek the counsel of this wise and compassionate woman. I was tempted but I couldn't. There was already more information in the public domain than was doing anyone any good. The problems I was lugging around like Jacob Marley's chains were not mine to share. I carried the trust and confidence of others and it was necessary to keep my trap shut. This was not a problem for me. The rule, code and motto which has served me well all my life is: 'Don't tell anybody anything, and if you have to say something, say nothing'. So instead of weeping on Betty's shoulder and pouring my troubles out, I bit the lower lip and said that I was grand. In fact, to explain the breathlessness and the hair standing on end I said that I had been out for a jog.

'A jog?!' she asked. She sounded surprised like I had told her that I had been elected Pope. Her eyebrows were raised into the 'are ya coddin' me or wha'?' position.

Even though I regard Betty as the exception to her sex – partly making up for the rest of them - I bridled at her attitude. I may not be in first flush of youth but in a certain light I reveal an athletic lissomness. Even Doctor Lawlor - who is otherwise an idiot - remarked on the firmness of my calves, the time I strained myself after falling off my bike into the canal.

'Yeah,' I said. 'A jog. It's like runnin'.'

'I've heard of it,' she said. 'I'm just surprised tha' *you* have. Do ya have one o' dem runnin' machines at home?'

'I have *not*. I'm not a bloody hamster.'

'So ya were runnin' in the *street*?' If she had added 'stark naked and playing the national anthem on a mouth organ,' she couldn't have sounded more incredulous - if that's the word I'm looking for.

I thought of telling her to go feck herself, but some things are just not done in the Daymo, and telling Betty Magowan to go feck herself in her own pub was one of them. So I didn't.

The problem that I couldn't share with Betty, which led to me having to hide under the Horgan matrimonial bed, was all Joe Horgan's fault. If I tell you that Joe is the greatest pestilence inflicted on mankind since the Black Death, you should understand that I do so as one of his oldest friends and admirers.

Joe and me have been pals since we cowered under the Christian Brothers' lash together. We were in the same class all the way up, suffering the dedicated attention of as fine a range of screwballs as ever applied themselves to the improvement of Dublin's unwashed and uneducated. Most of the brothers were of the Wackford Squeers' school of teaching, believing that the fastest way to communicate with a boy was through his pain receptors. Others were just eccentric, deluded, certifiable or some combination of the above.

We started with Spud Murphy, the classic boot camp NCO charged with knocking new recruits into shape. Spud introduced us to regular doses of the leather for offences like walking and breathing, but judged by Spud to be the wrong kind of walking or breathing. He showed extraordinary creativity in adding to the list of possible felonies. His philosophy was that if a boy did it - or indeed if he didn't do it - it was likely to be a punishable offence. I remember Joe once getting belted for saying 'Good morning Brother

Murphy' which Spud judged to be an attempt at sarcasm – which in all fairness, it probably was.

After Spud, we had Brother Scully (aka Smiler), a humourless rosy-cheeked little swine who lectured us constantly on the importance of having prayer, porridge and prunes in our daily lives. 'Pray boys that you never suffer constipation' was his constant cry. From his endless references to it we assumed that he was a major sufferer. The Lord seemed to be deaf to his supplications and the prunes didn't work either, because in our years in the school he never lost his pinched and pained expression.

Then there was Brother Butcher (unimaginatively known as 'the Butcher') who believed that any boy who couldn't wield a hurley stick like a rapier was a waste of space and food. We were steadfast in our disinclination to participate in the great Irish game mainly because it looked suicidal, but also because the Butcher was so keen on it. Reverse psychology you see! If he banned it, we would have given it a go. Instead we sold our souls to the devils of Manchester United, preferring to hone our soccer skills in the streets to hacking lumps out of each other on the school's muddy playing field. The Butcher regarded us as heathens and traitors. He regularly told us that we were unworthy of the freedoms our forefathers had won for us from 'na Dubh Sasanaigh' (the Black English). With spit flying he would turn the colour of beetroot and yell: 'Ye're nothing but corner-boys - corner-boys and bowsies. In all my years in this school ye're the worst yet.' We were delighted with this accolade until we discovered that he accorded it to every class he had.

In our final year we had Brother Foley (aka Stinker). To his credit Foley realised that we were by then beyond redemption so he didn't try much. He lived only for garlic and MGM musicals. His breath could melt marble but he could sing 'Old Man River', 'Singin' in the Rain', and 'They Can't Take That Away From Me' like an angel. He used to organise an end-of-year show which was just about the only thing in our school career that got our enthusiastic support. Stinker recognised talent and gave me the part of Curley in a production of Oklahoma. It being a boys school, the part of Miss Laurey was played by a skinny little rat from the first year called Spike Byrne. I often blame Spike for me taking up with Peggy. After singing love songs night after night to Spike, Peggy seemed like Marilyn Monroe to me.

Outside school Joe and me played for the same soccer team – the mighty Rockmount Rangers where the Under 16s went totally unbeaten the year we played for them. Mind you the two of us and a few others were touching twenty at the time. We had to give it up because sideburns and moustaches were all the rage at the time and our hairiness started to attract comment from the mammies of the opposition ninnies.

We did our apprenticeships together in Cassidy's and soldiered on as tradesmen for a few years. That ended when Joe had a falling out with the foreman, a man named Gerry Kane, known as Genghis Kane. Joe called Genghis an ignorant pig-faced bogtrotter - which was a fair and accurate description. Genghis countered that - in his considered opinion - Joe was the laziest and most useless painter he had encountered in a long career during which he had met many leading examples of the type. This was also nothing but a true and fair description of Joe, so you might say that this was nothing but straight talking between colleagues. Our Marian tells me that it's encouraged nowadays to give such honest feedback in annual staff appraisal sessions. Apparently they're trained to do it. It clears the air and leads to harmony, team bonding and general apple pie. It might have been fine if Joe and Genghis had had the training and if they had taken time out to reflect on the other's views and how each might strive to be better people. But that didn't happen. Joe felt miffed. He compounded his initial offence by throwing a bucket of green emulsion over Genghis. I remember our leader standing before us with the paint running down him and an expression like Wile E. Coyote after something has exploded in his face. Joe had his brushes in his bag and was heading for the door before Genghis had recovered enough breath to sack him.

We chased young wans together with very limited success, except once with two nurses who had a flat up in Phibsboro. We were hoping for tea and a biscuit and ended up getting the full soup to cigars. In the bleak years that followed, as we traipsed around dance halls, lucky to get a dance, we often wondered what magic had worked that night. Whatever the combination was of moonlight, Old Spice and female desperation, it never happened again. At the end of another unsuccessful Saturday night we would look at each other and say: 'Well, we'll always have Phibsboro!'

I was with Joe the first night I met Peggy at the pictures when love blossomed in front of the flickering screen. I have long ago forgiven him for not bashing me over the head and locking me somewhere until the madness passed. Such is life. I married Peggy, and Joe married Teresa the following year. It was just something you did as it was expected. You were on a conveyor belt that over a few short years brought you from short trousers to long, red lemonade to pints, and living with your Ma to being married, dead and buried. Nobody would have thought you were gay if you weren't married, because homosexuals hadn't been invented. The holy state of matrimony was where we were all headed like lemmings. Or am I thinking of lemons?

'No sign of a mot yet?' would turn into 'No sign of a ring yet?' after you'd gone out with the same one twice. Then it was a hop, skip and a jump to 'No sign of a child yet?'

I was like the frog in the boiling water. If you dropped me into married life with Peggy I'd have hopped back out like I'd been electrocuted. But the slow process of visits to the pictures and the few pints afterwards cooked me nicely.

Joe met Teresa when he was doing a job in a clothes factory behind Bachelors Walk. She was a seamstress and was always messing around with clothes, cutting bits off and adding buttons and bows. She made most of her own stuff which gave her a unique look. Ostentatious you might call it. I don't know if it was better or worse than what other young wans were wearing but Peggy thought it was worse. Teresa's clothes did have the benefit of distracting away from her nondescript features. She looked like someone you'd see through a wet glass. Peggy said that she looked like a photo-fit compiled by a committee. The one thing that was clearly discernible on Teresa's mug was habitual dissatisfaction. She was never a ray of sunshine or the life and soul of any party.

Teresa was small and Joe was big, so that from a distance they looked like an adult taking a child for a walk. She was romantically inclined and used to go on like they were Rhett Butler and Scarlett O'Hara. Peggy said it only worked if the parts were played by Boris Karloff and Lassie. Teresa used to call Joe 'Honey Bunch' when she wasn't even trying to be funny. It made me want to vomit but Joe didn't seem to mind. In fact I think I once heard him calling her 'Sugar Doll' but I'm not a hundred per cent sure so I'll give him the benefit of the doubt.

They manufactured three chizzlers - Elizabeth, Isabelle and Desmond (known in the Daymo as Lizzy, Izzy and Dizzy). Elizabeth married a big culchie called Matty and at the time I'm talking about they lived out in the wilds of Clondalkin. Isabelle was in England studying some codology or other, and young Des was shacked up in a room in Fenian Street with a redhead called Eimear. They claimed to be actors although Hollywood was taking its time signing them up. The strength of their vocation was enough to keep them from getting out of bed to do anything else. They put on 'street theatre' which involved arsing around Grafton Street pretending to be Juno Boyle and the Paycock. But give tourists a shawl, a head of red hair and a bit of dialogue about *the whole worl' bein' in a terrible state o' chassis*, and they think they've died and gone to the real Ireland. The essential next step of separating them from their euros is why God gave the likes of Dizzy and Eimear the gift of the gab.

But I'm telling you so much about the early life and times of Joe Horgan that I've nearly forgotten what it was I was telling you about in the first place. It was about how Joe landed me in the brown and smelly stuff.

Five or six nights a week Joe and me used to rendezvous for a few pints in Magowan's with Paddy Mulhall, Barney Pugh, Miley Magee and Eugene Larkin. Others came and went but we were the beating heart, the core and the very vortex of Magowan's. In fact it was the six of us who were the founding fathers of the Magowan's Golf Society. And it was the Golf Society that led to the problem between Joe and Teresa, so I'm not digressing when I tell you about the Society's creation.

Peggy wasn't very encouraging when I took up golf, even though she had been on at me to get out of the house and lose weight - loosely summed up in the phrase: 'Frank, I wish ya'd get yer fat arse outa here!'

I remember one Saturday lunchtime I was practicing my swing in front of the living room mirror. I knew that I needed to work on my stance so the mirror was handy. The only problem was that when I looked up to see if I was looking down, I wasn't – if you follow me. I tried to explain some of the finer points of the game to Peggy.

'It's seems the wrong way round 'til ya get used to it,' I explained.

'Wha' does?' she asked.

'The grip,' I said. 'The way ya hold the club. The normal way is the other way round.'

She was sitting at the table reading some rubbish magazine. She looked about as interested in the intricacies of the recommended grip as a doberman would be in a plate of carrots. But 'nil desperado' is my motto so I didn't give up.

'Derek – yer man tha' gave me the lesson – he says tha' I'm a natural,' I said.

'A natural!' she sneered, barely looking up from the magazine. 'If they make a golfer outa you I'm goin' for a trial with Manchester United!'

Peggy sometimes thinks that she's Oscar Wilde and I make it a rule to ignore her cack-handed wit. Reacting only encourages her. I didn't even flicker a muscle to show that I had heard her.

'The way ya do it is a nice easy swing,' I explained. 'Nice an' easy. Ya get nowhere by chargin' up an' lashin' into it.'

'I've bin tellin' ya tha' for years,' she said.

I continued to ignore her. I knew that it was pearls before swine but I pressed on with my masterclass on the correct way to line up a golf ball - or 'addressing it' as we in the game say.

'Feet apart; knees slightly bent; head down; eyes on the ball; arms straight; gently pull back ...'

I put the club into reverse and slowly drew it back from a ball that was on the floor in front of me in an egg cup. Naturally I didn't intend to hit it - I am not an idiot! It was only a demonstration swing, my aim being to glide serenely over the ball and take the applause from the invisible gallery. But I slightly miscalculated and the ball took off like a bullet out of a gun. The problem is that the business end of a golf club is very far away, so it's hard to know exactly where it is and what it is doing at any particular time. The ball hit all four walls and the ceiling but somehow missed the mirror and the window. Even the egg cup hit two of the walls. The ball also hopped off Bertie's head as he slept peacefully on the sofa. He voiced his outrage and confusion by leaping up and howling, like a cartoon dog who had been dreaming innocent dreams about rabbits, when the big rooster guy sneaks up and whacks him with a mallet. Peggy jumped up in synch with Bertie and poked me in the chest with a finger of steel.

'Frank, if ya don't get yerself an' that stick outa here, I'll shove it so far up yer arse tha' ...'

I was going to point out that the implement was called a club and not a stick, but I wanted her to stop poking me so I didn't.

'Alrigh', alrigh',' I said. 'Give over, will ya?'

I backed out of finger range.

'I'm goin' out in a minute anyway. Joe's comin' to pick me up. We're goin' up to the drivin' range to hit a few buckets.'

'Ya migh' find it easier to hit buckets,' she said, always the smart-arse. 'It's a pity ya wouldn't go an' kick one.'

I muttered a short prayer in reciprocation.

'Don't tell me tha' Joe Horgan is takin' up golf an' all!' she said. 'Does he know that there's walkin' involved?'

While she spoke she kicked Bertie. He had been continuing to loudly voice his grievance at having his beauty sleep disturbed. Peggy's kick had the desired effect. He shut up and sat in a corner watching us closely for signs of further assaults on his person.

'Y'are highly whimsical,' I said. 'In point o' fact, Joe is a very fine golfer. Anyway, ya can drive aroun' in these golf bogie things so ya don't have to walk if ya don't want to.'

'Jaysus!' she said. 'They're mad if they let *you* drive them. They wouldn't if they knew about you an' tha' poor cat ya killed. Y'are a feckin' maniac behind a wheel.'

'Tha' was an accident,' I said.

'Well why didn't ya go an' explain tha' to the Guards when they were lookin' for the culprit? Instead o' hidin' away like a girl an' gettin' poor Mick to drive tha' pile o' junk to England!'

She was referring to the incident when I had acquired a motor vehicle with a view to making occasional family jaunts into the countryside. When I was still mastering the finer details of driving there was a small accident. Technically it might have been construed that I had broken some nitpicking laws relating to licences, insurances and road safety. I am not a lawyer but I know how these things can be twisted. Mounting a kerb and causing a feline fatality might be viewed as an offence if not considered in the proper context.

'The Guards!' I said in a tone to suggest that I need say no more, but I did anyway. 'I wouldn't trust any o' them as far as I could throw them. If I was thick enough to confess to accident'ly runnin' over a cat – accident'ly mind you……'

'*Accident'ly!*' said Peggy, '- wi' the cat sittin' on the pavement doin' nothing' bu' lickin' its arse…'

'… *allegedly* on the pavement,' I said, keen not to yield points which were not fully supported by the evidence.

'Alleged by a crowd o' people at the bus stop tha' ya nearly killed as well. How could I have held me head up in Tesco's – married to a mass-murderer?'

Peggy liked to over-dramatise every tiny little situation.

'*If* I was to assist the Guards with their enquiries regarding the cat they'd pin every unsolved crime in the Daymo on me. It's wha' the buggers do. They'd lock me up in the Joy an' throw away the key. Then how would ya be fixed? Eh?'

I thought that would shut her up, but she looked less horrified than wistful at the prospect. She sat down and picked up her magazine.

'Will ya be back after y'ave hit yer buckets?' she asked.

'Well no, not straight back,' I said. 'We have a meetin' after - in Magowan's.'

'A meetin'? In Magowan's?' she sneered. 'An' wha' meetin' would tha' be? The Dublin Philosophical Society? Or is it the Nobel Prize Committee?'

'If ya mus' know, it's a meetin' o' the Golf Society Committee.'

'The Golf Society Committee!' she spat the words out like they tasted bad. 'Any excuse! Yis're jus' goin' on the lash - as per bloody usual.'

I moved to correct her.

'It is not boozin' as usual. Magowan's is the nominated Society club house. It's normal for the Committee to meet in the club house for all official meetin's. An' ya can hardly go in an' use the club facilities an' not buy a drink now, can ya?'

It was like trying to explain the principles of civilisation to a baboon. The rule of law, universal suffrage and the requirement to buy a drink in a pub – these are the things that set us apart from savages.

'This's an important meetin',' I told her. I didn't feel I had to justify myself but I wanted her to know that I was not dealing in trifles.

'We're goin' to be appointin' the Officers.'

'Officers!' Peggy made a noise that sounded like a laugh but she doesn't laugh much so I can't be sure.

'*Youse lot! Officers!*' She made the noise again. It was like a cistern filling up

Over her head I could see Joe pulling up in his Toyota. He had gone into the taxi game when he discovered that he could get paid for sitting on his arse.

'Ah, my chauffeur!' I said.

I shoved the three iron I'd been using into the golf bag and humped the whole thing onto my shoulder. I gave Peggy a few cheery bars of 'I'll be home for Christmas'.

'Well, tha's Christmas spoiled then,' she said.

'Ah no,' I said for clarity as it was still summer time. 'I'll only be a couple o' hours. I'll be back in time for the tea.'

'How will we cope?' she asked Bertie. 'We'll be countin' the seconds an' minutes, won't we?'

If Bertie had a view, he kept it to himself.

Chapter 2

It was my idea to set up the pub golf society. I was having a sneaky aperitif one lunchtime in Kinsella's and I saw that they had one. My motto has always been: 'what's good for the goose is good for the gander'. Kinsella's has no more claim on the finer things in life than Magowan's, so I thought - why not? When I made enquiries of the proprietor / barman / chief bottle washer – in short Ned Kinsella Esq. himself - he was fulsome in his enthusiasm.

'Ya can get into every golf club in the country,' he explained. 'They're delighted to have ya - an' why wouldn't they when y'are bringin' a coachload o' fellas who'll pay for the golf an' dinner, an' spend more money in the bar?'

'Our crowd've bin all over the country. It's bin great gas. Off in the mornin', fry-up on arrival, golf, then a meal an' a few scoops. We stop off somewhere on the way back to take on fluids an' we're back in time for a session here.'

Weighing the scheme up I could see no flaw. Grub, fresh air, gentle exercise, supporting the economy, enjoying the comradeship of one's friends and neighbours, and a load of pints. What was there not to like?

I had never played golf on a proper course before. I'd put in many notable performances in the pitch and putt arena so I fancied that I had the knack. The Flynns have always been natural sportsmen so I knew that I'd have no problems. Still - just to be on the safe side - I organised a lesson. The young lad who taught me said that he had never seen anyone swing a club like me. At the end of the lesson I mooted the possibility of a further session, and he was amazed that I was even thinking of such a thing. He said that in his professional opinion there wasn't anything he could teach me.

In putting the idea to the lads in Magowan's I was confident it would be carried by acclamation. The regulars are always up for anything that might be a bit of gas and the seal of approval was duly awarded without any dissention. Barney said that he would give his right arm to play, and Betty promised to put up a trophy if we organised a match against Kinsella's. This upped the stakes a bit. Now prestige and honour were at stake. It didn't matter whether we were talking about golf, football or tiddly winks, there was no way that we could countenance the possibility of being defeated by another pub.

Ned Kinsella had told me that Societies have to be established and organised properly. He said that things have to be done by the book or the golf clubs wouldn't let you in. He said that there have to be responsible people in charge. I could see the sense in that. You wouldn't want to let a bunch of messers from the Daymo loose on your property without someone in charge with a chair and a whip. You would want to be dealing with a responsible, sensible person. Therefore I knew that I would have to take a prominent position on the committee myself.

It was naturally assumed that Paddy Mulhall would be President, because his son-in-law could get membership cards printed for nothing at his place of employment when the boss wasn't looking. It was also in deference to Paddy's position as the suppository of all wisdom and as the father of the house in Magowan's. He was the longest serving customer and, in accordance with the rules of primo genuflex, some deference was due. He was never the sharpest knife in the drawer – he wasn't even the sharpest spoon in the drawer – but he did exude a certain to-the-manor-born authority. I put this down to the fedora he always wore which awed us lesser mortals who were without the courage to wear such a thing.

I decided to be Captain. I could see that my leadership skills would be needed to inspire, mould and cajole the members into a team which would become a legend in the annals of pub golfery.

I had Joe pencilled in as Secretary because he is my buddy and he would back me up if there were any disagreements.

Eugene Larkin was the obvious choice as Treasurer, as I figured he would lose his job in the Civil Service if he ran off with the money. Eugene was some kind of clerk in the government department that deals with trees and fishes. Why trees and fishes rather than shrubs and sheep, I have no idea. Eugene was in his late forties and still lived with his widowed mammy. Somehow or other he had avoided the holy state of matrimony even though he had a good pensionable job and didn't look like Quasimodo. In fact, compared to the average Daymo male, Eugene was a select specimen. You might even call him good-looking if you go for that tall, full-head-of hair, straight teeth, and lack-of-beer-gut look. He was always well turned out - probably a requirement of the clean office job. He was sociable, polite and inoffensive. The only thing that was wrong with him - if you want to be picky - was that he was an awful gobshite. If asked what he did for a shekel, he would say: 'Department o' Forestry an' Fisheries.' Then, after looking around to make sure that no one was listening would give a wink and add, with an air of deep mystery: 'At least tha's wha' it says on me I.D. An' I can say no more than tha' now, can I?'

Late one night when he had a few jars in him he told me confidentially that he really worked for Irish Intelligence. I nearly bit the top off my glass.

'Irish Intelligence?' I asked. 'I never heard o' tha'.'

'No, well ya wouldn't, would ya?' he said. 'It's secret. It's our equivalent o' MI6 or the CIA. Bu' we don't call it tha'. It's known in intelligence circles as 'The Unit'.'

'The Unit!' I repeated. 'Jaysus, Eugene – an' *you're* in it?' I tried to make it not sound like that was about as believable as him being in the Rolling Stones.

'Well between you an' me Frankie, I am – but ya have to keep it to yerself. Lives could be at stake.'

'Ah yeah,' I said. 'I know tha'. 'Wha' do ya take me for anyway? Ya know ya can rely on me. I won't breathe a word. Not a word.'

I couldn't wait to tell the lads.

'Tell us this,' I said. 'Do ya have a secret number? Ya know - like double-o-seven?'

'Dublin seven?' he asked.

'No,' I said. Why would ya be called after a feckin' postal district. 'Double-o-seven. Ya know. Like James Bond in the fillums – Dr No, Muckraker an' all dem.'

'Ah no,' he said. 'We don't have numbers. Too obvious. We have code names. I'm the Falcon.'

'The Falcon?' I said. 'Tha's a bird, isn't it?'

'Yeah,' he said. 'A bird o' prey.'

In fairness Eugene did have a nose like a can-opener. If he wasn't the Falcon he could only have been the Parrot. I managed to keep my face straight only by sticking my hand in my pocket and pinching my leg hard.

'Jaysus Eugene! Code names an' all! Like Broadsword an' Danny Boy,' I said.

Wha'?'

'Y'know – Clint Eastwood an' Richard Burton.'

'I haven't seen it,' he said, even though it's on the telly every second week.

'We've bin issued wi' these special phones. They work like ordinary ones but they have hidden cameras. They can even do vidjos.'

'Go 'way,' I said, marvelling at the wonderful world of espionage. I thought that all mobile phones could do that but I kept it to myself. It's not my area of expertise and I didn't want to look a fool - like I did the time Joe told me to try the new Halal rashers, and I got Peggy to ask for them in Brady's butchers. She had a go at turning me into rashers when she got home.

★★★

The Falcon, Joe, Paddy and me convened that afternoon for the inaugural meeting of the Golf Society's committee. Paddy called the meeting to order and we gathered around a little rectangular table in the bar with one of us on each side of it. Paddy wore his hat at an angle that exuded authority like a beacon. If that hat could talk it would have said: 'don't mess around with me.' He had planted himself on the upholstered bench by the window making that the head of the table. He had a little wooden hammer that he must have borrowed from a child's carpentry set. He banged the table with it.

'As the President I hereby declare the first meetin' o' the Magowan's Golf Society open,' he announced like he was addressing a stadium. Not for the first time, it struck me that Paddy suffered extraordinary little pain at the sound of his own voice.

'Hold on a minute Paddy,' I said. 'Ya haven't bin appointed yet. Tha' has to happen in the meetin'. Ya have to ask for nominations.'

'Bu' we agreed that I was goin' to be President,' he said.

I thought he might get belligerent and throw his hammer at me so I rushed to calm his troubled waters.

'Yeah, I know tha' Paddy, bu' ya need to be proposed an' seconded, and then voted in by a majority o' the members present. It has to be done righ'.'

Joe nodded in agreement after I gave him my special look. Paddy hissed like someone had pressed a valve on the back of his piggy neck.

'Ah in the name o' …!' he said. 'I never heard such a load o' shite in me life. Righ'! Do we have any nominations for the position o' President o' the Society?'

'Would you be willin' to do it Paddy?' Joe asked.

Paddy let out more air.

'I feckin' said tha' I would, didn't I?'

'Righ',' said Joe, having cleared that up. 'I nominate Paddy Mulhall.' Eugene said that he would second the nomination.

'Are there any other nominations?' Paddy asked, glaring around and daring us. I was nearly tempted but I was too near him.

'Tha' bein' the case,' he said, 'an' there bein' no further candidates, I hereby declare myself – Paddy Mulhall – duly elected as President.'

'Hold on,' said Joe. 'We haven't voted on it. We need to have a vote.'

Paddy's hat seemed to be moving on its own, like the lid on a boiling pot. His voice raised a notch.

'Wha's the point in havin' a bleedin' vote if there's only one feckin' candidate?'

'I'm entitled to exercise me vote,' Joe said.

'Tha's right Paddy,' I had to agree. 'Even in Russia they get a vote although there's only one gangster to vote for.'

Paddy glared at me.

'Not tha' I'm suggestin' tha' you're one o' them!' I added.

'Ah for feck's sake,' said Paddy. 'All in favour o' me bein' President?'

The three of us put a hand up.

'Righ',' Paddy said, writing something down on a sheet of paper he had produced from his pocket.

'Is tha' the minutes o' the meetin'?' Joe asked. 'Cos if it is, tha's my job. I'm the Seckertary.'

Paddy jumped to his feet and leaned over at Joe. Luckily there was the table between them.

'Y'are not the bloody Seckertary, or anythin' else, until after y'ave bin nominated, seconded an' voted for like I had to be. So keep yer trap shut Joe Horgan until y'are asked.'

'Strike tha' from the minutes,' I said.

'I'll strike you in a minute,' Paddy said back at me. 'Do we have any nominations for Seckertary?'

'I nominate Joe Horgan,' I said.

'Tha's very nice o' ya Frank,' said Joe.

'Not at all,' I said.

'Do we have a seconder for Joe as Seckertary?' asked Paddy. 'Eugene will ya put down tha' feckin' newspaper an' second Joe, or we'll be here all day!'

'Wha'?' asked Eugene who had been reading the Herald. 'Oh righ', yeah. Fire ahead.'

'Seconded by Eugene Larkin. All in favour?'

We stuck our hands up. Paddy shoved his bit of paper and a biro over the table at Joe.

'Now ya can take the minutes, Mr Seckertary,' he said.

Joe got up and went around to Paddy's side of the table, and sat down next to him. Paddy gave him a look to show that he was not keen on this invasion of his personal space. He shuffled along the bench away from Joe. Joe shuffled along, cosying right up to him. If you could have looked up from below it would have looked like a single arse with four cheeks. Paddy gave up trying to escape and returned to the agenda.

'Society Captain next,' I said to be helpful.

'Feck off,' Paddy said. 'I know tha'.'

'Do we have any nominations for Captain, God help us?' Paddy asked. I didn't much like his tone. Unpresidential, I thought.

'I nominate Frankie Flynn,' Joe said.

'Good man Joe,' I said. 'Eugene – second me like a good man.'

'Jaysus, I dunno Frankie,' Eugene said. 'I haven't read yer manifesto. What're ya goin' to do for the ordinary workin' member?'

'I'll give the ordinary workin' member a good root up the arse if he doesn't get a move on,' Paddy said. His patience was now thinner than a hoor's negligee.

'Keep yer hair on,' Eugene said. 'Righ', I second Frank. Bu' don't forget me when y'are in yer big job Frankie Flynn, d'ya hear me?'

'All in favour?' Paddy asked, and again all the hands went up.

I went around the table and squeezed in beside Paddy on the side opposite Joe. Paddy looked at me like I was trying to interfere with him.

'Wha' in the name o'!' he said but left it at that.

'Tha' jus' leaves the Treasurer,' Paddy said, 'an' then we're done'.

'Ya mean the Honorary Treasurer,' Eugene said.

'What are ya on abou'? Paddy asked.

'The Treasurer is always called the Honorary Treasurer,' Eugene explained.

'Why?' I wanted to know. 'It's not the Honorary President or the Honorary Captain.'

'Well it has to be the Honorary Treasurer. Isn't that right Joe?' Eugene asked.

Joe confirmed that Eugene was absolutely correct. I gave him a dirty look as I didn't require his role as yes-man to extend beyond myself.

'Do we have a nomination for the *Honorary* Treasurer then?' Paddy asked.

'I nominate the Fa... Eugene Larkin,' I said.

'Seconded,' Joe said and the hands shot up in auto-vote mode without being asked.

'Jus' bear in mind tha' I may not always be available for meetin's. Y'know, if I'm called in to deal with emergency situations. I'll say no more.'

'Da-Na – Da-Na-Da-Na – Da-Na-Na,' I warbled, giving them a blast of the Bond theme.

Eugene looked like a spy with a licence to kill and an inclination to exercise it.

On behalf of the Committee Paddy told Eugene that we would be happy to accommodate whatever crises might befall the State's trees and fishes.

'Righ', so tha's it,' Paddy said. 'President, Seckertary, Captain an' *Honorary* feckin' Treasurer all appointed. Now wha'?'

While Eugene was shoe-horning himself in on the bench beside Paddy, Joe and me, I asked: 'Did ya bring the membership cards, Paddy?'

'Yeah,' he gasped, struggling to breathe in the cramped space. 'I have them here.'

With great difficulty he managed to produce a bunch of cards from a trouser pocket. There were about two hundred of them. They felt warm and damp after their recent confinement. The name of the Society was across the top, and there were two little cartoons, one of a man hitting a golf ball, and the other of a pint of stout. In the middle was a space for the member's name, and on the back was an advertisement for a Chinese takeaway. Joe was like a man encountering the Mona Lisa.

'Jaysus, they're gorgeous,' he said. 'Fair dos to yer son-in-law. Did he do the designin' an' all?'

'Yeah,' said Paddy. 'But I told him wha' to put on them.'

'Wha's wi' the Chinese takeaway?' I asked.

'Ah ya see the way it is,' Paddy explained, 'is tha' the son-in law goes in there and the fella gives him extra noodles. It seemed only fair.'

We nodded our agreement.

'There mus' be a design award tha' yis could win,' Eugene said.

Paddy looked at Eugene trying to decide whether he was taking the piss. Eugene was, but he maintained a look of studied earnestness. Paddy let it go especially as the full weight of the Committee was becoming unbearable.

'Wha' are yis all doin' sittin' on top o' me for?' Paddy wanted to know, like a rugby player regaining consciousness and finding himself at the bottom of a collapsed scrum. We all looked at him, surprised at the question. Joe said:

'We're on the Committee aren't we? We're entitled to sit behind the table.'

'Tha's bloody ridiculous!' Paddy exploded. 'Yis're like children.'

'We're entitled,' Joe said. 'It's a well-known fact tha' the Committee sits behind the table. I'm surprised at you not knowin' tha'.'

Paddy wanted to take a swipe at Joe but he couldn't move his arms. He just managed to wriggle a hand free to bash his little hammer down. This was either to show that he was still in control or was a cry for help. The only effect was to spill the fresh pints that Betty had supplied in response to me giving her the eyebrow shortly before.

'Ah Jaysus, Paddy,' I said. 'Will ya go aisy for feck's sake?'

'Righ',' he said, clearing his throat and addressing the room. 'I hereby declare that the Magowan's Golf Society is open to receive applications for membership.'

'Wha' are ya talkin' abou', Paddy?' Eugene asked. 'There's nobody here only ourselves.'

It was late Saturday afternoon and the bar was about as crowded as clergy night at a strip club.

'It'll be a couple of hours before they stir out,' Betty said. 'I told Frank tha' yis'd have to put up a sign. Yis can't expect people to be inspired, y'know!'

She drew a shape with her hands so that we would know what a sign was. The Committee considered her idea and it was decided that it had merit, although Paddy muttered that she had no business making suggestions as she wasn't an elected officer of the Society. Betty provided a sheet of paper and a few coloured markers, and a sign was created. The headline declared the formation of the Society and the detail advised interested parties that they could enquire about membership by phoning Paddy and giving his number. We examined the production and the unspoken thought was that there was a lot of white space left crying out to be filled with something.

'Put down afternoons an' evenin's only. I don't be available in the mornin's,' Paddy said - the lazy bastard.

'An' say tha' the decision o' the Committee is final, and tha' no correspondence will be entered into,' Joe suggested. 'We don't want any head-the-balls.'

It was agreed that this was the right professional air to adopt to discourage applications from undesirables. The notice was ceremoniously taped to the wall near the jacks where it would be seen by all who passed that way. We stood before it like the shepherds come to worship at the stable.

'It looks good,' Eugene said.

'We shoulda put 'Men Only' on it,' Joe said.

This gave us pause for thought.

'Ah no, I think we're alrigh',' Paddy pronounced after reflection. 'Sure they wouldn't be interested. Women don't play golf.'

'Yes they do,' I said. 'I've seen them on the telly.'

'Tha's not the same,' Paddy said. 'They play a different thing. It's shorter. It's a bit like pitch an' putt. They're not allowed to play with the men anyway.'

'Yeah, bu'… I dunno,' Joe said and we nodded that he might have a point.

'Wha' if we put the word *'Men's'* in the middle?' Eugene asked, and we agreed that it was better to be safe than sorry. Paddy stepped forward with a marker and amended the poster.

And so it was that the Magowan's Men's Golf Society was born.

★★★

Our first outing was to the Dunsheelin Golf and Country Club somewhere in the wilds of County Wicklow. It was fantastic craic. No, hang on, it was better than that. It was high grade, mainlining, top shelf craic. The event broke records in all the key disciplines – drinking pints, slagging each other off and acting the maggot. We had thirty two participants including all of the officers of the committee.

And there was golf, although a casual glance from an undiscerning observer would have told him that this was not the Irish Open. We were short of the right gear. We looked like the first episode of Dad's Army before they got their uniforms. I wasn't too bad myself: the trousers off my faun suit blended reasonably with the speckley brown pullover our Marian bought me for Christmas. Joe said that I looked like a huge turd. He had a pair of chinos and a new shirt from Penneys that had cost him seven euro. I told him he'd been robbed. Only Eugene really looked the part. He had the golf shoes, the single little farty glove, the sun visor - even though there was no sun – the stripey trousers and a shirt with a crocodile motif. He looked like a cake made by a child.

The trio of Paddy Mulhall, Miley Magee and Barney Pugh caught the eye. You would never have guessed that they were setting out to play golf or any other sport. Paddy was wearing the same outfit he wears weekdays, Sundays and holy days of obligobly. This was no surprise as he once got trapped in his own clothes for three days due to a zipper malfunction. This made him forever suspicious of new stuff so has been wearing the same gear for years. Miley was dressed like he was going to an interview, complete with jacket, shirt and tie. Barney looked like he'd got dressed in the dark. He was wearing a pair of green corduroy trousers and a flowery shirt that he said was his, but which I'd definitely seen on his missus.

All participants had managed to buy, borrow or steal some golfing hardware. Other than Eugene's, the clubs looked like they had been mouldering in the backs of sheds and charity shops for years. Eugene's were more like a canteen of cutlery from Brown Thomas's window display. If I had asked him he probably would have told me that it was a special issue from the Unit, and that his sand wedge doubled as a rifle. Barney only had a five iron.

'It's all ya need,' he said. 'The rest of it's a load o' bollix.'

I could see his point. There wasn't much difference between one club and another, and most of the lads would have managed just as well with a shovel or a hurley stick.

'Bu' what'll ya do when ya get on the green?' I asked out of scientific interest. 'Won't ya need a putter?'

'Putter me arse,' he said. 'I'll use the back o' the feckin' thing.'

The sense in what he said was proven by the fact that he came third in the competition. I guess that he didn't wear himself out dragging a bag of clubs behind him and agonising over which one to use. He just marched up to the ball and without breaking stride gave it a clatter before continuing onwards. This was typical of Barney's general philosophy in life. He had progressed effortlessly through school, never coming near any qualification. We used to say that the only letters Barney would ever have after his name would be RIP. In his working life, his efforts were rewarded by being fired or made redundant almost as fast as he could get people to employ him.

I didn't do so well myself on the course as I kept losing balls. I started off with a box of twelve that I bought brand spanking new from the pro shop. By the seventh hole they were all gone so I withdrew from the field and headed for the bar. As I was coming in some twerp asked me if I had had a good round. He looked about twelve years of age, was dressed like an estate agent, and wore a badge informing anyone who cared that he was Darren O'Loughlin, Banqueting Manager.

'A good round?' I asked him. 'Are ya jokin' me or wha'? How could I have a good round withou' golf balls?'

He struggled to answer and while he was trying to think of something stupid to say I gave him further feedback.

'Tha' course is a disgrace,' I told him. 'The only place the grass is cut properly is on the greens. On most o' the rest of it there's only bin a half-arsed attempt. Aroun' the edges ... have ya seen it?! It looks like it hasn't been cut in years.'

'Yes, but ...' he said.

'Ya can 'yeah bu'' me all ya like,' I said. 'It's still a disgrace. An' wha' abou' the fourth hole, eh?' I asked him. 'Wha's tha' all abou'. It mus' be the best part of a mile long, an' then when y'are nearly there, there's a big feckin' lake right in front o' the bleedin' flag! Tha's ridiculous!'

'Well you see, the thing is ...'

'It's ridiculous! Whoever decided tha' was a good idea obviously never tried it. There mus' be a million golf balls in tha' lake. There's three o' mine in it anyway. Tha's prob'ly how yis make yer money. Yis prob'ly wait until everyone is gone home and then ya go out with a net, and sell the balls to the next bunch o' mugs who come along.'

He ran up the white flag, realising that he wasn't dealing with any ordinary fool.

'Thank you sir,' he said. 'I will ensure that your points are put to the Greens Committee for consideration.'

I felt good that I had that off my chest. I felt even better when I heard later that Miley had lost a nine iron in the same lake when he forgot to keep a hold of it.

★★★

After dinner we had the presentation of prizes. Joe ran away with the first prize because he cheated. He came in with a scorecard that Seve Ballesteros would have been pleased with. Joe's technique was to exclude any shot where he missed the ball or where it landed anywhere he hadn't intended. He contended that these weren't really his shots and therefore were ineligible for inclusion in the count under the rules of the Royal and Ancient, as interpreted by him.

Paddy made a speech where he insulted everyone present - as expected of him as President. Then he told several jokes, all of which we knew and could tell better than him. He was heckled in our usual good-natured fashion with one of the lads jocularly throwing a bottle at him. It missed by a mile, proving that it was thrown only in jest. If there had been malice intended, it would have been on target. However, it was taken as a cue by the assembly to start throwing whatever was to hand. Throwing is like singing or laughing – once one starts everyone has to join in. In seconds the air was filled with bread, potatoes, items of cutlery and a chair. This upset Darren, our Banqueting Manager. He approached Joe, as Society Secretary, and asked him to exert his authority to restore order. Joe wasn't sure if such a delicate task was strictly within the armpit of the Secretary's job description. As a natural liberal, he was disinclined to interfere with the members as they got on with enjoying the event in their own way. Also, Darren hadn't said 'please'. After giving the request the nano-second of consideration he thought it deserved, he pronounced his verdict.

'Feck off,' he said. 'They're only messin'.'

'Well, if you won't do something,' Darren said, close to tears, 'I will have no option but to call the Guards.'

At this moment Miley hit an apple with a three wood and it exploded across the room into a thousand bits. This was regarded by the membership as a very impressive trick, and a new game involving fruit and golf clubs started. The lads lined up across the end of the room with a selection of apples, pears, and oranges and commenced firing. It was like being inside a fruit blender on full power. I saw Barney and his five iron addressing a banana and I was interested to see the result, but was distracted by Darren yapping more about calling the Guards. Joe took a slug out of his pint before responding.

'Tell them tha' if they're only goin' to send a couple o' lads in a squad car, they might as well not bother.'

In fact the services of the constabulary were not required as the supply of fruit ran out, and Darren refused to replenish it. There was no real harm done. The room had been turned into a fruit cocktail but there was no structural damage. Darren was so relieved that his worst fears had not been realised that he was willing to forgive and forget. He even shook my hand as we left and he thanked me again for my helpful comments on the state of the course.

'Y'are grand,' I said. 'We'll be back next year.'

He seemed to swallow something jagged but managed a wan smile.

'An' remember wha' I said,' I said. 'Give yer gardener a good kick up the arse, an' get him to cut tha' grass.'

The consensus was that the day had been a great success – it was everything and more that Ned Kinsella had said it would be. We had the cooked breakfast, the dinner, and the few convivial pints in the clubhouse. Paddy drank gin and tonic, not because he liked it, but because he thought the members would expect it of their President. On the way back we paused to give custom to a boozer in a one-horse town where the horse had long-since got bored and left. There was only one other customer who looked like he had recently died. He didn't say a word or move a muscle while we were there, and there were clear signs of putrefaction. The barman had to stir himself from a coma to serve us but once he got going, the old skills came back to him. I led the troops back into Magowan's like Caesar re-entering Rome after a successful day out in Gaul. Betty welcomed us like the fond parent of a family of prodigal sons.

But I'm getting ahead of myself again and forgetting to tell you about Celestina - which makes as much sense as writing a murder mystery and forgetting to mention the murder. Celestina was one of three waitresses serving us in Dunsheelin. They dished up the soup, the meat and two veg, followed by the choice of rhubarb crumble or fruit. Nobody had the fruit, making it available for the game described above.

Celestina was all legs, lips and make-up. She was a female designed for thrills and good times and not for cooking or child-bearing. She had hair the colour of a red-setter, and enough white teeth to equip a crocodile. Her bosoms wrestled to burst free of their constraints while her backside swung as she moved like a hypnotist's watch. She stood out from her two colleagues like a rose on a dung hill. When W S Gilbert wrote of the maidens with the homely faces and bad complexions he had this pair of gargoyles in mind. Like Celestina they were kitted out in regulation waitress white shirt and black skirt, but they weren't fooling anyone. These women were built for the big gansies and boots required when cleaning out byres and pigsties. Their hands bore the marks of ploughing, sowing and reaping, with not a sign of a manicured fingernail. Yoked to a plough the two of them would have given a Massey Ferguson a run for its money. While one of them was dredging bits of vegetation from the bottom of a soup tureen an involuntary comment escaped me.

'So I'm getting' the scrapin's o' the pot, am I?' I asked.

'Y'are lucky,' she said. 'All the besht shtuff is down the bottom. Now ate up an' shut up.'

I did as instructed.

I noticed from where I was sitting that Eugene was giving Celestina the full benefit of his silky charm. Eugene often confused his raving heterosexuality with a vocation. Even without being able to lip-read I could tell that he was bullshitting about his secret work for the nation. She hung on his every word paying no heed to other customers in need of drink, spuds and other essentials. As we were leaving, I saw him whispering something to her. She laughed and gave him a playful little dig, quite different from the haymakers dispensed by Peggy.

'Good man, Eugene,' I said as we walked over to the bus. 'Y'are in there, are ya?'

'Ah now, Frankie. Ask me no questions an' I'll tell ya no lies!'

'I know,' I said. 'If ya said anythin' ya'd have to shoot me. But tell us this: where's she from? She's not local stock.'

'No, she certainly isn't - she's a Narusian.'

'Jaysus, Eugene,' I said. 'Ya'd want to mind yerself - in your line o' work. She might be one o' them honey traps. A Mata Hari. Tryin' to find out the secrets o' the Department o' Fisheries - like wha' yis put in the batter. Ya might reveal all in the throws o' passion.'

'Go feck yerself,' Eugene said, delighted.

As it turned out he had no reason to be delighted because it was Joe who shifted her. Joe who is like a sack of coal that has lost all pride in its appearance. Joe who - apart from Teresa, who doesn't count - showed as much previous interest in the opposite sex as I have in having my nipples pierced.

I am known in Magowan's as 'old lynx eyes', and I would have sworn on a stack of bibles that Joe never exchanged a word with Celestina that day. But communication happened somehow, sending me down the slippery slope that ended under Joe's bed.

Chapter 3

On reflection I think it was Joe's car keys that did it. There has always been a type of woman who goes weak in the head at the sight of a man with a car key - even if neither the man nor the car are the latest models. Joe and the Toyota were frayed, battered and smelled like a charity shop on a hot day but both were functional. Where Celestina came from, ownership of a donkey with its own straw hat may have been the mark of the more affluent road user. When Celestina spied Joe with his Toyota key fob she will have heard echoes of *Some Enchanted Evening* with strangers' eyes meeting across a crowded room. The Dunsheelin room was definitely crowded but I don't remember remarking on the evening being enchanted in any way. While Eugene was trying to dazzle her with tales of international intrigue she only had eyes for Joe's key dangling from his trouser loop. She must have made her move while I was preoccupied with Darren or with the tureen operative.

I didn't notice when Joe started shaving every day, nor did I pay any attention to his new shirts. I don't take note of that kind of thing. If Joe had come into Magowan's dressed as the Emperor Napoleon I might have said something, otherwise my motto is that a man's toileting and tailoring arrangements are his own business. I did notice when he started smelling funny and mentioned it to him.

'Jaysus Joe,' I said. 'Ya smell like a cheap hoor's bedroom. Wha' is it? It smells like a mixture o' Dettol an' boiled sweets.'

He told me that whatever it was, it smelled better than me. As I had raised the subject, he went on to suggest that I would do the Daymo a favour if I took a wash myself every few months.

He also recommended that I spray some industrial cleanser under my oxsters to counteract my powerful manly secretions. I took all this as part of the normal cut and thrust of discourse in Magowan's and left it at that, but a week or so later I sensed that something was really up. He had done something extraordinary with his hair. It was more than just a cut – he had had it *styled!* He denied it of course. He swore that it was the usual ten euro job that we all got up in the blind barber's, but I knew that he was lying.

These were definitely signs but I didn't know of what. What code book deciphers what it means when a man who has won slob of the year for years suddenly starts spraying himself with unguents and turning his head into a topiary exhibit?

When he went AWOL I couldn't shrug off his oddities any longer. Like the rest of us, Joe is a man of regular habits. Since starting the taxi scam he worked most days and on Friday and Saturday nights. He would be in Magowan's the other five nights. Now suddenly there he was: gone, absent and missing, with a big empty space where he normally sat. Paddy Mulhall voiced all of our concerns.

'Is Joe Horgan after dyin' or wha'?'

'What d'ya mean?' Barney Pugh was puzzled as usual, reckoning that we would have noticed if Joe's name had appeared in the Herald's deaths columns.

'Wha' do I mean? Wha' the hell do ya think I mean? Where is he? Is the ground after openin' up an' swallyin' him or wha'? We haven't seen hide nor hair of him since the Sunday before last.'

I agreed: 'Yeah, an' even then he had the one pint an' was gone. It wasn't even ten o'clock!'

This may not strike you as remarkable but a keen observer of custom and practice in Magowan's would recognise such behaviour as bizarre. It was like a camel arriving at an oasis after a lap of the Sahara and rather than having a full humpful, settling for a quick sip and rushing off. We discussed every reason we could think of to explain the mystery - that Joe was off the drink - that he had some dread disease - that he was on some mad diet - that he had found religion - even that it might be part of some odd game or ritual. We dismissed them all as more ridiculous than each other. The truth - that Joe had turned into a Don Wan - never occurred to us.

Miley Magee dropped the bombshell a few days later. He testified that he had seen Joe in the Toyota with a dolly bird on the front seat beside him. There was nobody in the back where female taxi customers are normally billeted. A man might jump in beside the driver for the sake of camaraderie, but a woman never would. I was somewhere between confused and stunned.

'Bu' I don't get it,' I said. 'Wha' would Joe Horgan be doin'…?'

Paddy Mulhall rubbed his hands together, delighted.

'Bejaysus!' he said. 'There's life in the oul dog yet, wha'?'

'Will ya give over?' I said. 'Joe Horgan wouldn't…' I couldn't think exactly what Joe would or wouldn't do, other than that it wasn't whatever Paddy was suggesting. 'I mean to say! It's Joe Horgan we're talkin' abou', for God's sake!' was the best I could come up with.

After careful consideration Paddy and Miley agreed with my analysis. It was inconceivable that Joe could be up to shenanigans. There had to be some other explanation. We were jumping to conclusions. Who could know why women do anything? We agreed that maybe they sit in taxi front seats and we just hadn't noticed. But the larva of doubt had burrowed itself into the warm and nurturing soil of my noodle where it grew into a big fat question that cried out for an answer.

★★★

The crying out became unbearable by the Saturday afternoon after we received Miley's report. Unable to bear it any more I went around to Joe's house to beard him in his den. Visiting

Joe at home was a momentous thing to do but desperate situations call for desperate measures. Daymo men interact with other Daymo men in the pub, or occasionally by arrangements made in the pub, at a football match or suchlike. We do not pay social visits on each other. This is the Daymo and not a setting for a Jane Austen novel. We only venture into the family home to pay our respects after a death. Generally the first time I get inside another man's home is to see him laid out amongst the bottles of stout and the ham sandwiches. The matrimonial home is the preserve of the female of the species. Only resident males are permitted on the premises, and at that only on sufferance.

I walked past the house twice before I gathered the courage to skip up the garden path and ring the bell. Joe opened the door and I guessed that Teresa wasn't in because she's far too nosey to hang back and not come to check out a visitor.

'There y'are,' I said.

'Where else would I be?' he asked. I had to concede that he spoke nothing but the truth so I elaborated.

'We haven't seen ya in Magowan's for a while. Paddy thought ya might be dead. We saw nothin' in the Herald about a hooley an' we were terrified tha' we were after missin' it.'

'Ya can tell them all tha' I'm still here. I hope they won't be too disappointed.'

'They'll be disgusted, bu' they'll get over it. Where've ya bin anyway?'

Joe looked uncomfortable - like Ginger Celtic, the Daymo's provider of dodgy satellite television services, when you ask him for a receipt.

'Look Frank, ' he said. 'Come in for a minute. Teresa's not here.'

We went through to the kitchen and he put the kettle on.

'Do ya want a spring-sprong?' he asked.

'Go on then,' I said, taking a pink one and two white ones out of a jar he put on the table.

'Why don't ya eat the lot o' them?' he asked.

'Ah no,' I said. 'I'm watchin' me weight.'

'Are ya?' he asked.

We talked about Manchester United until Joe had the tea made. Then we sat down to what you might call an uncomfortable silence. He was examining a spoon like he'd never seen one before and I helped myself to a few more biscuits just to pass the time. Eventually he coughed and wiggled like he was trying to shake his vocal chords into action.

'Do ya remember the golf day?' he asked. 'Out in Dunsheelin?'

I confirmed that even at my advanced stage of senility I could remember back a few weeks.

'Do ya remember the waitresses?'

'Which one?' I asked. 'The ones tha' looked like the love children o' Lon Chaney an' a buffalo or the other one?'

'The other one,' he said. 'The one with the red hair. An' the foreign accent.'

'An' the fine thrupenny bits?' I asked.

'Yeah her. She's from Narusia. Her name's Celestina.'

Joe choked a bit on the name, his voice spluttering and dying away like an old lawn mower. He examined the spoon again as his complexion turned tomatoey. Relaxed and at ease he wasn't.

'Celestina,' I said. 'Tha's a funny name. Sounds like a make o' car.'

He didn't offer a view on whether he thought that the Ford Celestina might sell.

'Well, go on then,' I said. 'Don't keep me in suspenders. Wha' about Celestina wi' the big chest?'

Joe shot up like he'd been stabbed in the arse by something pointy. He brandished the spoon at me like an offensive weapon.

'Don't you speak about her like tha' Frank Flynn, or I'll feckin' well ... I'll feckin'...'

From the way he was holding the spoon I could guess what he might do with it if I persisted in speaking of Celestina in a loose and offhand way.

'Calm down,' I said. 'Take it easy. Sit down. Sit down. Talk to me. Wha' happened?'

I know from watching police negotiators in films that you have to calm down armed aggressors. I was facing a spoon rather than an AK47 but the same principles applied. Joe sat down, embarrassed. He dropped the spoon onto the table and if I could have got my foot up I would have kicked it out of his reach like they do.

'Well ya see, I got chattin' to her at the golf,' he said. 'She's only bin in Ireland a few months an' she's seen nothin' o' Dublin - only the bit between where she lives an' Dunsheelin. She gets the bus. She's no car like, so she's stuck. An' she's very shy so it's hard for her to meet people - new friends like. All her friends an' her family are in Narusia.'

Joe's verbal constipation had suddenly turned to dysentery.

'Oh righ',' I said, just to keep up my side of the conversation.

'Well I told her tha' I might be able to show her a few places on me days off – wi' me havin' the car an' all. An' she said tha' it'd be too much trouble. Bu' I said tha' it'd be no trouble at all, an' she said if I was sure...'

'Fair do's to her,' I said. 'Very polite. Ya don't always get tha' with foreigners. There were a couple o' young fellas in the paper shop yesterday. Spanish or somethin'. Turks maybe. They were foreign anyway... Well the carry-on o' them...'

Joe wasn't interested in hearing the full particulars of the incident. He ignored me and carried on.

'So I've jus' been bringin' her to see the odd place. Y'know. Bray. Howth. Into town. Into a few o' the pubs.'

Now he had stirred my interest. Being an authority on the City's drinking establishments I was interested to know which pubs Joe had chosen in which to entertain the young lady.

'Which pubs?' I asked, cutting to the main issue.

Joe looked embarrassed again. He and I have had many detailed conversations about the relative merits of Dublin boozers. We would agree on all the essential aspects. In our view there are three broad categories: Good pubs where the pint is satisfactory, the clientele is sane and there's football on the telly; tolerable ones you might duck into for an emergency pint to get away from the wife in a shopping centre, or if it started to piss rain when you were passing; and the rest put on this earth to cater for scangers, tourists and juveniles. Typically the last group serve food, play loud music and the drink is fit for neither man nor beast.

'A couple o' places in Temple Bar,' Joe said, deeply ashamed. 'She wanted to go there...'

He was like a young lad in confession admitting to interfering with himself. I told him that it was alright if that was what the lady wanted. But it wasn't alright and we both knew it.

'An' we went into Dirty Face Macs,' he muttered in a low voice.

'Dirty Face Macs!' I echoed, astounded. 'Ya went into Dirty Face Macs?! *You*?!'

'It was only the once. Celestina heard about it an' she wanted to go. I told her it'd be shite bu' she wanted to go anyway.'

Dirty's is a late-night joint which is strictly for youngsters getting out of their tree on shots, slammers and stickies. It is the chosen destination for hen and stag gatherings. The ambiance is guaranteed to induce deafness, blindness and madness or your money back. The only people over thirty in there are middle-aged men trying to pick up something which would require a course of penicillin to remedy.

'Did ya enjoy it?' I asked, mercilessly rubbing the salt in.

'I did not,' he snapped back. 'It's a wojous kip. We only had the one drink and we were out.'

He was like a man before the court hoping that his offence would be treated as an out-of-character lapse, and that his previous good behaviour would stand to him.

'So how many times have ya been out with Semolina since the golf?' I asked.

'Celestina!' he corrected. 'Oh, I dunno. A couple - maybe nine or ten.'

'Nine or ten!' I said. 'In a few weeks! Jaysus Joe!'

'Maybe it wasn't tha' much,' he said. 'She has no one here. I'm the only one she really knows. An' I have the car.'

'Ah well then yeah,' I said. 'The car!'

Sarcasm is my weapon of choice when a whack over the head with a brick is not immediately available.

Joe realised that he was arguing a lost cause. You can't go running around town with a redhead and expect pillars of the community to tell you that it's grand. You certainly can't if you're patronising places like Dirty Face Macs!

'Does Teresa know?' I asked, knowing the answer.

'She does *not*,' he said, wielding the spoon again in a menacing way. 'An' you're not to tell her either. Y'are not to tell anyone. I don't want this all over Magowan's.'

'Wha' do ya take me for?' I asked. 'Frankie Flynn is no informer. "In one ear an' out the other" is my motto. "Hear no evil; see no evil; speak no evil," - tha's me. "Wha' goes on tour, stays on tour". Wha' I always say is...'

He didn't want to hear what I always say.

'Yeah, righ', righ',' he said. 'Ya've made yer point. Jus' keep yer big trap shut, tha's all.'

I didn't much like his attitude but I let it pass. He was a comrade needing support and it was for me to provide the steadying arm.

'So wha' are ya goin' to do?' I asked. 'I mean ya can hardly ...'

'I know tha',' he snapped. 'I need a bit o' time, tha's all. I can't jus' dump the girl...'

'No,' I said, but I didn't see why he couldn't.

I wanted to ask how far the relationship had developed – were they exchanging cake recipes or bodily fluids - but Daymo men are not equipped with the vocabulary to ask questions like that. Anything I could come up might sound insensitive, leading to me having a teaspoon removed in the Northside General. I figured that I was unlikely to get a straight answer anyway, so I let it go.

'I saw Eugene givin' her the ol' Double-O treatment,' I said. 'I thought she'd be another notch on his lamp post by now.'

Joe grinned.

'Yeah, tha's wha' he figured too. Celestina thought he was a right daw. He was talkin' shite abou' him organisin' security for a state visit o' the Narusian President.'

'Jaysus,' I said. 'I wouldn't bet tuppence on the man's chances if Eugene is lookin' after him. Wha's he comin' to Ireland for anyway?'

'I dunno. Maybe there's a sale on in Arnott's or he wants to catch the Leinster Final. It's wha' they do, these fellas, isn't it? He'll have his photo takin' with our lad on the lawn outside the Awras, make a speech abou' the historic ties tha' bind our great peoples together...'

'Well, *you're* doin' yer bit for Irish Narusian unity, anyway,' I said, risking the spoon.

'Then a big dinner up in the Castle for all the aleckadoos, an' back to the airport. Job done.'

'He'll be lucky if we don't lose him in the Arrivals Hall with Eugene involved,' I said.

'I said to Celestina tha' Eugene couldn't organise an orgy in a hoorhouse, but she didn't get it. She said tha'd be an easy thing to do.'

'Foreigners can be very literal,' I said. 'Them fellas in the shop … I told them tha' they were as thick as sixteen breadboards laid end to end. Wastin' me time. Tryin' to measure it out they were.'

Having shared amazement at the cultural divide between the Daymo and the rest of the world, I got back to the agenda.

'So d'ya think we'll see ya anytime soon in Magowan's?' I asked.

'Ya will o' course,' he said. 'I jus' need to sort this out first, tha's all.'

'What'll I say to the lads in the meantime?' I asked.

'Ya can tell them whatever ya like, as long as ya tell them nothin',' he said. 'Say tha' I'm gone off to join the Foreign Legion. Say tha' I've been abducted by the Moonies or by the Presentation Sisters. I don't give a shite. I'll leave it to yer fertile imagination.'

'Y'are askin' me to lie?' I asked, trying to look affronted.

'Now ya have it,' he said. 'Now ya better feck off before Her Nibs gets back. If she finds ya, she'll give ya the third degree, an' I'd back her interrogation techniques over your ability to keep yer gob shut any day.'

I tried to look affronted again as he shepherded me to the door but it's hard to do it when your mouth is full of spring-sprongs.

'Ah Jaysus Frankie - ya hungry ghet - y'are after atin' all the biscuits!'

It wasn't me who spilled the beans about Joe's extra-marital activities. I am certain that everyone I told was sworn to absolute secrecy but somehow or other the word got out. I was being badgered for confirmation by everyone in Magowan's who hadn't anything better to talk about. As Joe's loyal comrade and confidant I said nothing. At first anyway, but once the horse has bolted there's not much use in denying that the stable door is wide open. One evening I was sipping a restful pint when I was accosted by Iggie Farrell. Iggie is a God-fearing man, ignorant in manners and knowledge, the kind who is the backbone of the Daymo. If people were supermarket trollies, Iggie would be the annoying one with the dodgy wheel.

'Eh, c'mere Frankie, is it true wha' I hear abou' tha' bopey dollix, Joe Horgan?' he asked.

I put on my Fu Manchu inscrutable face.

'I don't know wha' y'are on abou',' I said.

'Will ya go 'way outa tha'!' he said. 'Aren't the two o' youse as thick as thieves? He wouldn't scratch his arse without gettin' a second opinion from you on whether it was itchin' him or not!'

Although flattered to be considered the man with the inside gen, omertà is my watchword.

'Ah now, Iggie,' I said. 'Joe's business is no one's bu' his own.'

'I hear tha' he's after takin' up with a bit o' fluff - a proper Marilyn Monroe. Is tha' righ'? There's hope for us all, wha'?'

Iggie rubbed his hands together until I thought he might combust. Any fire would have been extinguished by his salivation at the prospect of romance. Unfortunately, hope for him as an attraction to the ladies was zero. Any female left in possession of even one of her senses would give him the thumbs down. If Iggie had ever been fair of face or full of grace it was a long time ago. He had bad teeth, greasy hair and smelled bad. He looked like someone used to sleeping rough because that's what he did most nights. Marie Farrell pulled up the drawbridge at a certain hour, and if Iggie wasn't back by then – and he often didn't make the curfew - he had to sleep in the shed.

'I can say nothin' Iggie,' I said. 'Me lips are sealed.'

'I hear she's from Holland,' he said.

'Narusia,' I said.

This impressed Iggie.

'Narusia! Y'are not serious! Wha's he doin' with a wan from Narusia?'

'I don't know wha' he's doin'! An' wha' difference does it make where she's from?'

'Well, I dunno,' he said. 'It's jus' very interestin', tha's all. Narusia! Well doesn't tha' bate everythin'?'

Iggie was as impressed as if Joe had acquired the magical powers.

'Well I suppose if y'are goin' to give it a go, ya may as well go exotic, wha'?'

Iggie rubbed his hands together trying again to get a fire going. He took a slug out of his pint to dampen down his exotic Narusian thoughts. At that point Paddy Mulhall came in with important news that Manchester United had signed a new winger. This was naturally given emergency priority in the order of business, relegating Joe's love life to the back burner.

I don't want you to get the idea that Magowan's is full of crusty old conservatives dedicated to the preservation of some outdated moral code. Oh contrary - Magowan's is a bastion of acceptance, liberality and tolerance. Whoever invented diversity, equal opportunities and all that cod probably came to Magowan's first to learn how it was done. No view or practice is outlawed. In fact the more outrageous or stupid it is, the better we like it. Oddness is grist to our mill, oil to our wheels and salt to our chips. Nobody will ever enquire into the details of a man's relationship with his god, his wife or his inspector of taxes. The unspoken rule is: let he who is always on time for mass, tells his missus the unalloyed truth, and is straight with the Revenue Commissioners, cast the first stone. Jokes and remarks about the fair sex in general are acceptable, but are usually verboten if about a named female. It is regarded as indelicate to refer disrespectfully to a real lady who might turn out to be someone's missus, sister or mother. The resulting bruised feelings could lead to bruised bodies and worse.

Of course there are limits even to tolerance. We are not savages. Our liberal instincts wished Joe the best but there was a niggling feeling that what he was doing threatened civilisation as we knew it. We expected leading members of the Daymo community to have their dinners with their missuses and then to assemble in Magowan's to talk shite. Where would we be if everyone decided to give the dinner and Magowan's a miss and to go cavorting with Narusians? The details of Joe's relationship with Celestina which were then in the public domain were still sparse. I was confident that a jury of Joe's peers would judge that he had gone temporarily bonkers. Being fair-minded they would allow for this aberration in the course of life's journey. The bit of eccentricity and colour might even add to his standing. Provided he got back on track he would be welcome to return to the fold. Of course if they found out about Dirty Faced Macs he was screwed.

★★★

Early on the Sunday evening a week later Joe strolled into Magowan's. I know it was early because Songs of Praise was on the telly. There weren't many in and Betty greeted Joe like a lost lamb.

'Ah there y'are Joe,' she said. 'Did ya get let out early on parole for good behaviour?'

This was her polite way of asking him where the feck he had been but he wasn't saying.

'Howya Betty,' he said. 'Pint please. Frank - yerself?' I nodded affirmation. 'Two,' he said, and Betty went into a blur of action.

'So how's it bin goin'?' I asked. 'Did ya sort out the other thing?'

'Yeah I did,' he said in a voice that sounded like it was bubbling up through soup.

'Good man,' I said. 'It's for the best.'

'I've left Teresa. I've moved in with Celestina.'

When Betty came back with the pints she must have thought we'd been visited by Medusa. Joe had stopped talking and I was staring at him. The only thing moving was my jaw which was swinging like a lantern in a strong wind. Joe paid for the pints, and when Betty had discreetly withdrawn, I steered him over to a corner table.

'Jaysus, Joe,' I said. 'Y'are not serious?'

'I am serious,' he said. 'I was goin' to end it with Celestina but, y'know, I jus' couldn't do it.' Joe looked at the floor and went the colour of the Man U home shirt as he muttered: 'I love her, Frank. Tha's the be-all an' end-all of it.'

What was I supposed to say to that? Congratulate him? Wish them a long and happy life together? Sing him a few bars of 'A Nightingale Sang in Mountjoy Square'? I thought for a second that he was pulling my leg, but a close examination of his tortured mug, which was a casserole of emotions, told me that he wasn't. His mouth was wobbling around like a bicycle going over potholes, as his feelings competed for control of it. For a horrible moment I thought he was going to cry. This was not the stuff of normal Magowan's banter. I didn't want to hear it, and now that I had, I didn't know how to deal with it. My repertoire of cutting wit would not serve in this situation. The pint suddenly tasted rancid and my stomach felt like I'd stepped into a lift and the cables had been cut. My brain was flapping around like the film had reeled to an end and the projectionist had gone on his break. Eventually some words found their way out.

'Ah, well then...' I said. I suspected that more was required and after a few moments of agonised silence I managed: 'How's Teresa about it?'

'She's not best pleased.'

I remembered how Teresa reacted the time we had the weekend batter on the Isle of Man. The sea crossing back to Dublin didn't agree with Joe after he had done his best to drink the island dry. He spent most of the trip lying in a pool of fluids, most of which were his own. He was in a very bad way when we got him back to his door. Rather than offering him the consideration and care that he obviously needed, Teresa set about gutting, filleting and roasting him on the doorstep. She said things that no loving wife should ever say to her beloved. She wouldn't even let him into the house until he had taken off most of his clothes and put them in the bin. I don't mind admitting that it shook me, and I am a man used to suffering at the hands of an indignant woman. My imagination couldn't stretch to how Teresa would respond to this new and graver offence.

'What did she say?' I asked in wonder.

'Say? She didn't *say* anythin'. She roared. She screamed. I'm surprised ya didn't hear her. She said I was a revoltin', disgustin' dirtbag. Tha' she hoped I'd die roarin'. Tha' if I got crabs, scabies an' AIDS it'd be too good for me.'

I nodded. Grim, but no worse than might be expected.

'I went back to get me stuff this evenin'. She'd left it all out in the front garden packed in a few boxes.'

'Tha' was thoughtful.'

'Me clothes. Me books. Me records. All covered in paint - stuff I had left over from doin' the hall an' stairs.'

'A sort o' creamy colour?' I vaguely remembered from my recent visit.

'Yeah, magnolia.'

'Jaysus!' I said. 'An' wha' about the kids? Did ya tell them?'

'Teresa did before I had a chance. Lizzy rang me on the mobile an' ate the face off me. I haven't heard from the other two yet. No one in here knows anythin', do they Frank?'

I swallowed something sharp and lumpy.

'I think there might be some talk. Bu' I never pay any heed to fellas gossipin' like oul wimmin.'

At a time of crisis, a man needs a friend to console him and to help him get rat-arsed. I recognised that we had reached such a point in Joe's life. I ordered supplies in the form of two more pints and a couple of large Jemmies. They disappeared like the dew on a hot morning. Joe reciprocated and the pattern having been thus established, we were off. After we'd sunk a few and I judged that Joe was sufficiently mellowed, I made gentle enquiries re his new arrangements.

'So are ya, eh, like livin' with Semolina?' I asked.

'Celestina,' he said. 'Yeah, she has a little flat in Ringsend. It's over a shop.'

'An' there's jus' the one, eh, bedroom, is there?' I asked.

'Yeah, there's not much to it. A sort o' kitchen livin' room, a bedroom an' a jacks. If she breathes in I have to breathe out. We watch the telly from the bed. We even have our dinners in the bed half the time.'

I imagined this Narusian bird of paradise, wearing something slinky and pinky, nestling amongst the pillows beside Joe in his vest and Y-fronts. It didn't seem right - not in any moral sense - it just seemed wrong, like beans and custard or strawberry flavoured crisps. Once again, I was struggling to keep up my end of the conversation.

'Wha' sort o' shop is it?' I asked.

'I think it's a travel agent.'

'Tha's handy,' I said. 'I mean for her gettin' back to Narusia an' tha'.'

'Yeah. She's talkin' abou' bringin' me over to meet her family.'

I was thinking that Joe might get on well with her father as they would be of a similar age.

'Ah she's a great girl, Frank. She gets so excited when I come in, y'know. She's very affectionate. Very demonstrative.'

'Peggy's the same,' I said. 'She can't keep her feckin' hands off me half the time!'

'Celestina does things tha' I never came across before. I don't know if it's Narusian or wha'. I mean, did ya ever hear this one? I have to lie on me back wi' me legs danglin' over the…'

'Ah there y'are Paddy.' I was relieved to be spared further details of Joe's bedroom aerobics by the arrival of Paddy Mulhall.

'Howya Joe!' Paddy said. 'I hear yer wife's after throwin' ya out.'

'Wha'?' asked Joe. 'Where did ya hear tha'?'

I examined my conscience and was relieved to find that I'd been with Joe since I found out, so it probably wasn't me who had blabbed.

'Mary got it off from Barney's missus. She had it from the fat bird in the pork shop – whasshername? Ya know the one?'

We nodded that we did.

'I suppose Teresa found out abou' the floozie? Ya can't keep tha' kind o' thing under wraps. It's like tryin' to hide fish – people get the whiff of it.'

Paddy gave Joe a broad grin and what might have been intended as a knowing wink. Joe's face registered a dozen emotions, all of them unpleasant. His colour went from pink to red to a greenish black in a few seconds. No one likes to hear that their darkest secrets aren't secrets, or to have their beloved described as a floozie. By now Joe was nicely marinated in stout and strong spirits and was listing slightly to starboard. To order his thoughts sufficiently to formulate a caustic response was beyond his capabilities. So he did what any red-blooded Dubliner would do in the circumstances. He took a swipe at Paddy. He missed and the momentum caused the pints and chasers we were then working on to hit the floor in an explosion of broken glass. There are pub proprietors who will smile indulgently at customers engaging in combat. They say it adds atmosphere and character. Betty Magowan is not one of these. Her strict rule regarding violence on her premises is that only she is allowed to administer it. Before the glasses even hit the floor Joe realised that he was on a red card. Betty came round the bar bearing mop, dustpan and a stern expression.

'You,' she said to Joe. 'Out! Now!'

'An' another thing,' said Paddy. 'Y'are sacked from the Golf Society. We can't have the Seckertary shaggin' waitresses wherever we go. Not to mention assaultin' the President!'

Joe paused in his walk of shame to have another lunge at Paddy but Betty got in his way.

'Wha' did I tell ya?' she asked him. 'Get out! Y'are barred.'

'Ah Betty,' I said, in an appeal for clemency.

'*You* keep yer trap shut unless ya want to go with him.'

I did, as I didn't.

Chapter 4

Joe's exclusion from his normal circles was complete and comprehensive. As well as being evicted from the marital home and excommunicated from the Golf Society he was permanently barred from Magowan's. Betty's initial barring might have been rescinded in the light of a new day as such things often are. I have been barred many times myself and always manage to win Betty's favour back with a few honeyed words. Unfortunately Joe had compounded his attempted assault on Paddy and the destruction of pub property by telling Betty that she was an effing cow. Not the sort of thing to say to a publican whose hospitality you hope to enjoy in the future. Drawing on my own experience I recommended that he throw himself on the mercy of the court, pleading provocation, drunkenness and insanity. But Joe is proud and stubborn as well as thick, and he refused.

'I wouldn't go back in there if Betty Magowan got down on her bended knees,' he said.

That seemed unlikely.

'Ah Jaysus Joe,' I said. 'Jus' tell her tha' ya were on antibiotics or somethin'. She'll be grand.'

'Feck off,' he said. 'I'd only end up beatin' the crap outa tha' excuse for a human bean, Paddy Mulhall.'

I realised that in his current frame of mind Joe would not make a success of any rapprochement I might try to broker, so I shelved it for the moment. But my heart was heavy. Joe was Robin to my Batman, nut to my bolt, Sullivan to my Gilbert. We were a team. I trusted him to agree with me unquestioningly and often uncomprehendingly when I was surrounded everywhere else in life by Peggy and others who delighted in quibbling with my every utterance.

There was also the inter-pub golf competition to think about. I had challenged Ned Kinsella to a match and he had accepted. The honour of Magowan's as well as my status and esteem rested on a positive result. Joe's personal loyalty to me, as well as his dishonesty and deviousness on the golf course, would be crucial in stacking the cards in our favour. Without him I would be depending on the raw talent of our team and I shuddered at the thought.

As well as these concerns I was upset that Joe's life was breaking apart like a cream cracker under a hammer. He had lost his home, friends and family, and replaced them with a dolly bird living in a flat the size of a dog's kennel. The vultures had already gathered and were picking over the remains. He was hardly gone through Magowan's door before Paddy had appointed Miley Magee as temporary secretary pending a full meeting of the Society. 'Presidential prerogative' Paddy called it when I objected. He said he was entitled to do it under the rules of Habeus Corpus or the Geneva Convention or something. Without Joe to back me up I had to swallow it. Miley Magee! We might as well have appointed Bertie. At least Bertie pays attention when I'm talking and shuts up when I kick him.

One evening a few days later I met Joe in a pub near Grafton Street. It was a place used by civil servants, bankers and other culchie chancers who had come to Dublin to grab all the handy jobs. Joe called it neutral territory; I called it no-man's-land. It was one of those places offering that authentic Dublin pub experience that no real Dubliner would recognise. We were surrounded by dicks in suits, obviously work colleagues who couldn't stand the sight of each other but afraid to go home in case they would miss something. They laughed loud and long at every half-arsed joke, the best of which wasn't worth a smirk. Joe struggled to get served, as a man who looked like the love child of a pig and a buffalo monopolised the barman.

'Can I get three pints of Hyno? And a gin and tonic. Make that a large one. Oh hold on … are you sure Barry? You might as well. Oh well, a single then. What's Aoife drinking? A dry white wine. Is it the Peeno or the Chardonnay? Peeno, right. Aisling, are you ready for another? Good woman. What is it? A pint of Magners – on its way.'

When the barman had produced the drinks and tried to get paid, the puffallo was deep in conversation with another braying fool about rugby.

'He shouldn't even be in the team, Pawrick. He's well past it. It's time for new blood.'

The barman managed to get his attention. 'Good man. How much is that?'

After rummaging in various pockets, he produced a card, changed his mind, and offered another one. The barman had to go and get a machine and between them they had to type in the collected works of William Shakespeare before the transaction was finished. By this stage my tongue was hanging out so far I could taste the carpet. Joe had two pints bought and paid for and we had them nearly demolished before the other shower had even lined theirs up.

'Listen, Frank,' Joe said. 'Let's get out o' this kip. Come back to the flat an' we can have a drop there.'

I raised an eyebrow a half inch. Demands for me to make house-calls were becoming more frequent than I wanted.

'Wha'? I said. 'D'ya mean now?'

'No I was thinkin' maybe o' Christmas the year after next. Look, jus' finish tha' an' c'mon. It's not far. We can get a bus aroun' the corner.'

I was already further away from the Daymo than felt right. The idea of heading further into the wilderness didn't appeal to me at all. I felt like Cinderella at about half eleven.

'Ah Jaysus Joe,' I said. 'I dunno. Peggy'll be worried…'

We both knew that this was untrue. Peggy takes to her crypt every evening without any thought for my whereabouts. It is not until the following day that she might entertain herself by remarking upon the hour of my return, usually with some exaggerated comment about me having made enough noise to 'wake up half the bloody street'. Not that I'm complaining! Miley Magee's wife has the unacceptable habit of staying up well past midnight just to continue whatever she was berating him with when he left.

'Alrigh',' I said. 'Do we need to buy in provisions?'

'No, we're grand,' Joe said. 'I got some when I was doin' the shoppin' in Tesco's.'

This was a stab to my vitals: a grown man reduced to traipsing around Tesco's foraging for life's little essentials. Joe realised what he had said and blushed. I felt for him and almost put my arm around his shoulders to administer a supportive squeeze. But I didn't. Young lads these days snuggle up to one another at every excuse like penguins in a storm, but men over a certain age still observe the rules regarding personal space. Joe and me were well over that age.

★★★

By the light of a silvery moon, because the street lights were all smashed, I examined the outside of Joe's love nest. It was a grey block straight out of 1950s Eastern Europe so Celestina will have felt right at home. The shops on the ground floor were wrapped in shutters which the local artistic community had spray-painted with more enthusiasm than talent. I thought that the northside of Dublin had cornered the market in dodgy neighbourhoods, but this place took grimness to new depths. The only thing that sparkled was the wall-to-wall carpet of broken glass. On the stroll from the bus stop we encountered a man who offered to fight us both for no better reason than that we were there and there wasn't much else going on. Another citizen lurked in a doorway administering some intravenous stimulant.

Joe produced a key and let us through a battered door between two shops. Inside, he rummaged in the dark and found a button on the wall. When prodded this produced a dim yellow light which fizzed through a bad connection. We found ourselves in a narrow hall, serving as a pram parking area and leading to a flight of concrete stairs.

'Come on, quick,' Joe said. 'The timer only gives a few seconds.'

We shuffled past the prams and Joe led the way up the stairs taking them two at a time. He got another key ready as he went, and just managed to get it into a lock before there was a click and we were in inky blackness. I tripped over the last step and crashed into Joe as he opened the door of the flat causing the two of us to crash through it like Laurel and Hardy.

'Hello Joe!' I heard Celestina's voice as I removed my head from Joe's arse. 'Did you have nice time with your friend?'

We were in a room that served as living room and kitchen. Celestina was getting up from a settee and coming towards us. She was wearing a tee shirt and the smallest pair of knickers I have ever seen. They would just about have fitted an emaciated Barbie or might have served as an eye-patch on a fully grown human. I could hardly see the point in wearing them at all. They were literally overshadowed by her bosoms which were leaping around like a couple of excited puppies. She grabbed Joe and gave him a big slobbery kiss like she was trying to get control of a melting ice-cream. Embarrassed, he managed to extricate himself.

'Celestina,' he said moving out of the way to reveal me lurking behind him. 'Frankie's come back for a nip o' somethin'.'

She seemed very pleased to see me – more than I'm used to anyway. Before I could get my bearings she was wrapping her arms around me and kissing my cheeks in a foreign way. I didn't know where to look, or what to hold on to as she waltzed me to a chair opposite the settee.

'You are very welcome, Frankee,' she said. 'It is very nice to see you again.'

'An' it's very nice to see … to meet up with you again too,' I said. 'Y'are lookin' … Is there any chance o' tha' drink Joe?'

'Yeah, no bother,' Joe said, disappearing to wherever the drink was stored.

Celestina sat on a settee opposite me. I examined a spot on the wall behind her. It had signs of damp which I found very interesting.

'Did you have good time in bar?' she asked, forcing me to drop my gaze a bit. I tried to organise it so that I could take in her face at the bottom of my range of vision and nothing else.

'Are you okay, Frankee?' she asked. 'Is something wrong with your …?' She indicated the neck area.

'Wi' me neck? Yeah – a bit o' sciatica, maybe.'

'Sy-at-ick-a?' she repeated.

'Yeah – it's a curse. The Flynns have always been martyrs to the oul sciatica. Ah, good man Joe.'

Joe was back like a St Bernard with a couple of go-large whiskies. He had the bottle under his arm, on standby for refills.

'Here we are,' he said, as indeed we were.

'Sláinte,' I said, and then feeling that some kind of toast was called for, I said: 'Here's to yis. The best o' luck an' all tha'.'

Joe nodded and raised his glass. He sat down beside Celestina and she snuggled up to him. She threw a few legs across his lap and put an arm around his shoulders. Joe had his drink in one hand and rested the other on her leg. And I don't mean her ankle – I mean the bit just south of her homogenous zone. I hadn't seen anything like it since Big Daddy and Giant Haystacks used to wrestle.

'So how is family, Frankee?' Celestina asked me and I had to think for a minute what she was talking about.

'Who? Ah Yeah ... they're grand... they're all grand ... they haven't brought the police to the door anyway ... tha's the main thing wha' ... ya can't ask for more than tha' now can ya?'

It was her turn to look confused.

'The police? You have trouble with police?'

'Don't mind him,' Joe said.

'You Irish! I don't understand. You say funny things.'

'It's called talkin' shite,' Joe said. 'An' ya can always tell when Frankie's talkin' shite cos ya can see his lips movin'.'

That killed the conversation. If they didn't want witty banter they'd called in the wrong man. The silence was so total that you could have heard a dust mite fart. Joe and I were not used to talking in the presence of females and I found it particularly awkward that this one was all over him like a boa constrictor. There was nothing to do but concentrate on the drink so we took to sucking it up like wildebeests after a hard day on the veldt. After a while things started to go fuzzy and I found it easier to focus if I leaned my head to the side and closed one eye.

'Your sy-at-ick-a again?' Celestina asked.

'It's his impression o' Long John Silver,' Joe explained. 'Isn't tha' righ' Frank?'

'No, it isn't,' I said putting on my dignified voice. 'It's cos I am ever-so-slightly pissed.'

I tried to get to my feet, just to see if I could, but the Ringsend gravity was too powerful. I fell back onto the chair as though I was attached by a bungee. Joe laughed.

'Ya better stop here. Ya can kip on the settee. Make yerself at home. It's Liberty Hall here. I'm goin' to bed.'

Given that I was incapable of much movement there was little more to be said. Joe unwound Celestina's arms and legs from around his neck, got up and wandered out of my range of vision. My brain grappled with the problem of how I was going to explain to Peggy where I had been. It drew a blank. Celestina stayed where she was in front of me.

'You are very good friend, Frankee,' she said. 'Joe, he loves you very much.'

I didn't know whether to correct her use of the language or to say that I loved him too, so I just grunted.

'His wife, she not very good to him,' she said. I grunted a bit more.

In my communications with Peggy I find that grunting serves me very well. It can signify agreement or disagreement and so I stay out of trouble without even having to listen to her. I figured that it might do the trick with Celestina too.

'Joe is very passionate man. He needs passionate woman. Woman who knows ways to love a man. I think his wife does not know it.'

I managed to squeeze out a bit of dialogue.

'Ah no. Teresa wouldn't … ya know … there was never much o' tha' … not in the Daymo anyway … maybe a bit more now, since people got the central heatin' …'

I waved my arms around a bit to add depth to my view. Foreigners like that class of thing and I had no further details to add.

'Joe – I think – he is like great river of love,' she said.

I went back to noncommittal grunting. I've heard Joe described as many things – a great river of piss or bile maybe - but not love.

'Like great river with dam. When I meet him, is like dam opens and all love bursts out. Great flood of love.'

I started to feel sick as the room did the hokey-kokey and I was being forced to consider Joe's previously unimagined prowess in the fandango department. Celestina was appearing in multiple versions of herself like she was on a telly with vertical hold problems. I excused myself and managed to tack a course to the jacks. I don't know how long I was there as I slept for a while standing up. When I returned Celestina had gone. Presumably she was tending to Joe's enormous river.

He had offered me the hospitality of the house, but where was the turned down duvet and the chocolate on the pillow? All I had was a two-seater settee which would have accommodated Bertie in comfort, but Bertie is less than two foot long in his socks. He is also a dog with low standards regarding where he is willing to lay his head of an evening. I had a go at several positions – lying with my legs hanging over the end; sitting with my legs stretched along the thing; lying at ninety degrees with my legs turning at the end onto the chair. All were varieties of crucifixion. I eventually resorted to lying on the floor and suffered my worst night in captivity since the time in my youth when I went camping in Enniskerry and forgot the tent.

***

'Wha' d'ya mean ya stayed at Joe Horgan's?'

It was around lunchtime the following day and I had managed to return my mortal remains to base. I was feeling like death warmed up, and I badly needed tea, sympathy and a rasher sandwich. Instead, Peggy was giving me a cross examination that would have been ruled inhumane in North Korea.

'I told ya,' I said. 'Joe invited me back, an' we got talkin', an' the last bus woulda bin gone ...'

'Ya went to tha' place where he's shacked up wi' the quare wan? I've heard it all now!'

'I wanted to talk to him an' he doesn't come into Magowan's since Betty ...'

'I've always said tha' Betty Magowan'd serve drink to Nick the Divil if he had the price of it, so I'm glad to hear tha' she has some standards. She's dead righ' not to serve Joe Horgan. And *you* – consortin' wi' the pair o' them!'

She made a face like she'd tasted something putrid. Then she changed tack.

'Why didn't ya ring an' tell me? I was worried sick. Ya've no consideration.'

Responding to this charge could only plunge me further into the soup. The honest answer was that calling her hadn't occurred to me and if it had I wouldn't have bothered. Peggy's picture of herself anxiously fretting for her beloved was not credible. However her allegation that I lacked consideration for her feelings was reasonable. I would have been happy to plead guilty to all charges if I thought it would have got me off with a caution, but that was unlikely.

'I thought ya'd be asleep,' I said as this was more or less the truth. 'I didn't want to bother ya.' This was not true but I thought it struck the right note. It worked to the extent that Peggy lifted her metaphorical foot off my windpipe.

'So he's livin' there?'

'He is, yeah,' I said.

'Disgustin'. He should be ashamed of himself.'

'Live an' let live – tha's my motto,' I said.

'Teresa Horgan won't be able to hold her head up in the street. God love her!'

Peggy was relishing the prospect of witnessing Teresa not holding her head up in the street. She had never been a close buddy of Teresa's.

'Well it was hardly Teresa's fault tha' Joe decided to go off on a sabbatical,' I said. 'It could happen to any woman. Ya have to be fair!'

'I know wha' I'd a done to him.'

I decided not to ask in case she provided a demonstration.

'Ah well ...' I said.

'Don't you 'ah well' me, Frank Flynn! An' you goin' an' spendin' the nigh'! God knows wha' y'are after bringin' back. Take yer clothes off an' I'll burn them.'

'Ya will an' yer arse,' I said.

I was wearing several much loved items and even in my weakened state I wasn't going to hand them over. In need of rest and figuring that the rasher sandwich was unlikely, I went off to bed. I was like a wounded beast of the jungle staggering off to find a quiet place to lie down and recuperate. I didn't bother undressing as I hadn't the energy, and in case Peggy carried out her threat to set fire to my trousers and accessories.

★★★

While I was restoring F. Flynn to operational condition, Peggy sloped off into town to harass the butchers, bakers and other tradespeople. As she was proceeding down O'Connell Street, dragging her knuckles along the gutter behind her, who should she see in the taxi rank opposite the Gresham Hotel but poor old Joe. She ambled over to shoot the breeze with him.

'Listen here to me you,' she greeted him.

Like me, Joe was not in the full of his health, but he managed something like a welcoming smile, assuming her to be a member of the taxi-using public. The smile disappeared like snow in an oven when he realised who it was.

'Don't you be goin' an' draggin' Frank Flynn into yer hoorin',' she said.

'Wha' are ya on abou' Peggy?' he asked.

'Ya know damn well wha' I'm on about. Ya had him out wi' ya all night - up to God knows wha'.'

At this point Joe lost the faint grasp that he normally has on his senses. In a misguided attempt to protect me he went for the 'deny everything' defence. This is the tried and tested default position to adopt when accused of anything. It buys time while the accused tries to come up with something better. But on this occasion, strange though it may seem, what was called for was the undiluted truth.

'I haven't seen Frank for over a week,' he said.

To give him credit, Joe is a masterful liar. He could tell you that Ballyfermot is the favoured holiday destination of the Arab princes and you would believe him. It is a skill that serves him well when he needs to persuade tourists that his route to the airport is a short cut when they pass some landmark more than once. There are hundreds of people in America who will tell their friends that there are two statues of Parnell and two Custom Houses in Dublin.

Anyway his honest-to-God-cross-me-heart-and-hope-to-die expression stopped Peggy in her tracks. She fixed him with the death stare that always makes me confess to the charges in hand, and to ask for other offences to be taken into consideration. But Joe didn't flinch. She turned the power up to max and tried again and Joe didn't even blink. The man has incredible powers.

'Ya were out on the gargle with Frank las' nigh', an' he's only after gettin' back this lunchtime.'

'It's nothin' to do with me, Peggy,' he said. 'I'm tellin' ya tha' I haven't seen him. I was workin' las' night.'

Any normal person would have left it at that but Peggy is super-suspicious by nature. And knowing Joe for as long as she did, she wasn't going to buy any story from him without a full cross-examination.

'Ya look a bit shook,' she said. 'Ya don't look like a man who went straight to bed after his cocoa.'

The cock didn't crow as O'Connell Street doesn't stretch to live poultry, but the bugger denied me for the third time anyway.

'Listen, I'm tellin' ya Peggy,' he said. 'I wasn't with him. He was prob'ly in Magowan's with Paddy an' Miley an' them.'

Peggy ran out of questions and rested her case. She left him to his taxiing and resumed her quest for pork chops and Fairy Liquid. The problem was that she was now a woman with unresolved questions and when Peggy has unresolved questions she sets about resolving them. Such a situation is rarely in my interests. So as I lay in my bed with a proprietorial grip on my trousers, sleeping the sleep of the pure and dreaming the dreams of the innocent, I knew nothing of the tsunami of trouble that was heading my way.

Chapter 5

When I woke up I felt like a new-born lamb – a bit shaky on my feet but ready to face the world. The raging storm that had been going on between my ears had subsided to occasional squalls. I pottered downstairs and made tea and a cheese and pickle sandwich. Bertie saluted me with a wagged tail and if I had one I'd have wagged it back. Although my troubles were many and varied I felt more than a match for them. I like to think that I have few equals when it comes to planning strategies and marshalling resources to achieve objectives. When objectives know that they are in my sights they invariably come out with their hands up.

Turning to the Joe situation I felt that it was grim but solvable. The thing was to act and to act fast before the concrete set. As I chewed on my sandwich a plan began to hatch. Chewing often has that effect on me as it jiggles up the grey cells. Joe was suffering from a temporary blindness probably brought on by the dazzling Celestina. I figured that normal vision could be restored by laying before him all that he was missing: viz – wife, family, pub and pals – not necessarily in that order. Simply reminding him of these pearls would be insufficient. I had to lure him in, show him the goodies, and let him taste the pints and smell the roses, so to speak. Teresa would be key to the plot. She needed to be primed to strew roses in his path, make him his favourite dinner, and have his slippers warming by the fire. It wouldn't work if he was to be met with angry words, bitterness and recrimination. And this would be Joe's likely reception if Teresa wasn't carefully coached and maybe drugged. To think is to act is my motto, so I dumped the cup and plate in the sink and set out to make yet another bloody house call.

The distance between the Flynn and Horgan households is no more than three minutes even for a drunk with his bootlaces tied together. For me it was as fast as tele-transportation.

'Howya, Teresa,' I said when she opened up. Of course she will have been very surprised to see me but she stood aside and nodded that I should come in as though I dropped in every day.

'I was just wonderin' whether ya were alrigh',' I said putting on my best bedside manner.

'I'm not great,' she said and the self-pity started to brim around her eye-balls. I choked down the natural desire to tell her to get a grip and instead reached for the sympathy ladle.

'You an' Joe!' I said. 'It's ridiculous. After all the years yis've bin together … like Mickey Rooney and Judy Garland.'

'He's a bollix,' Teresa corrected me. Even during bad patches Judy never called Mickey a bollix. As quick footed as a mountain goat, I altered my approach.

'Ah well, he's tha' alrigh',' I agreed figuring that Teresa was more likely to dance to my tune if she was singing from the same hymn sheet as me. Psychology, you see. I produced some anti-Joe sentiments of my own to establish my bona fides.

'He's an awful gobshite,' I said. 'How the louser could walk out on a lovely home like this – an' on a lovely wife like you…' I forced myself to say.

Teresa was never my mug of tea. She was okay as far as she went, which wasn't far. She was a small woman but not in any petite or pretty way. Although perfectly functional in all key areas, like a Swiss penknife, she had nasty sharp edges and pointy bits.

'I did me best, Frank,' she said. 'Ya know tha'. I always did me best.'

'Ah, I know ya did,' I said, accepting her word for it.

'I reared his kids, kep' his house, gave him his dinners ...'

I nodded to acknowledge each of these significant accomplishments.

'Ya were always great,' I said. 'He didn't deserve ya.'

Having established this common ground - that Joe was a dick of the first water - I planned to gently steer the conversation around to his good points. I wanted her to remember his winning smile, his kindness to animals and his prowess at changing light bulbs. I wanted her to think fondly of the days when she ran her fingers through his hair, and he said those romantic things that men only say during the mad period of courtship or when drunk. From there it would be a short hop, skip and jump to engaging her in a plan to get those good times rolling again.

To my horror Teresa started to sniffle and immediately this light drizzle turned into a flood of tears and snot. The safe course of action was for me to remember an urgent appointment to see a man about a dog and to head for the hills. But the chivalry of the Flynns and my commitment to the mission in hand would not allow it. Without reference to me, some automatic pilot put one of my arms around her shoulders. My other hand fished a paper hanky out of my pocket and pushed it at her.

'Here, this is clean,' I lied.

'Glurk,' she said in thanks.

'No bother,' I said, and I may have added 'there, there,' as I rubbed and patted her back. I'm not sure why I was doing this but it felt like the required treatment. She did much blowing and spluttering into my hanky as I rubbed and patted like I was hoping for a genie to appear. Eventually a sobby hiccuppy noise, like a car running out of petrol, indicated that Teresa's well was running dry.

'Thanks ... hic ... Frank ... hic ... y'are ... hic ... very good ... hic.'

Her voice and breathing slowly returned to normal as we stood, me still with my arm around her, administering occasional rubs and pats. I was afraid that if I stopped she might have a relapse. Teresa rested her head on my chest and I gave her a little nuzzle with my chin. She sighed and said 'Ah Frank', and I said 'Ah Teresa,' just to be chatty.

She looked up and kissed me on the cheek. Her head had returned to its base on my chest before the full horror of what had happened hit me. Her arms had found their way around me and she gave me a little squeeze. This was beyond my wildest nightmares. How had I got myself into this - and more importantly how was I to get myself out of it? Before I could even begin to draw up a plan I was overtaken by events.

We were in our clinch just by the front door when it was transformed into a large and loud drum. Somebody on the other side was giving it a vigorous going over with what sounded like a battering ram. Think of the approach taken by the police in the execution of a dawn raid and you will have the picture.

In spite of the banging I could hear the words *'Teresa Horgan'* being yelled at a high volume. I could hear them because they was issuing from the powerful larynx of Mrs P. Flynn and when Peggy yells she aims to be heard.

'Teresa Horgan, are ya in there?'

I had assigned my brain the tricky task of calming Teresa down before moving on to the delicate Joe rehabilitation work. These missions had already been shelved due to Teresa's misinterpretation of the situation. And now this!

At the speed of light, instructions were issued for all leave to be cancelled amongst my grey cells. Alarm-bells were ringing and grey cells were donning fire-protection suits and rushing to action stations. The Chief Engineer cell was shouting: 'she cannae take any more Captain.' All non-essential services were shut down. I desisted from breathing and my heart probably stopped. Continence lay in the balance for a few seconds, and was maintained only after a vote recount. As the mental processes shot up to Mach 5, the real world went into slow motion.

In a flash I perceived how the situation could be misconstrued by anyone who was bad-minded enough to do so. Peggy was just such a person. If she found me here with Teresa I would have much explaining to do and Peggy was unlikely to give me enough time to do it. If by any chance she had seen me and Teresa looking like Doris Day and Rock Hudson in Lover Come Back, I was already doomed.

In such circumstances the natural response is for fight or flight. The brain considered the first option and dismissed it with a hollow laugh. Instead it issued immediate mobilisation orders to the leg department. I thought of the back door but Peggy was very capable of trying both sides of the house, so effectively she had me surrounded. Peggy's voice was still echoing when I was heading up the stairs at speed, employing the silent running technique of a Red Indian. Through arm-waving and some basic folk-dancing, I communicated to Teresa that she should delay opening the door until I was out of sight.

Hiding under a bed might strike you as a cliché unworthy of a man of my resource. However, I suggest that you would have done no better given the time available and the facilities offered by the average Daymo bedroom. I briefly considered diving into a wardrobe, but I would only have fitted if I had decanted the contents onto the floor, which might have given the game away. So I limboed under the bed in the style of a greased ferret. Once there I adopted a Cistercian silence and listened for enemy movements.

I was in a world of dirt and fluff. Teresa's commitment to the war on dust was clearly less than Peggy's. Peggy has disturbed many a peaceful lie-in by turfing me out of the scratcher for the purpose of vacuuming invisible dust particles. If Teresa had ever done such a thing, it wasn't recently. Again I reflected on Joe's stupidity in not knowing when he was well-off.

I could hear voices from below but not what was being said. The volume suggested that the drawbridge had been lowered and that Peggy was now on the premises. I hadn't had time to tutor Teresa on what line she should adopt. They were never bosom buddies and it seemed unlikely that Peggy would have dropped in for tea and a chat. Whatever reason Peggy had for calling was unlikely to have been in my interests. I needed Teresa to be guided by a woman's instinct for the protection of life and to say nothing about my presence.

The talking went on for a while, giving me a straw to clutch. But women talk whenever they're breathing and without necessarily listening to each other. For all I knew they were having a ritual babble about shopping and the weather before Teresa would get around to saying: 'By the way, if y'are lookin' for Frank, he's upstairs.'

The faint candle of hope spluttered and died when I heard the voices grow louder as they came up the stairs. Teresa seemed to be objecting to something and Peggy seemed to be telling her to 'feck off' if 'Feck off, Teresa' can be construed as such.

A couple of doors opened and closed before Peggy and Teresa came into the room in which I was holed up. I heard the wardrobe being investigated and congratulated myself on not being in it. But Peggy was following my tracks like a bloodhound. Her feet came towards the bed. She got down on her knees, leaned over and looked in at me. The exertion of the search had winded her so that she was breathing like something in the winners' enclosure at Leopardstown.

'Come out from under tha' bed, ya little shite!' she said.

Now you know the entirely innocent circumstances that led to me being under the Horgan bed. Peggy was not the kind of woman to suspect innocence where there was any possibility of guilt. Such was her negative view of human nature that her default position was always to assume the worst. She claimed that this was justified by a life living with me but this view could not be supported by the facts. Peggy is capable of finding me guilty of felonies even where there is zero evidence and I have a cast-iron alibi. Once she accused me of something when she knew I couldn't have done it as I was with her at the time.

'So ya say,' she said implying that my saying it made it doubtful.

Finding me hiding under another woman's bed would be solid proof of guilt – guilt of what would be of little relevance. She might inquire into that after sentence had been passed and executed.

★★★

But like Houdini in his prime, I had defied the odds and escaped from Peggy's clutches to the sanctuary of Magowan's. Now I needed to lie low for a bit to plan my next move, as well as to give Peggy time to calm down and not reach for a blunt instrument at the first sight of me. The problem was that I wasn't in the habit of going on the lam and I didn't have a safe house to which I could retreat. Staying with either daughter was out of the question. Angela and Tommy have more kids than I would want to share a county with. Anyway, as Peggy's second home, the place would have been as much a refuge for me as a dog's house would be for a cat. Marian and her 'partner', Susan, have a two bedroom flat and the second bedroom is spare. Their relationship is perfectly fine with me but there are limits. I would struggle to sleep a wink in an adjacent bedroom. Live and let live is my motto, but every little noise would make you think wouldn't it? Anyway Marian was very likely to sympathise with Peggy and to hand me over to her custody.

The night chez Joe and Semolina was a night too many for me and I wasn't going back there. I'd have been more comfortable sleeping on a bench in Stephen's Green. And as I've explained earlier, the worlds of pub and home in the

Daymo do not overlap, so the missuses of other Magowan's stalwarts would never countenance a house guest.

The only possibility was Eugene Larkin, a.k.a. the Falcon. He did not have the burden of a loving wifestill living at home with his old mother. Ma Larkin knew me since I was in short trousers and used to regard me fondly. I hadn't seen her for a few years and understood that she was housebound. Whether this was due to age and infirmity, or by direction of a court, I didn't know. As I went through my options, the shortlist boiled down to Larkin's and the park bench, and Larkin's won.

The great thing about Magowan's is that if you sit there long enough – and I usually do – all the world passes by, and so it was that evening. I had hardly finished identifying Eugene's as my preferred refuge when the man himself appeared before me. I gave him one of my winning smiles, and regretted that I couldn't present him with slippers, pipe and an evening paper. I did what I could.

'There y'are, Eugene,' I said. 'Ya'll have a pint?'

'Thanks Frank,' he said. 'I'll have a vodka an' red, thanks very much.'

I ordered this ordure for him. Normally I would have commented on what such a drink said about a man's character. It wouldn't have been complimentary, so in the circumstances, I bit my lip.

'How're things at work?' I asked.

'Desperate busy,' he said. 'The boss was givin' out to me today for goin' aroun' the office with me mickey hangin' out. I said to him: 'If y'are goin' to work me like a horse, I may as well look like one!"

I laughed more than this was worth, reckoning that being an appreciative audience would do my cause no harm.

'I suppose ya mus' be busy at this time o' year alrigh' – wha' with the trees growin' an' the fishes migratin' an' all tha'…' I said.

He looked at me like I was jabbering Greek. Then he gave me that shifty look to check nobody was listening, in the manner of George Cole in the St Trinian's pictures. He leaned in towards me and whispered: 'The Unit is after bein' assigned to look after the Narusian President on his visit. Top priority. The Minister wants to do some deal to do with turf-fired generators. So he doesn't want any messin'.'

'Not like with tha' American politician?' I asked.

The dignitary to whom I referred, a US Senator, had been subjected to questioning by Gardai because he looked dodgy. There had to be an official grovelling apology assuring the US that we do not regard all African-Americans as dodgy. The truth is that the Gardai operate an inclusive and equal opportunities policy with regard to dodginess and anyone who isn't a big thick culchie is liable to fall within the armpit of their definition.

'Yeah, tha' was a disaster. He was jus' lookin' at buyin' somethin' in Brown Thomas's, an' the next thing he knows he's in a cell with a couple o' Guards lookin' up his arse.'

'It's all part o' the céad míle fáilte,' I laughed.

'I've been put in charge o' the visit,' Eugene said. 'Access all areas - every resource at me dispersal - the whole shimozz. Do ya get me?'

I nodded that I did, but I didn't.

'I'm on call twenty four seven,' he said.

I assumed that this was the number of his fancy phone with the camera.

'So wha' have ya got to do?' I asked, being polite. I didn't give a fiddler's what he had to do, but I am a man who has listened to Paddy Mulhall for hours at a stretch, so I can take it.

'There's a load o' prep work before the visit. Monitorin' dissidents. Lookin' down manholes. Checkin' wha' he'll be eatin'.'

'Don't forget to look under his bed,' I advised, my recent experiences still fresh in my mind.

'Good tip. Thanks.'

'Ya'll be workin' long hours so?' I asked.

'Every hour tha' God sends.'

'Yer Ma'll be lost without ya,' I said.

'Yeah, I suppose she will, bu' she'll have to lump it. Wha' can I do?'

'I might be able to lend ya a hand,' I said, recognising an opening where I see one. 'I need to keep a bit o' distance between me an' Peggy for a few days. If ya have a spare bed, I could come an' be company for yer Ma when y'are out.'

'Wha's up with Peggy?' he asked.

That's the thing with spies – always asking bloody questions.

'Oh it's nothin',' I said. 'Ya wouldn't understan' - bein' single an' all. Every now an' again in a marriage ya need to allow one another a bit o' space to think, reflect, find yerself...'

'An' not find you!'

'Now ya have me,' I said. 'Y'are very perspicacious. So wha' d'ya think? What about it?'

'Yeah, we could do tha'. We've loads o' room. Me Ma has always had a soft spot for you. She says y'are a harmless poor fecker.'

I wasn't too pleased at being called harmless. The persona that I try to cultivate for general consumption is early Clint Eastwood – tough and reliable, but you wouldn't want to mess with me. 'Harmless' isn't the effect I aim for, but I wasn't going to dispute Ma Larkin's view with my rights of residence in the Falcon's nest still in the balance.

'She was always a gas woman,' I said. 'So we're set all then. I'll jus' come home with ya when we're done here.'

'Wha' tonigh'?' Eugene asked. 'Have ya no luggage nor nothin'?'

'No,' I said. 'It was kinda a sudden thing. I didn't even have a chance to pack me toothbrush an' a change o' drawers.'

Eugene laughed: 'Y'are an awful man an' no mistake! But ya would be helpin' me out. The Ma is not as good on her feet as she used to be. She needs help gettin' to an' from the toilet – tha' class o' thing.'

I nearly cancelled the booking when I heard that. There was little I could conceive of as being worse than conscription as toilet attendant to an old woman. In my experience, people in their dotage throw modesty to the winds, and are capable of revealing what should stay forever hidden. But after my previous night sleeping like a fakir I badly needed the full eight hours on a regulation mattress. Eugene was running the Last Chance Saloon and I wanted in. So swallowing my pride with a dash of bile, I lied that I would be only delighted to make myself useful.

★★★

I've known Ma Larkin all my life. She used to go to bingo with my mother, and in the summer they used to sit in the park in Mountjoy Square knitting woolly jumpers, mittens and balaclavas. I itched from birth to sixteen when I could at last afford to buy clothes that weren't made out of sheep cast-offs.

In her declining years Ma had lost some of her powers, but the trace elements remained. She was a tall woman, now stooped to the shape of a boomerang. Her voice was high-pitched like a cat on helium so that when she spoke you expected the sound of shattering glass. She smelled of cough sweets and Friars' Balsam.

'So Peggy thrun ya out did she? ' she cackled after I had arrived with Eugene. He had gone off to his secret command bunker leaving her to entertain me. 'Fair fecks to her!'

'She did not,' I said. 'I decided tha' I'd let her cool her heels for a bit, tha's all.'

'She shoulda thrun ya out years ago – ya were never worth the space,' she said amiably. 'If I'd a married ya, I'd a killed ya on the weddin' night an' danced on yer grave every day since.'

'Yeah well,' I said, 'lucky tha' ya didn't then.'

'Lucky for you! I'd a smothered ya in yer sleep, or poisoned ya.'

I wasn't much enjoying this witty banter on the many and varied ways she would have done away with Frankie. The tea she had given me tasted funny. It smelled of Vim, Flash or other concoction guaranteed to eliminate all known germs. I put the cup aside as she continued her eulogy.

'I've known ya since ya were shittin' yella - ya were always a useless gobshite.'

'Thanks very much,' I said. 'If I ever need a reference I'll give ya a shout.'

'What'll we do if she comes here lookin' for ya? Do we tell her tha' we haven't seen ya, or fling ya out? Then yis can kiss an' make up.'

'I'd be all for feckin' ya out,' she answered her own question. 'Jus' for the laugh!'

She had a good cackle at that, delighted with herself. In fairness, I could see that there might be entertainment possibilities for the neutral observer, but I wanted to dampen down enthusiasm for cheap thrills at my expense.

'I can't see Peggy combin' the Daymo lookin' for me, but if she does, it might be better to say nothin'. She's not a great respecter o' private property when her dander is up,' I said.

She nodded her agreement. 'Wha' did ya do to upset her so much tha' ya have to go into hidin'?'

'It's nothin',' I said. 'Jus' a little misunderstandin'. I'll sort it out in a day or two.'

She looked at me, clearly requiring further and better particulars in return for lodging rights.

'Peggy thinks I'm after takin' up with another woman.'

Ma started to make a noise like an old-fashioned kettle boiling.

'*You*?!' she hooted. 'Wha' would *you* be doin' wi' another woman?'

She just about managed to get this out before being overcome by a series of shrieks, rattles and wheezes. Her face went the colour of a septic boil as she slapped her sides, apparently trying to beat discipline back into her body. She produced a hanky from her sleeve to staunch the flow of spit that was dribbling through the hairs on her chin.

'Jaysus,' she said, when she had regained some control,' tha's the best laugh I've had in years. Frankie Flynn with another woman!'

The thought set her off on another round of the spit and wheezing routine. I was already fed up with it and didn't see what was so funny. There were mangier specimens than me playing at away grounds - Joe Horgan for example.

'Who's it supposed to be anyway?' she managed to spit out one time she came up for air.

'Teresa Horgan,' I said.

This nearly killed her altogether. She was shrieking so much that a neighbour might have thought murder was being committed. But I figured that the neighbours were probably used to her.

'Ah no, stop, stop! Teresa Horgan! Why are ya botherin' wi' a little drink o' water like her? Ya want somethin' ya can get a hould of. Frankie, y'are some eejit…'

'I told ya … I didn't …'

'C'mere help me up outa this quick.' She was still struggling to get words out between the snorts and wheezes.

'Ah no, there's a bit after gettin' out! Look wha' y'are after causin'. C'mon, get a move on.'

I went over to where she was sitting and very reluctantly gave her my arm. She hauled herself up and leaned on my shoulder.

'This way,' she said. 'The jacks is out through here.'

I must have looked unenthusiastic about the mission because she added: 'Ya needn't worry. Jus' get me in there - I can wipe me own arse.'

Eugene reappeared at this point and assisted in the process of shoving his mother out into the hall and through the toilet door.

'Yis seem to be gettin' on well,' he said when she was safely installed. 'Sounds like yis were havin' great craic.'

'Yeah,' I said. 'Great craic altogether. Where the hell were *you* anyway?'

'I had to check in with the Unit. We've gone Code Amber on the visit.'

I must have looked blank.

'It means tha' we have to stay close - be ready for action stations at all times.'

'Jaysus,' I said. 'Wha' other codes are there?'

'Well, there's Turquoise. Tha' means tha' everythin' is grand.' An' there's Magenta.'

'Magenta!'

'Yeah. It's a sort o' rosy colour.'

'Is it?'

'Magenta means tha' there's a clear an' present danger.'

'Like in the fillum? Why don't yis jus' have green, orange an' red?'

'Nah. Too obvious.'

'I suppose y'are righ',' I said. 'No one's ever goin' to guess wha' turquoise, amber an' feckin' magenta mean.'

The clear and present danger that we faced at that moment was Eugene's Ma calling that she was finished and needed help.

'Frank!' she called. 'Frankie Flynn! Fire in the hole! C'mere Frank, I want ya.'

'Ah what's she callin' *me* for?' I asked Eugene.

'Ah y'are a novelty. Tha's all. She's fed up annoyin' me. Go on, she only wants a hand out of it.'

'Frankie!' she called. 'Will ya bring paper? There's no paper in here.'

I could hear her cackling like a huge steam-powered hen.

'Don't mind her. She's jus' gettin' it up for ya.'

'Jaysus!' I said wiping damp off my forehead. 'I haven't had enough drink this evenin' for this kind o' feckology!'

'FRANK!' she yelled. 'Have I to sit on this toilet all nigh'?'

The Flynns have done their bit down the generations. There were Flynns at Athlone and Wexford. There were Flynns on the barricades in 1916. But no Flynn sticking his head over the parapet felt more fear than I did as I eased open that lavatory door. I had only half an eye open for what sight might await me. To my relief she was leaning on the sink, properly dressed. She cackled again, delighted with herself.

'C'mere, gimme yer arm,' she said.

She latched onto me like a lioness onto a sick antelope's neck and we returned to the living room bouncing off walls and door frames as we came. Eugene was sitting reading something but I was too distracted to see if it was a file of state secrets or the Herald.

'Goodnigh' son,' Ma said. 'Me an' Frankie are goin' up to bed.'

She must have felt my arm trying to wrigglefree.

'Don't panic. Jus' get me up to me boudoir an' ya can feck off for yerself. Ya look too knackered to be of any use anyway. Tomorra nigh' maybe - we might give it a lash, eh – the two of us? Me a poor oul widda woman, an' you separated from yer wife. We might as well make the best of it, wha'?'

'Y'are very funny,' I said. 'Anyway, I might be gone by tomorra.'

I didn't expect to be reconciled to Mrs F that quickly but I hoped that I might find some billet other than this madhouse. I had had enough of Ma Larkin's wit and of the Falcon and his secret codes. I pushed her into her bedroom and retrieved what was left of my arm which had had all the blood squeezed out of it.

'Aren't ya goin' to tuck me in?' she asked. It was only the ancient chivalry of the Flynns that stopped me from saying something unbecoming. She kicked off her slippers in a coquettish manner, to reveal toe nails that a vulture would have been proud of. As she moved to unzip her skirt I ran for it.

Back downstairs I asked Eugene if he had a bottle of anything medicinal in the house. He had no whiskey but produced some hooch that he brought back from a foreign assignment, about which he could tell me nothing. It tasted like drain cleaner but did help to bring my heart rate down to a gentle canter. After a pint or so of it I was able to look life in the eye again without wanting to cry.

How many films have you seen where the hero is being chased by the bad guys and the good guys at the same time? He's usually a CIA agent that the Rooskies are trying to bump off because that's what they do, but so is the CIA because they think that he's done something iffy, but he hasn't. He's out on his own, battling everyone, relying on his own genius to beat the lot of them. Well that's exactly the way it was with me. If ever a man's cup had runneth over with bilge, that cup was mine. My motives and actions had been only of the noblest, and where had it got me? I was a hunted man, up the flipping creek without a paddle or even a spare pair of socks. A lesser mortal would have crumpled but the Flynns are men of steel. We take the cards dealt to us by Fate – even if Fate is dealing them off the bottom of the pack. We coolly assess what we have, we formulate our plans, and we act.

I needed a little time for Peggy to come off her war footing and to allow round table talks. I felt that I could persuade her that I was not the Casanova of the Northside. Restored to base I could then get back to the business of reconciling Joe and Teresa and getting Joe reinstated to the Golf Society committee. The fixture against Kinsella's was only weeks away, and the honour of Magowan's and of me personally were at stake. There was training to do, tactics to be developed and dirty tricks to be planned. And here was I trapped with James Bond and his mad mother.

I helped myself to a final dose of Eugene's drain cleaner. I bid him goodnight and retired to the spare bedroom, carefully wedging a chair under the handle in case Ma thought to amuse herself by inflicting some new terror on me in the night. I badly needed sleep – the stuff the poet Keats described as the soft closer of our eyes and the low murmurer of tender lullabies. Some other chap, whose name escapes me, spoke of it knitting up the ravelled sleeve of care. Anyway, they knew what they were talking about. Barricaded into Eugene's box room, and fortified with his booze, calm descended and optimism surged. I felt that shares in Flynn Enterprises might have been at rock bottom but the only way from there was up. I told myself that, rested and refreshed, I would line my problems up and knock them over like dominoes.

Well, I was wrong. Worse was to come.

Chapter 6

E ugene was up and off to HQ at some ridiculous hour when even the larks were pressing the snooze button. As he was not amongst those present, I had only Ma to provide light chat over the breakfast table. I hoped that she might have turned into a kinder old dear overnight, but she hadn't. Before I could even sit down, she was acting like a plantation owner who had conferred the favour of bringing me indoors for light household duties.

'Frank, is the tea not ready yet? ... what are ya doin'? ... I can't drink this! ... can ya not even make tea? ... an' where's me toast? ... I'm an old woman an' me days are numbered ... there's only so long I can wait for toast y'know.'

I fervently wanted to turn her into toast. A search of kitchen presses failed to turn up any rat poison, so I had to rely on the outside chance that she might choke. But it was not to be. I could have given her broken glass sandwiches and the old dinosaur wouldn't even have noticed.

'What're ya sittin' down for? There's me smalls in a basket in the corner o' me room. Put them in the washer will ya? An' ya needn't be sniffin' at them either. There was a thing in the Sunday paper abou' perverts doin' tha'. I don't want ya gettin' any cheap thrills in this house.'

I didn't dignify that with a response and just trudged off to find the basket of which she spoke. I dumped the contents into the washing machine like it was plutonium.

'Well, put powder in an' switch it on. It won't do itself! Number one. The boil wash.'

I twiddled some knobs and the thing came to life.

'I've a few other things tha' need doin',' she said.

'Well ya can get stuffed if ya think ...' I started.

'Don't *you* speak to me like tha',' she said. 'Y'are not so big tha' I couldn't reach up an' give a good slap, ya pup.'

By now I had had enough of Ma's caustic wit and was willing to risk everything to escape. Peggy's normal habits were well enough known to me that I could give her a wide berth. Dublin is not the biggest city on earth but it's big enough to steer clear of someone using basic fieldcraft. Before Ma could set me further chores, I bid her goodbye.

My destination and place of safety was the premises of J. P. Twomey, Turf Accountant. With Ma Larkin out of my face, my plans and stratagems presented themselves again for consideration. In my experience there is no better environment for sifting evidence and drawing conclusions than a bookies shop. As in a library, heads are lowered in study and people speak softly for fear of disrupting the mental processes. Indeed was it not in Twomey's that I had analysed the weights, pedigrees and trainers of the runners in the previous year's St Leger? And had I not picked the winner at sixteen to one? The animal crossed the finishing line doing cartwheels and was giving interviews before the second horse came into sight.

As a limbering up exercise I thought I would look through the day's runners and riders to see if there were any attractive investment opportunities. Thus absorbed, I did not notice Joe Horgan until he was within my personal space. He came bounding up like a spaniel to a dead duck.

'Ah, Joe,' I said – or something to that effect - wondering what had prised him from his transportation duties. 'Wha' has ya in here?'

'You, ya dirty little shit,' he responded.

You will have noticed an informality in the way Dubliners greet one another. This is normal, acceptable and part of the character and charm of the place. It is a matter of taste and skill to avoid going too far and causing offence. On this occasion, Joe had either got it badly wrong or there was something bugging him. I wasn't used to being addressed in this way (apart from by Peggy of course), and I needed further details before responding.

'Eh?' I asked.

'Don't you 'eh' me, ya back-stabbin' sleveen ghet. Y'are lower than a snake's belly, so y'are.'

This was useful insofar as it elaborated on Joe's strong feelings but the cause of his animus remained unclear. I thought of saying 'eh' again, but went for something more detailed that might get me to the heart of the matter.

'Is there somethin' wrong with ya?' I asked.

'Yeah, an' there'll be somethin' wrong with *you* when I'm done with ya.'

He illustrated what he had in mind by grabbing me by the shirt front and bouncing me off the wall. This caused a news-sheet setting out the day's racing at Dundalk to rip away from its moorings and flutter to the floor. J. P. Twomey employs minions to serve the punting public and one of these gave voice to advise on J. P.'s policy regarding brawling on the premises.

'Eh, lads,' he said. 'None o' tha' in here now.' Then in the spirit of 'going the extra mile' in customer service, for which Twomey's is renowned, he added: 'If yis want to bate the shite outa each other, yis'll have to go outside.'

Joe seemed to think that this was not an unreasonable request and tried to drag me towards the door. I preferred to stay in Twomey's and so benefit from their policy re violence. I locked my arms around a radiator pipe and planted myself in the manner of a mighty oak. Joe had a go at dislodging me but found it was impossible without ripping the radiator off the wall. This would have been frowned upon by the watching staff. Having achieved a stalemate I asked him again what had caused this schism between two pals of cradle days.

'I heard about you an' Teresa, ya louse,' he said.

'Eh?' I asked again, feeling that such a handy little word deserved a further outing.

'Have ya no decency in ya? I'm hardly gone an' y'are in there. Y'are disgustin'.'

I was going to quibble that philanderers in glass houses should not be throwing stones, but I was too agog at the import of what he was saying.

'Hang on,' I said. 'Me an' Teresa? What are ya talkin' about? Who told ya tha'?'

I expected that it must have been Peggy and thought that I could get him to see reason by showing him that his informant lacked objectivity, being generally bent on my ruin.

'Teresa did,' he said.

'Eh!' I said again. In fact, I may have ejaculated it.

'Stop sayin' 'eh'!' he said. 'I went aroun' to pick up some things an' she told me. She said tha' you an' her have been givin' one another the glad eye for years. Tha' ya couldn't wait to get yer paws on her. An' stop gawpin' at me with yer mouth open. Ya look like a letter box.'

Such was my nonplussedness that I had indeed been gawping. By a force of will I shut my mouth and started to babble.

'Tha's ridiculous!' I said. 'Teresa! Are ya mad?! I'm not Cary Grant, but I'm not desperate either.'

I could see immediately that I might have phrased this more tactfully. My aim was to convey that the chivalric code of the Flynns did not permit dallying with other men's wives. I did not wish to imply that Teresa was a gargoyle unlikely to attract the admiration of any male with sufficient eyesight to distinguish a bus from a bicycle. The inferred insult was that Joe had signed up with this creature, had begat three kids with her and, by implication, that his taste was up his arse.

Joe narrowed his eyes and took a step back in the manner of a chap about to take a swing at another chap. I babbled on, hoping that some random point might give him pause. For a start, I put it to him that by transferring his devotions to Celestina, he had compromised his position as Teresa's squire and champion.

'I mean Joe – feck it – ya took off wi' Semolina an' gave Teresa the bum's rush.' He was still in the strike position so I babbled on. 'An' if I was lookin' for a new suit, I wouldn't go for one tha' *you'd* been wearin' seven days a week for years, now would I?'

This didn't have the desired calming effect either.

'I'll wring yer bleedin' neck,' he said, making hand gestures demonstrating just how he would do it.

'Now lads, if yis don't give over, I'll have to call the Guards,' the Twomey operative stated from behind his bandit screen.

'Righ',' said Joe. 'I'm goin'. But listen to me Frankie Flynn. Ya better keep lookin' over yer shoulder, cos I haven't done with ya yet. Not by a long chalk.'

As he slammed the door behind him, I swallowed something that felt like a raw potato wrapped in sandpaper.

★★★

My planning session in Twomey's hadn't gone well. Joe's attempt to rearrange my body parts had been too great a distraction. I couldn't even give attention to the day's racing which normally has hypnotic power over me. Giving it up as a waste of time, and feeling that a new refuge was needed, I emerged furtively into the street. All my senses were on alert in case Joe was lurking in a doorway with a snooker ball in a sock. I looked. I listened. I even sniffed. The world appeared to be Joeless as well as free of Peggy and other predators. I slunk along Capel Street going I knew not where. My usual haunts were probably being staked out by the enemy and therefore too dangerous. I was like a piece of flotsam bobbing on life's ocean and barred from all friendly ports. As the poet

Davies might have put it: "What is this life if full of care, we can't go to Magowan's or even Kinsella's?" Feeling exposed on the main boulevard, I dropped into the warren of smaller byways around the fruit market.

The locals in that quarter are a unique subset of humanity. Their families have been supplying Dublin with fruit, veg and fish since the Vikings developed a taste for fish, chips and peas followed by apple pie. In more recent times they have developed lines in illegal cigarettes, fireworks and Christmas novelties. Keen inter-breeders, they never venture far from their neighbourhood, where the support of a cousin is never far away. A life in the open air has given them the complexions of mountain goats, while the need to promote their goods in a boisterous marketplace has developed in them the carrying voices of ship fog-horns. They are doughty negotiators and can pass off damaged fruit as perfect, or counterfeit goods as the real thing, with aplomb.

I found what I needed in the shape of a pub called the Nugget. Inside, the place was as dark as a confessional. There were windows, but if they had ever been cleaned it wasn't recently. Using instinct and experience more than sight, I made my way from the door to the bar. Half a dozen local men were leaning on it like cattle feeding from a trough. Each had an elbow on the counter, leaving the other arm free for pint manipulations. Their arses stuck out like protective bollards. They were giving their full attention to a horse race on the television and ignored my arrival. Three old biddies sat side-by-side at a table by the wall like an interviewing panel. They gave me the evil eye, obviously knowing that I was not a blood relative. I edged up to the bar but the arse formation wasn't yielding. Eventually, by hopping up and down, I caught the barman's eye.

'Yeah?' he asked. In that short syllable he managed to convey that he didn't like the look of me and would be happy if I would turn around and go away. I felt as welcome as a Shinner at an Orange picnic. I gave him my brightest and sunniest smile.

'A pint o' stout please. When y'are ready. No rush. Thanks very much,' I said.

He considered where he might find offence in my little speech, and looking disappointed that he could not, went to pour the pint.

The race on the telly ended. A man at the end of the cattle herd broke formation and turned to look at me. This wasn't the kind of furtive glance you might flick at a stranger. This was the full up and down suspicious appraisal of a cow protecting her calf from a possible predator.

'A grand day all the same,' I said, as the alternative 'Who the hell d'ya think y'are lookin' at?' didn't strike me as a great idea.

He didn't answer but continued to eye me like a cow considering a charge. He nudged the man next to him and the nudge rippled along the trough. They all slowly swivelled to join the first guy in giving me the once over. I admired the choreography of it. The first guy, who I took to have a leadership role, spoke.

'Wha's bleedin' grand about it?'

When he put it like that I could see that my airy description was hard to justify. The weather had been weaving like a drunk all day between sun and rain. It was impossible to identify the current status. The bit of daylight getting through the manky windows was the colour of a miner's phlegm. Anyway I guessed that this gent was not really interested in a meteorological conversation. The situation was the equivalent of Clint Eastwood entering a saloon and being met by Eli Wallach and associates – although Eli never brought the herd into the bar. I was afraid of spooking these guys and being flattened in a stampede.

I was rescued by our genial host returning with my pint. As I paid, I thanked him in terms that would have been overdoing it if he had saved the life of my only child.

'Ah tha's great,' I said. 'Thanks. Thanks. Sláinte. Good luck. Grand. Good man. Thanks.'

I took a slug. It was the worst pint I've had in a life during which I have suffered many bad ones. It was stale, flat and warm. Dishwater with a squirt of washing up liquid would have had more life in it and tasted better.

'Lovely,' I said appreciatively. 'A great pint, tha'. A great pint altogether. Gorgeous. Thanks.'

The barman seemed satisfied with the positive consumer review. He growled and sidled off, leaving me with Eli and his bovine buddies.

'Y'are not from aroun' here,' Eli said. I felt that he should have said 'from these here parts' but I didn't correct him.

'Ah no,' I said. 'The Daymo. I live in the Daymo.'

One of the others piped up: 'Wha'd bring a fecker from the Daymo in here?'

He seemed surprised and suspicious. I shared his feelings. What indeed would bring anybody into this dump? I could have tried to wring sympathy by providing them with details of the outrages which I had suffered - but I discarded the idea. I thought that a speech commencing: 'If you have tears, prepare to shed them now,' would likely be met with 'No, we haven't,' so I went with: 'Ah I was jus' passin'. I've seen this pub many's the time and I always thought I mus' come in sometime. Ya know the way it is?'

They didn't know. Heads were not nodding in understanding. I tried to list the attractions of the establishment to the discerning drinker. A marketing consultant would have had his work cut out, but I gave it my best shot.

'It's very handy an' accessible,' I said - meaning that it was on a street, and that it had a door so that you didn't have to enter via the chimney. A slight eyebrow movement from Eli encouraged me to believe that he had not fully considered this benefit before, so I pressed on.

'An' it's cosy … an' relaxed,' I said. I figured that rats and other vermin would probably find it so. After that I was stumped. I had another go at the foul-tasting pint. I detected notes of paraffin and old cheese that I had missed in my first sampling.

'The next time y'are passin',' Eli said … I waited for his warm invitation … 'keep goin'.'

The others laughed at his ready wit and I joined in respectfully.

'Ah well,' I said. 'It was nice, anyway, jus' the once…'

'Lovely of ya to drop in,' Eli said. 'Now rev up an' clear off.'

I downed the pint as fast as I could so that some of it trickled down under my shirt collar. I gagged on the last of it. Muttering an au revoir to my new friends, I thanked the barman again, and stumbled towards where I thought the door was. One of the three witches spoke as I went past.

'Y'are not goin' are ya?' she asked. 'Ah don't. Sure y'are great gas!'

I was relieved to escape, but my relief didn't last long. I was still a fugitive. I muttered to myself that even the foxes have their holes and the birds have their nests but I had bugger-all nowhere to hide. Inspired by these ecclesiastical thoughts, I ducked into St Mary of the Angels in Church Street which was to hand. It was doubtful whether St Mary or indeed the angels would look after me, but they were likely to be less belligerent than Eli et al.

I don't know if you've ever been inside a Dublin church outside the normal Sunday mass times? It was a new experience for me. Most good Irish Catholics limit their church attendance to the bare minimum of mass on a Sunday. The rule is that if you arrive before the Gospel and stay until the start of communion, you get the necessary heavenly credit. In my youth, men would venture no further than just inside the church door. Latecomers would find it impossible to get past the throng at the back, while the body of the church would be empty. At the Pro-Cathedral worshippers extended the church jurisdiction to the railings on the far side of the street, where they would peruse the Sunday papers during the less solemn bits.

To my surprise, the place was doing a roaring trade in the middle of a weekday. The faithful present consisted mostly of pensioners. I've noticed that people tend to get more religious when they realise that the meeting with their Maker is pencilled into His diary. They consider how the interview is going to go and start to sweat. Reviewing their stories so far they wonder how they are going to put a gloss on the murkier bits. Their lifelong strategy of bullshitting may not work with the All-seeing One. Just because the Lord once walked amongst us doesn't mean that He'll be impressed with: *'Ah ya know how it is yerself.'*

There was a lot of serious explaining and apologising going on, with enough candles burning to roast a hog. Eyes were closed tight as lips mumbled prayers learned in school. Rosary beads were clutched like lifebelts in a hurricane.

I shuffled into a pew beside an old crone. She had a head of curlers tied up in a scarf and was still wearing her slippers. She was obviously in such urgent need of repentance that she hadn't time to work up the effect a lady likes to achieve before presenting herself in public. I whacked my knee off the bench and muttered a little prayer of my own. The woman desisted from her chat with the Almighty long enough to give me an uncharitable look. If you could be damned with a glance then I was on my way to the fiery furnace. I shuffled up into her personal space just to annoy her, but half a second later was reversing away when I hit her BO force-field.

At least I felt safe. There was no chance of Eli and the lads coming to shoot the place up. Even if God – for a laugh - guided Peggy's or Joe's footsteps there, they wouldn't get physical on sacred turf. But while the calm was pleasant, I am a man of action and must be up and about my affairs. Also, the hard flat bench was disagreeing with my backside, which is neither flat nor hard. I got up to do a tour of the side altars and other attractions. Before getting far I was accosted by a finalist in the Uriah Heep lookalike competition. His coat had seen years of continuous service without troubling a dry cleaner. His hair was dirty and his skin a patchwork of grime. He ambled up to me deferentially.

'God bless ya sir!' As he whispered these words he bowed to me like I was royalty. I grunted an acknowledgement that was meant to convey: 'Hello. Now go away.' The subtlety of my response was wasted as he took it as an invitation to converse.

'St Anthony,' he said. 'I swear by St Anthony. He's yer only man. Anythin' ya want – ask St Anthony.'

'Is tha' a fact?' I asked, thinking that a bar of soap would be a good request.

'It is,' he said. 'There's others who are mad on St Jude or St Bridget, an' *she'll* have truck with no one bu' Laurence O'Toole.' He pointed at the curlers and slippers lady. 'The best o' luck to them, I say, bu' I never look any further than St Anthony.'

I tried to get past him but I couldn't.

'So whatever ya need, go no further than St Anthony.'

'Thanks, I'll do tha',' I said. I was going to ask for his name so that I could tell St Anthony who had recommended him, but before I could he continued.

'I was jus' prayin' to him now – askin' him for a bit o' help like – an' I opened me eyes an' there ya were. It was like a miracle! I gave him thanks, I don't mind tellin' ya.'

'Wha' did ya thank him for?' I asked, suspicion growing in me like a balloon.

'For sendin' ya.'

'For sendin' *me*? St Anthony sent *me*?' I asked.

'He did. God bless him!'

I had had no instructions from St Anthony or anyone else but decided that I'd better go along with this lunatic in case he was in possession of a weapon.

'An' wha' did he send me for?' I asked, fearing that I knew the answer.

'God bless ya for askin' sir,' he said. 'God bless ya. Oh I'm terrible afflicted, so I am. I've had no luck all me life. I was given up by me mother an' raised in an orphanage. An' when I was sixteen the nuns put me out with only the clothes I was stood up in.'

I was as one with his mother and the nuns as it was also my intention to get rid of him at the first opportunity.

'An' I've suffered all me life wi' me back. Oh somethin' desperate! So I could never hold down a job - though I tried - God knows I tried.' He drew closer to me, so that I got the full benefit of his personal magnetism. 'An' do ya know wha' I'm goin' to tell ya? I haven't got tuppence in me pocket at this minute. Not tuppence!' He made it sound like an achievement. Before I could come up with a response, he continued in a confidential whisper. 'So, if ya could spare me anythin' at all sir – anythin' at all - I could get somethin' to eat up in the Richmond.'

'Sorry,' I said, abandoning my church tour and heading for the door. 'I'm short meself today.'

He followed me into the porch, his voice rising as we got closer to the noise of the street.

'Even a few coppers?' he tried.

''fraid not,' I said trying to shake him off, but he was following me like a guided missile.

'An' me after tellin' ya me life story!' he said. 'Ya have to give me somethin'!'

At this point we had fully emerged onto the pavement. He wasn't going to give up the chase and got fully in my way as I tried to make a break for it. I loudly told him to bugger off and gave him a gentle push to assist him in doing so. I may have thrown in some juicy remarks about his general appearance, about him being a pain and a nuisance, and maybe even about St Anthony. He took it all in his annoying Heepish way and tried to mooch his head onto my shoulder. This did not make me warm to him and I gave him another push to maintain a distance. He made whinging noises like a cat with a cold. A crowd of devout ladies had gathered without me noticing.

'For St Anthony,' he pleaded as he tried again to get close to me.

'Feck you an' St Anthony,' I replied pushing him off with a good shove. He tottered backwards and landed on his arse.

'Tha's a disgrace,' I heard a voice say, followed by a chorus of agreement.

'Ah, the poor divil! God help him!' said another. The poor divil sniffled as he realised that he had a sympathetic audience. He stayed on the ground making the cat noises and producing a very pathetic overall effect.

'Ya should be ashamed o' yerself,' an oul wan with a face like a boxer said.

Laid on top of all my other troubles, the injustice of being castigated by this mob weighed on me like the proverbial final straw. I lashed out.

'Feck off the lot o' yis - an' mind yis're own business, yis malignant oul cows,' I said. Even as I spoke I thought I might be overdoing it.

'Did ya hear tha'? Did ya hear wha' he said? he bloody cheek o' him.'

There was general assent that they had all indeed heard me.

'An' outside a church!'

There was also consensus that this did indeed make my offence all the more heinous. One or two blessed themselves.

'I only asked him for the price of a cuppa tea,' whined the St Anthony devotee. 'Then he insulted me. An' he hit me!'

He gave a few more sniffles.

'Ah, God love him,' said the boxer. 'Give him somethin',' she said to me. It was more an instruction than a suggestion.

If you have a picture in your mind of me surrounded by a few frail old ladies in shawls, replace it with a pack of yellow-eyed she-wolves, foaming at the mouth, ready, willing and able to tear me limb from limb.

'I've no change,' I said, pulling out my wallet and showing that only notes were present. This was a school-boy error.

'That'll do,' said one.

I reluctantly pulled out a five euro note.

'Wha's he goin' to get for five euros in this day an' age, ya miserable bastard?' one asked.

There was a chorus of agreement that more was needed. Twenty was proposed, and after a short debate - in which I was not invited to participate – the proposal was carried by acclaim. I quickly handed over a crisp blue note before there was a higher bid.

'Thanks very much,' the recipient said, jumping to his feet in a manner which suggested that St Anthony had worked a miracle on his back. 'God bless ya. I'll be able to get meself somethin' nice t'eat for me tea.'

'I hope it chokes ya,' I whispered to him out well of earshot of the rabble.

Chapter 7

Exhausted by the dangers lurking around every street corner, and having failed to find any alternative, I slunk back to the Larkins. Eugene had not yet returned from his espionaging so I was left to the mercy of Ma's hospitality. I must have been wearing my cares on my sleeve because she felt moved to comment on them.

'Wha's wrong wi' ya?' she asked. 'Ya look like a snake with a sore throat.'

'It's not jus' Peggy tha's gunnin' for me,' I told her. 'Joe Horgan heard the shite about me an' Teresa an' he wants to kill me as well.'

She laughed.

'Don't mind him,' she said. 'He's only a gobshite.'

'Tha's not much comfort to me,' I said. 'Wha' difference does it make whether I'm murdered by a genius or a gobshite? I can't even have a pint in peace without worryin' tha' he's goin' to come in an' mash me into the carpet.'

'Did ya try explainin' to him tha' it's a load o' nonsense?'

'I did. But he was squeezin' me windpipe at the time so it was hard to get the message across.'

Ma made a sympathetic noise like a clucking hen.

'An' there's the golf match with Kinsella's comin' up, an' I can't even attend the committee meetin's. There are important decisions to be made. God only knows wha' tha' shower'll do without me. Apart from Eugene, o' course,' I added, catching her eye. 'Eugene'll be grand.'

'Y'are in it up to yer leeroadies righ' enough,' she laughed. 'I'll tell ya wha'. I'll look into me crystal ball an' see if I can come up with somethin'.'

'Would ya?' I asked and I was genuinely hopeful that she might.

It might seem strange that I would look to this old witch as a counsellor but she could be very resourceful when put to it. I remember the time she rescued my mother from a looming disaster with the Department of Social Welfare. My Ma was claiming sickness benefit while she was working as a cleaner. This was due to a simple misunderstanding in that my Ma thought that there was no way the Department could find out.

Ma Larkin went with her to a hearing in the Custom House. It transpired that a Social Welfare official – a Mr Bolger – had been following my Ma around. He had more information on her movements than my Da ever had. He had times and dates of when he had seen her letting herself into the premises of Kirwan and Associates, equipped to clean. She had resigned herself to having the proverbial book thrown at her but Ma had other ideas. In a performance of which Rumpole would have been proud, she suggested mistaken identity. When Mr Bolger said that this was impossible, she cast doubt on his powers of sight, pointing out that the alleged offences were committed during the hours of darkness, and that he relied on glasses. She further subtly suggested that his damaged eyesight may have been caused by a cocktail of venereal diseases. Without directly accusing him, she suggested that he was well-known to ladies who sold their warmth and affection in the Grand Canal area. She pointed to his admitted enthusiasm for following women around after dark.

Mr Bolger had arrived at the hearing in a relaxed and confident mood. As far as he was concerned, this was an open and shut case. He was not at all ready to defend himself from attack. We later learned that he and the presiding official - a Mr Finnerty - were not mutual admirers. Mr Bolger thought that the senior man was a pompous, conceited fool, promoted above his abilities. Finnerty's view of Bolger was that he was a disrespectful upstart who needed to be kept in his place. Ma's outrageous attack on Bolger delighted Finnerty. In response to Bolger's spluttered denials, he said:

'These are most serious charges Mrs Larkin. We shall have to reconvene the hearing to allow more time to consider all the matters in proper detail.'

There was never a reconvened hearing and my Ma never heard any more about it. In my view, a woman who could snatch victory from the jaws of certain defeat like that was a woman you wanted on your team.

'I find it easier to think when I'm relaxed,' she said. 'Ya wouldn't run me a bath like a good man would ya? Put in some o' me salts. A couple o' scoops o' the stuff outa the box on the winda.'

I went as instructed, and had the bath running and the powder sprinkled in no time.

'Fillin' up now,' I reported back.

'Did ya put in me rubber mat so's I don't slip?'

I went back and slung in the mat.

'An' will ya get out one o' the big towels for me?'

I confirmed that I would, and I did.

'An' put a smaller one on the floor for me feet.'

I went back and laid out the small towel as instructed.

'An' will ya bring in a chair for me to sit on?'

The chivalry of the Flynns was being stress-tested but I managed not to say anything indecorous. I installed a chair.

'All is now ready an' waitin' Ma'am,' I said.

'Ah, tha's great,' she said.' 'Y'are a treasure. C'mere an' gimme a hand.'

We crashed into the bathroom with her using me as a human zimmer frame.

'If I sit on the chair here an' lean back into the sink ya can wash me hair,' she said.

'Ah c'mon now,' I said, feeling that lines were being crossed.

'It'll only take ya a minute.'

It took ten minutes. I was going down for the third time when she announced that the washing and rinsing procedure was ended and I could be dismissed. When I emerged I was wetter than the time I fell into the canal. I needed fortifying before I could contemplate the probable horrors in Ma's post bathing routine. I had just got the top off Eugene's hooch bottle when her high-pitched screech acted on me like mains electricity.

'Frankie!'

'Wha'?' I replied and if I sounded testy it was because I was.

'I've got an idea. C'mere.'

I went back to the bathroom with one eye open an eighth. Christians went into the Coliseum with lighter hearts. Thankfully the combination of powdery stuff and dirt was doing a good job in obscuring her essentials.

'Shut the door. There's a draught.'

I closed it reluctantly, but stayed close to it.

'I'm not scrubbin' yer back,' I said.

'Did I ask ya?' she spat back.

'I don't know where the soap is. Have a root aroun' an' find it for me.'

I must have looked alarmed because she continued:

'Not in the bath y'eejit. It's prob'ly over by the sink.'

I found the soap, handed it over and retreated to the door.

'Ya said ya have an idea,' I said.

'I have,' she said. 'Now tha' Joe's in love, the only one he'll listen to is the quare wan.'

'Celestina?'

'No – his Aunt Fanny! O' course Celestina, if tha's her name. Get *her* to tell him tha' y'are the best pal he's ever had – his only one prob'ly, the poor bastard! She can tell him tha' the bonds o' friendship are too strong for ya to be tryin' to get the drawers off his skinny little missus. A few o' the righ' words from her an' he'll leave ya alone. Until the next time ya do somethin' stupid anyway.'

I could see wisdom in her plan although delicacy would be needed. Certainly if he was going to listen to anyone, it would be Celestina. I gave the idea's tyres a few kicks and they seemed to be sound. A glow of optimism began to thaw the nuclear winter of my outlook. If Joe stopped pursuing me like the posse after Butch Cassidy, I could give my full attention to the golf. A reformed Joe, made to see sense, might even help to get me clemency and a full pardon from Peggy. My motto is that the darkest hour is just before the dawn, and I could just see the sun peeping over the horizon.

A string of bubbles rippled from the bathwater like celebratory champagne. Ma cackled and I joined in benevolently. A woman who could produce rescue schemes like hers could fart away to her heart's content with my blessing.

'It could work,' I said. 'I think it *will* work.'

'O' course it'll work. Men are thick. Ya can always get them to do wha' ya want through their bellies or their willies. Gluttony and lust – there's nothin' more to them than tha'.'

Feeling magnanimous I was not inclined to argue. Men – apart from Barney Pugh – are more complex than that, but I let it pass. My brain was already busy planning how I was going to tackle the course. It refused at the first fence.

'How am I goin' to get at Celestina?' I asked. 'I can't jus' go waltzin' up to the door. If Joe is there he'll have me gutted an' filleted before I can say howya.'

She sighed like a great Roman general needing to explain strategy to an enlisted spear-carrier.

'Well ya'll have to go an' see her somewhere else then, won't ya?'

I mused on the concept of 'somewhere else', shoving my eyebrows together in thought. In fact I gave them a good squeeze like I was wringing out a wet cloth, but nothing suggested itself. The words 'somewhere' and 'else' formed and reformed in my brain like coloured blobs in a lava lamp, but I got no further.

'Maybe the golf place where she works,' suggested Ma.

'How'm I goin' to get there?' I asked. 'It's out in the middle o' nowhere, an' I've no car.'

'Can't ya get a taxi?'

'A taxi?' I asked.' Do ya think I'm made o' money? Anyway, with my luck Joe'd be drivin' it.'

'Well I can do no more for ya,' she said. 'Anyways wha' are ya doin' hangin' aroun' in here for? Have ya no daecency. I suppose y'are waitin' for me to get up so's ya can get a good eyeful?'

I leapt through the door like a salmon and I can't remember if I opened it first.

★★★

I shared the problem later with Eugene. As I was effectively confined to barracks, I was pacing up and down on his carpet. He watched my movements like he was at a slow-motion tennis match.

'Ya could always get her at the Reception,' he said.

I raised an enquiring eyebrow.

'The Reception in the Four Provinces Hotel tomorrow. She'll be at it.'

I raised the other eyebrow so that all my eyebrow resources were fully deployed. With his training in codes and signals he understood that what I wanted was further detail.

'It's in Ballsbridge,' he said.

'I know tha',' I said. 'But wha's this Reception, and wha's Celestina doin' at it?'

'Ah,' the Falcon was now on the case. 'It's for the Narusian President. He's goin' to meet a gang o' people. The Minister for Foreign Affairs will be there with some Irish exporters – the lads who sell cheese an' stuff to Narusia. They're mad about Irish cheese over there. An' there'll be a few from the Irish Narusian community. They can chat to their great leader about how things are back in the home place while the Irish lads get stuck into the free bar. It'll be jus' a few specially invited Narusians wi' the situation the way it is in Narusia.'

'There's a situation?'

'There's always a situation. The north Narusians don't get on with the southerners. There was a kind of a massacre back in the nineteenth century and it still rankles. The south lads grabbed all the guns an' they decided it'd be a shame not to use them while they had them. Most o' the northerners have forgotten an' forgiven. These things happen in history. They know tha' in all fairness, if they'd had the guns, they'd a done the same thing. But there's a few diehards who sing the old songs an' nurse the old grievances. Ya know how it is.'

I nodded that I did. We Irish also like to cherish our old grievances.

'Somebody took a pot shot at the President last month. They missed but the word is that they might have another go at him in Dublin.'

'On the basis tha' we don't mind tha' class o' thing?'

'On the basis tha' they think tha' security might be lighter here. They won't know tha' the Unit has been assigned to the man's protection.'

'They'd shit themselves if they knew tha'.'

'Feck off. We'll be low key, but we'll be ready.'

'An' how is it tha' yer wan is gettin' into the gig?' I asked.

'I invited her.'

If I had had a third eyebrow I would have run it up the flagpole to join the other two.

'Ya invited her? For wha'?'

'Tha' time I was talkin' to her in the golf club. She told me where she was from an' I mentioned the Reception. She said she was a big fan o' the President an' I said I could get her in.'

'Ya were doin' the big fella.'

'I was jus' talkin' to the girl, tha's all.'

'I know wha' ya were up to ya dirty ghet, bu' Joe Horgan wiped yer eye for ya.'

'Tha' as maybe. Anyway I got her added to the guest list. Tha's all.'

'Can ya add me on as well?'

'Too late oul scout. It's all done an' dusted. Copies o' the list signed, sealed an' lodged with the Guards, the Department, the Awras, an' the Unit. No chance o' makin' any changes. I couldn't get Jesus in if he promised to make me an apostle.'

'Well, wha' use is it to me then?'

'Use yer head. It's a public place isn't it? Jus' sit in the lobby an' nab her when she shows up.'

It sounded simple but the fact is that I am uncomfortable in fancy surroundings. I always expect an under-manager to pop up and tell me to clear off. I tried to train myself out of the feeling by occasionally dropping into the Gresham or the

Shelburne for a shite. The staff were always the height of politeness, holding doors open for me and wishing me 'good morning sir'. The guy in the loo even used to brush my collar. Nobody ever tried to throw me out but I still never felt at home. It's hard to shake off centuries of oppression when the plain people were trampled on by the aristocracy.

★★★

When I had left home two days before I was planning only a fleeting visit to Teresa. I hadn't packed for an extended absence and by day three the clothes I was stood up in could have stood up on their own. I couldn't present myself at the Four Provinces looking like a pig farmer who had let even pig farmer standards slip, so in the morning I headed for the shops.

The Flynn tailoring arrangements are normally commissioned through Peggy. I outline my requirements or she notices losses and impairments in the course of her laundering duties. Then, acting as my agent she proceeds with full authority to acquire whatever is required. These needs are usually limited to socks, jocks and maybe a shirt. My outer wear is made up of vintage items which improve with age and rarely need replacing. But now I was in uncharted waters without even a boat. I needed a full ensemble from hat to boots and had no clear idea where to get it. The retailing maze that is the centre of Dublin is a closed book to me. Peggy has devoted herself to mastering its intricacies and can hold forth for hours on the relative merits of Dunnes versus Penneys. For me it is a hazardous river with occasional stepping stones which the wary traveller can use to cross. These stepping stones are the public houses with which I have made myself familiar for such emergency uses.

I considered asking Ma Larkin for advice but I guessed that she hadn't bought clothes since bustles were fashionable. Even if she knew, she would delight in sending me astray. The only thing to do was to fling myself in at the deep end. Therefore at the crack of ten I found myself proceeding along

Henry Street looking for clues as to which shop might trade in gentlemen's trouserings and associated items.

Arnott's window provided a clue. Mannequins were modelling the correct use, not only of trousers, but also of shirts, jackets and shoes. Large banners proclaimed that a sale was on and that many prices were reduced by fifty per cent. The clear suggestion was that the management had lost its reason and that only a fool would fail to take advantage. I am not a fool and was through the door before the men in white coats arrived to restore sanity.

The problem with such emporia is the infinity of the product range. In a public house your choice can be made and the business transacted before you even sit down. Pints and other options are provided in only a few standard measures. The variety and quantity required can be conveyed in monosyllables or even in basic sign language.

Arnott's Men's Department was the size of Belgium. There were whole provinces given over to shirts, swim wear and underwear. Trousers came in different cloths, colours, patterns, cuts, styles, and in every conceivable combination of waist and leg measurement. I have never seen men shaped like some of the combinations on offer and I have seen them all in Magowan's. Stringy McMahon is built like a mile of bad road while Two Dinners Holden once had to have the Fire Brigade to get him out of his bath. A sign for Sports Wear helped to narrow the field. If I had to invest in extra clothes I figured I could kill two birds by going for something in the golfing line.

I was rummaging along a rail of sale items when I was approached by an assistant. His name tag proclaimed him to be Kevin. He looked like he was working in Arnott's while waiting for his call up to the Corps de Ballet.

'Can I help you sir?' he asked.

'Yeah,' I said. 'I need a few bits an' pieces. Wha' size are these things?'

'Do you know your measurements, sir?' he asked.

I didn't. He pranced up and executed what is called a demi detourné in ballet circles. Using a tape measure with practiced assurance he manoeuvred me into various positions to establish the thickness of my neck, the circumference of my waist, and the shortest distance from my ankle to where the light disappears.

'This section here sir,' he said, drawing me to a place where the trousers were more generously waisted than the ones I had been perusing. But I was getting somewhere. The field was being narrowed although there was still too much choice. Golf gear tends to the gaudy but I am fortunate in being able to look good in anything. Price was going to be my deciding factor. With a speed that Kevin will have admired in allegro movements, I made my selection of trousers, shirts and a couple of pullovers. The shoes I was wearing would have to do as there was nothing in my size in the sales category.

Kevin looked like he might execute an échappé sauté in his excitement, but beat back the urge. Arnott's train them in self-restraint. He looked at me in clear admiration.

'Would you like to try them on sir?' he asked.

'They'll be grand,' I said. 'Bu' I want to change into these ones.' I picked a trouser, shirt and pullover combination which I thought had a pleasing complementarity.

'You're going to wear them now?' he asked.

'Yeah,' I said. 'Is tha' alrigh'?' – knowing full well that in Kevin's world the customer is always right.

'Yes, of course,' he said. 'The changing room is this way.'

He pirouetted and led me to the cubicles.

The trousers were a cream and red creation with the kind of stripey pattern normally found in top quality carpet. They nicely matched the shirt which also came in stripes – this time in a cheerful yellow and bluey blue. The trouser stripes went north south and the shirt went east west which was fortunate as I didn't want to look like a pedestrian crossing. The pullover was a V-neck in a tinned salmon pink.

The changing booth's mirror revealed an overall effect which was more than satisfactory. My old shoes looked out of place but I solved the problem by shuffling closer to the mirror where I couldn't see them. And the price was right. I was almost sorry that Peggy wasn't there to bear witness. It would have taken her a day to achieve what I had managed in minutes.

When I left the cubicle Kevin was standing in first position at the cash desk. Seeing me in my new finery he did a thing with his tongue like you do after licking a battery. A number of colleagues from the Arnott's troupe had joined him. They seemed to have nothing better to do than stand in a chorus line.

'Is everything satisfactory sir?' Kevin asked me.

'Everythin's grand,' I assured him.

'Very nice on you sir,' one of the colleagues offered.

'Thanks very much,' I said. 'It's not wha' I'd normally go for, but at these prices, eh?'

'Absolutely!' he agreed. 'There's nothing else you need, sir? Maybe a nice summer hat? A boater maybe?'

One of the others seemed to be choking on something. He excused himself and disappeared behind a rail of football shirts.

'Ah no, thanks,' I said. 'I've got more caps at home than I know what to do with. But, c'mere, I migh' take one o' them big umbrellas, if they're in the sale.'

An umbrella is often a handy thing to have in Ireland although I had never actually bought one before. My practice when it rains is to go into the nearest pub and ask if anyone has handed in a black umbrella. More often than not they have.

The chorus line confirmed that some golf umbrellas were indeed in the sale, and enthusiastically debated which one would go best with my outfit. I put the chosen one under my arm and picked up the bag holding the rest of my purchases and my old clothes.

'You're all set so!' Kevin said. He escorted me all the way to the street door, which was just as well as I would have struggled to find it. Holding it open, he gave me a final appraisal in the natural light.

'Very striking,' he said. 'Ask for me if there's anything at all you need in the future,' he said, and I promised that I would. You just don't get service like that anymore.

★★★

I got the bus over to Ballsbridge. As I was paying the fare, the driver asked me: 'Off to a funeral, are ya?'

Obviously the smart bastard was referring to the relative cheerfulness of my outfit.

'No,' I said. 'I'd only wear these to a funeral if it was yours.'

As I made my way up the stairs, he went onto his public address system.

'Dis is a health an' safety announcement. Passengers on de upper deck might wish to put on dayre sun-glasses to avoid damage to dayre eyesigh'.'

As I appeared at the top of the stairs I got a cheer and a round of applause. There was a cacophony of: 'Mother o' God!' 'Wha' in the name o'...' followed by a rendition of *Joseph and his Coat of Many Colours*.

'Alrigh'! Alrigh'!' I said. 'Yis're all very funny. Leave it alone now an' feck off for yerselves, ya shower o' shites.'

Needless to say they didn't. Dubliners don't need an excuse to take the piss. They are permanently primed for opportunities to make the smart remark. The bus people had hit the mother lode and they were going to make the most of it.

'Could ya tell me when we get to Stephen's Green – I'm after bein' struck blind.'

'Sorry pal – I'm speechless,' his pal spluttered, feigning a struggle to talk.

'Ah will yis leave the poor fella alone,' said a woman. 'He's after cheerin' me up. He's like a little rainbow.'

'Jaysus, maybe there's a pot o' gold! Hey mister, will ya stand up so's we can have a look under yer arse?'

'Did yis see the shoes?'

Necks were craned to examine my footwear.

'Jaysus! They musta run outa pixie boots in fairy land.'

I got off the bus before my stop as the driver was now leading the singing. *'He looks handsome … he looks smart … he's a walkin' work of art … in his coat of many colours …'* If I was to give him his due, but I wasn't going to, I'd say that his voice wasn't bad.

'Y'ave a voice that'd curdle diesel,' I said to him as I left. 'It's a wonder yer engine doesn't seize up.'

He just gave me a friendly toot and led a cheer as the bus pulled away. The passengers on my side all waved and I waved back in the Churchillian manner.

★★★

I got to the Four Provinces in plenty of time for the reception with the Narusian President. The foyer was full of well-stuffed Yanks manoeuvring around one another like bumper cars. Darting in amongst them were tourists of other persuasions and members of the south Dublin business mafia.

The counter staff had undergone the lobotomising that is needed to ensure the corporate standard of service. If you insulted their mothers and their mothers' mothers they would have thanked you and kept smiling. The porters were a different kettle of fish. They were doing the job, but on their own terms. They would take no more bullshit than would be justified by a hefty tip. When called upon to perform a task they did it – eventually. After finishing chatting with their mates they would stroll over to the lucky service recipient, every inch the equal. 'Now sir, gimme tha' bag … it's no problem at all …where are ya in from? … good man.' Then over the shoulder: 'I'll be back in a minute; I want to hear the end o' tha' story.'

Planted on a fancy sofa near the revolving doors, I was well placed to spot Celestina whenever she might arrive. My plan was to nab her and appeal to her better nature, hoping that she would want to stop me being turned into mince. If that didn't work, I was going to tell her that I had left a letter fingering Joe as the culprit in the event of my premature demise. I hoped that she would not want her future dealings with him to be through iron bars.

'Hiya buddy!'

A Yank with the dimensions of a box van lowered himself onto the sofa next to me. I grunted a reply that was meant to convey that I did not regard myself as his buddy, and that if he was to go away that would be fine with me.

'You taking this goddamn tour?' he asked. 'I didn't wanna, but my wife said 'Hell Bob, whadaya gonna do all day?' and I said 'Jus' lemme alone can't ya? What the hell do I want to go on another bus for? It just rains alla time in this goddam country. And there's never anywhere to pee.'

My heart softened slightly. I knew what it was to be under the spousal lash.

'I said I'd take a bath and a snooze, and she said 'We come all the way from Minnesota to Ireland so's you can take a bath?' Jeez!'

I gave him an understanding nod.

'Anyway, ain't we seen it all already? The GPO, the jail where the Brits shot those guys, the statue of Daniel O'Donnell... Say, have you just arrived? I haven't seen you with the group before.'

I started to say that I had indeed just arrived, but pulled up as I realised that for some reason he thought I was from his neck of the woods. Some instinct told me that it might be in my interests to go along with this. Fortunately I am known and admired in Magowan's for my skills as an impressionist. Drawing from my repertoire I gave him a bit of my Jimmy Stewart.

'Waaall,' I said. 'I guess you could say I've just arrived, yaaas. I got in from JFK on the red eye this morning. Me and my wife Murray.' Jimmy pronounced Mary 'Murray' when he was married to Donna Reed in It's a Wonderful Life.

He looked at me with a new interest.

'I don't suppose you know how the Vikings did?' he asked.

I guessed that he was referring to some sporting contest, but as I didn't know whether the Vikings competed in football, baseball or tiddly winks, I shook my head.

'Goddamn papers here are full of crap,' he told me.

'Yaaas,' I said agreeing with him. The most interesting part of any Irish newspaper is the deaths. The rest is just guff about politicians on the make, gangsters shooting each other, and celebrities I've never heard of doing nothing. If the gangsters would shoot the politicians and the celebrities, that would be worth reading.

'You from Noo Yawk?' he asked.

I didn't know where Jimmy's accent was from, so I settled for 'waaall, a few miles outside', which seemed to satisfy him.

While we were hobnobbing, I had neglected my mission to waylay Celestina and I hadn't been watching the door with the required concentration. I was only reminded by the sight of flashing blue lights outside, as a Garda motorcycle escort shepherded the Narusian President's limo up to the hotel's door. The car came to a halt and a couple of simians in bulging suits jumped out. They had curly wires going into their ears, and the anxious air I have only seen before in men who have arrived in Magowan's at last orders. They cleared the few feet of space between the car and hotel door, combing it for signs of assassins. When they were sure that there was nobody dodgy around – or at least as sure as you could be in Dublin - they opened the car door and made a two-man cocoon to usher the leader inside.

From what I could see, he was a weedy little scut with a tiny beard, about the size of a pocket in a thong. If I'd been talking to him, I'd have told him that he had missed a bit. He was moved through the hotel guests like the ball in a rugby scrum. When they reached a double-door marked 'Munster Suite', the gorillas shoved him through it like they were posting a parcel. Before the door closed I could hear a voice inside announcing the presidential arrival, followed by applause.

I suspected that Celestina must have slipped in while I was talking with the Yank. I didn't fancy hanging around until the shindig was finished so that I might grab her on the way out. It was also the case that I hadn't eaten a thing since breakfast. I'm not a regular attendee at receptions but I was sure that you can't have one without free food. Breaking away from the Yank saying that I needed to talk to Murray, I went to reconnoitre.

The President's men at the Munster Room doors displayed an attitude that said that anyone getting past them would do so over only their cold dead stiffs. They didn't look like the sort that might be susceptible to bullshit so I sidled past. Circling the perimeter of the Munster enclosure I found myself in a corridor around the back which was being used by serving staff to ferry food and drink into the reception. This was based on my observation of them disappearing with full trays through a door marked 'staff only' and returning empty-handed. This door showed no sign of men in suits but who knew what might be lurking on the other side? I walked past several times trying to get a glimpse inside. As well as being keen on fulfilling my mission, I was as hungry as a bear just woken after a long winter to find the cupboard empty. Salivating like Pavlov's pooch, I agonised over whether I should just dive into the room and risk it. I find that the more I hesitate over such things the harder it gets to make up my mind. Like that guy Hamlet said in the play 'the native hue of resolution is sicklied o'er with the pale cast of thought'. My resolution was pig-sicklied over with thoughts.

While I dithered, the waitering traffic dried up and I was left with the corridor to myself. I could hear nothing from inside the room as the walls were made from better stuff than whatever the Daymo is made from. At home, if I sneeze in bed the woman three doors down blesses me. But in the final analysis I am nothing if not a man of action. My motto is that an ounce of action is worth a ton of thinking. So I said 'feck it' and dived through the door. When I say 'dived' I mean that literally. I was expecting the door to need a good shove so that's what I gave it. But the thing turned out to be moored on light springs to allow it to flap backwards and forwards to facilitate heavily burdened waiters. At my first touch it flew away from me and crashed against a wall.

The momentum caused me to explode into the room like a cork from a bottle. El Presidente was in full speechmaking mode and I just caught a complimentary remark about the quality of Irish cheese. He was cut off by a sudden shortness of breath caused by me hitting him hard and square in the small of the back. Unfortunately the door was right behind where he was speaking and there was nowhere else for me to go. The audience was gathered around him in a respectful silence to hear his views on cheese, but the silence didn't last. The room erupted into gasps as the two of us hit the deck. He was back on his feet in a second but had lost his glasses. Like a drunk playing blind man's bluff he was jumping around swinging his arms like a windmill. I got to my feet embarrassed and keen to explain. Before I could, one of his swinging arms whacked me in the gob.

I don't know about you, but I react badly when I am whacked in the gob. I don't sit back and ask myself why the whacker did it, whether it was justified or whether it might be counter-productive to whack him back. The Flynns are hardwired to respond immediately. After shaking my head to check that all my teeth were still properly anchored, I clattered the President with a ripe one to the side of his head.

Incidents like this rarely take long but so much happens that the brain skips along like a squirrel through treetops. I was still giving most of my attention to the President who was on the floor snapping around my ankles. From the corner of my eye I could see two bulging suits trying to get through the mob to rescue their man. They were impeded by the keen Irish sporting crowd who were enjoying the fight. The locals weren't going to give up their vantage points easily. Anyway, they had glasses of wine and neither earthquake nor nuclear attack is likely to cause a Dubliner in possession of free alcohol to spill it. So a mere pair of onrushing quarterbacks would be no more troubling to them than a light breeze.

I bent down to push the annoying dignitary away from me so that I could better take stock of the situation. While down there I tried to gather up my belongings which had rolled away from me in the melee. They included my umbrella which Kevin had kindly wrapped for me.

'Look out,' some idiot screamed. 'He's got a gun.'

I laughed and the screamer did too. We both knew that he was just taking the piss. I figured that everyone would know that. I jumped up and waved the umbrella at the crowd and I may have said 'Ya feelin' lucky, punks, huh?' It was like Moses parting the Red Sea. As I swung the umbrella around they all dived for cover. There was a crash as glasses hit the floor. This told me that the idiots seriously thought that I had a gun.

'Ah, look!' I said, trying to show them that it was just an umbrella in Arnott's wrapping. This seemed to only make it worse but before I could explain further the President grabbed me by an ankle. I took to kicking him with my free foot to discourage his attentions, but this proved to be a mistake. Kicking with one foot made me completely dependent on the other to maintain my vertical status. Therefore the President could focus on this relatively weak point – my Achilles heel, so to speak. Showing more pluck than I would have given him credit for, he stuck to his task, eventually giving my ankle a good lug so that I came down like the mighty oak. The next thing I was aware of was the men in suits pointing armaments into my face, telling me to freeze, and words to that effect.

Members of the local constabulary appeared much sooner than they do when summoned to a fracas in the Daymo. With the assistance of the suits they trussed me up like a pork joint.

It was only as they led me away that I first sa Celestina.

'There y'are,' I said, but she just stared at me. If she wasn't nonplussed by events she was far from plussed. She may have considered it unwise to be exchanging idle chat with someone who was clearly so non grata.

I was surprised then to notice that there were so many cameras present. As I was leaving there were enough flashes to create a continuous bright light. Obviously the ladies and gentlemen of the press were there all the time, this being an important event in the life of the nation. Expecting that the highlight of the gig might be a notable cheese review, they were overjoyed to witness some real drama. Afterwards I saw some of their ridiculous headlines, including: *'Assassination attempt foiled by brave Narusian President,' 'Narusian dissident arrested by Gardai,'* and *'Fire-arm sent for forensic examination.'*

On the way to a dungeon in the bowels of what the papers called 'an undisclosed Garda station' (Pearse Street) I had time to analyse the success of the mission.

'Tha' didn't go so well,' I thought to myself.

Chapter 8

The whole thing might indeed have been laughed off as a misunderstanding if it wasn't for Bob B Schwenkmeyer, a realtor from Coon Rapids, Minnesota. I suspect that Bob B's father held the position of village idiot in Coon Rapids, providing the citizenry with amusement while they waited for the twice-a-day donut delivery truck. At some point when he wasn't at his work sticking lit sticks of dynamite up his arse, Dad managed to sire Bob B. This would have been in a tryst with a buffalo, giving Bob B his talent for bellowing rubbish while staring vacantly into the distance. He was a man who liked to talk loudly and at length, even when he had nothing to say. He was the reluctant tourist I had met earlier and this was the biggest thing that had happened to him since he had a thirty inch waist. There wasn't a policeman or a reporter to whom he was not willing to damn me. He convinced them all that I was an imposter, a spy and an assassin.

I was initially questioned by a couple of flatfoots who were in awe of being in the presence of Frankie the Jackal. Their questions were properly deferential. I believe that they came close to asking for my autograph. I was tempted to admit everything as I couldn't bear to see the disappointment on their little faces if I told them the boring truth. Then Inspector Jim Deegan came through the door, and the bonhomie went out the window. If you have read the earlier volume of my memoirs you may recall that I had previous dealings with this thug when I put him onto the trail of P. J. O'Connor and his drugs gang. Far from being grateful, he was convinced that I was a key mover in the organisation. Recognising my quick intelligence, he said that he couldn't believe that I was as stupid as I made out. I have always thought that a life spent amongst the criminal classes soured Deegan's view of humanity. He divided the world into the convicted and those against whom nothing had yet been proven. I can't imagine Deegan having a mother, but if he had, nothing would have pleased him more than to discover that she had some illegal motive in feeding and nurturing him. He would then have had her charged, tried and banged up without pausing for breath.

When Deegan came in, the two uniformed yokels naturally deferred to him. It seemed to me a shame that they should do so as Deegan was less a good example to young policemen as a horrible warning. He was the same six foot three, eighteen stone arse that I had met before. He was even wearing the same shiny grey trousers and brown jacket ensemble that were fit for the bin the first time I saw them. His face was like an untreated shot-gun wound. He peered at me and the light of recognition lit it up like someone had flicked a switch.

'Ha, ha, ha, ha!' he laughed. He even slapped his thigh such was his enjoyment. He leaned over the table to get a closer look at me, coming so close that I could count the ginger cactus plants growing out of his ears.

'Ha, ha, ha, ha! I don't believe it! Is this what half the policemen in Dublin have been guarding? Ha, ha, ha, ha!'

I was not impressed by the levity, and neither were his two junior colleagues. We were as one in our view that the business of interrogating a dangerous assassin called for a higher level of decorum.

'Well, well, well!' he said, composing himself. 'Mr Frankie Flynn, criminal mastermind! By Jaysus.'

'You know the suspect, sir?' asked Uniform A.

'I do,' he said. 'You may remember me putting away a drugs gang a while back? It was a big investigation. There was a bit of coverage,' he added modestly.

A bit of coverage! There was nothing else in the papers for weeks. I'd made the bastard famous.

Deegan's summary of our previous business was not quite the way I would have put it myself. He had no idea what was going on until I put him on to it. I had delivered O'Connor up with an apple in his mouth and a sprig of parsley up his arse. But I didn't want to get off on the wrong foot on this occasion by quibbling over the details.

'This eejit was in it up to his oxsters,' Deegan told the other two. 'The drugs were stored in his house but the place was cleared out before we got there. We couldn't pin anything on the bugger. The Commissioner himself said that Flynn must be either the smartest or the thickest criminal in the country. But, by Jaysus, this time we have you boy!'

'Ah, Inspector Deegan,' I said. 'Will ya give over! I'm glad it's yerself tha's in charge. Now we can get this ridiculous nonsense sorted out, an' all go home to our teas.'

Deegan ignored me and picked up some papers.

'Is this what we have so far?' he asked.

Uniform A confirmed that the dossier represented the total of their sleuthing to date.

Deegan got a chair and pulled it near to me, making a racket as he dragged its legs across the concrete floor. He sat on it backwards, close enough to me to flex his arm and hit me if he wanted. I reckoned that he had achieved high rank by being a very big oaf, in an organisation where that attribute was prized above all others. He was a bald man with clumps of red bristles growing out of and around his ears, like weeds at the edge of a field. His clothes had probably been bought during his youth, when he was a sketched outline of the man he had become. As he leaned towards me his trousers strained like a sail in a hurricane. At any second I expected them to give way, and for his arse to escape, filling the room and smothering us all.

'So what have you been up to this time, Frankie?' he asked.

'I'm sayin' nothin' til I see me solicitor,' I said. I had been reflecting on his 'this time we have you' statement, and thought that it would be hopeless to rely on fair play to get me out of there. My study of the law courtesy of TV told me that I had the right to remain silent and to have access to an attorney.

'Ah Frankie, Frankie!' Deegan said, patting me on the shoulder. 'We're just having a little talk here, you and me. We can do all that interviewing stuff later. Then you can have all the lawyers you want. Isn't that right lads?'

The two lads nodded to confirm that their leader spoke only the truth. Deegan referred to the notes again.

'It says here that you went to the Four Provinces, carrying a firearm with intent to kidnap, injure or murder the President of Narusia. That you evaded the security cordon by passing yourself off as a tourist at the hotel.'

'It wasn't a firearm,' I said. 'It was an umbrella. I bought it in Arnott's.'

Deegan looked at the other two.

'We don't know, sir. It was taken away by forensics. They're still examining it.'

'Do you think they'll be able to tell the difference?' he asked, and they all sniggered.

'And what about the fancy dress, Frankie?' he asked. 'Why are you done up like a fairy cake?'

'Eh?' I asked before remembering the dash I was cutting.

'Ah no, it's jus' wi' me not bein' at home – an' not havin' me own clothes – I needed to get some. An' I got these. In Arnott's. Wi' the umbrella.' 'There's a sale on,' I added to be helpful and in case it was important.

I could smell burning as Deegan's brain tried to deal with this new intelligence.

'You're not living at home? Why not?'

'Oh it's all a load o' crap,' I told him. 'It's all Celestina's fault. She's from Narusia, y'see. It was her tha' I came to see at the hotel.'

'You came to meet a Narusian national at the Four Provinces?'

'Correct,' I said. At last we were getting somewhere. 'Things had gone beyond a joke, Inspector. So I was goin' to meet up with Celestina, an' between us we'd put a stop to Joe an' his carry-on.'

Deegan looked like a bull dog doing the cryptic crossword.

'Is Joe the Narusian President? And was this Celestina an accomplice in the plan to assassinate him?'

'Wha'?' I asked.

I tried to rewind the last bit of the conversation to see where our paths had parted.

'No, look – I don't want to assassinate anyone. Except maybe Joe an' Peggy. An' I might throw Teresa in.'

Uniform A was scribbling away.

'Wha' are ya doin'?' I asked. 'Writin' to yer Mammy? Put tha' pen down an' pay attention.'

He put the pen down.

'Are there other people on your assassination list,' Deegan asked – 'apart from the President, and Peggy and Joe and Teresa? Who are these people anyway?'

'Peggy is me wife. Joe is me best friend an' Teresa is his missus.'

He seemed perplexed.

'And you want to murder them? Your best friend?' He didn't seem that surprised that I might want to kill the women.

'Only in a manner o' speakin',' I explained.

'We just got him in time,' said Uniform B and Uniform A nodded agreement. They had cheered up, reassured that they had a real psychopath on their hands.

Deegan leaned even closer to me. The trousers were going to give way at any time. It was like one of those underwater movies where the captain dives to a depth that the submarine is not designed to withstand. There is much creaking and banging as the structure struggles to take the pressure. Sweat trickles down the crews' necks as they await the implosion that will mash them all into fish food. I tensed, waiting for his arse to erupt like a huge spotty airbag - but by some miracle the trousers held. They must have been made out of titanium.

With bits of spit hitting me like shrapnel, he said: 'You must think that we're right gobdaws.'

That was exactly what I did think, but a bit of diplomatic lying seemed to be what was needed.

'No,' I said. 'No way!'

I tried to think of evidence to support this view but I couldn't. They had said or done nothing in my presence to support any proposition other than that they were as thick as slurry.

'You'd better start telling me the whole story,' Deegan said. 'The Narusians are demanding that the full rigour of the law be thrown at you. They're already pissed off that the maximum penalty here for attempted murder of a head of state isn't a firing squad. You can only get Life here.'

His manner suggested that he had much sympathy with the Narusian view.

'Life?!' I yipped. 'Whatayaonabou'?!'

'You're lucky they can't extradite you. I've heard stories about the jails over there that would make your hair stand on end. You'll have it relatively easy in the Joy and if you behave you might be out before you're eighty.'

'Would ya feck off,' I said. 'Y'ave had yer laugh. Now pack it in.'

Deegan sighed the sigh of a man used to dealing with the ungrateful recipients of his public service. Speaking to the other two he said: 'Put him away for now and we'll pick it up again later.'

To the enormous relief of his trousers, Deegan stood up and went out. A and B locked me in a cell where Dettol competed with piss for odour dominance. I hadn't been deprived of my belt or laces, so they either didn't regard me as a suicide risk or they didn't care. I had a mind to string myself up just to land them in it.

The cell designer was obviously a Zen philosopher of the minimalist school working on a tight budget. On the plus side it was peaceful and devoid of Peggy, Joe and Ma Larkin. The furnishings consisted of a concrete bed covered by a thin plastic mattress, and a metallic toilet with matching sink. There was a high window made from the thick glass usually used on pub cellars. Electric light came from a bare bulb covered in a wire protector. There weren't any entertainment opportunities. There was no way that even a little bird was going to get through that window so the chances of me becoming the Birdman of Pearse Street were zero. The only reading material was the collected thoughts of previous occupants which were scratched into the wall. These provided no stimulation or enrichment and were no credit to the Irish educational system. It was depressing that grown men could not spell common four-letter words. There was a time when Dublin's jails were full of poets and playwrights, but what I had before me was barely the standard of the monkey house. But as there was nothing else available I gave it my full attention. There was a shared view of one Sergeant Kelly, whom I had not met personally, but who stirred strong emotions amongst his guests. I won't record the comments verbatim, but the tenor was that Kelly was from the same stable as Deegan. Indeed some scribes felt that they knew Kelly well enough to guess at the character of his mother. I thought that she might have been a kindly soul sucking on her pipe and spitting into her fire, oblivious to her starring role in these ruminations. I was trying to make sense of a particular hieroglyphic when the door rattled and Uniform A appeared with a polystyrene cup containing milky tea. He had guessed how I liked it and guessed wrong.

'Tae,' he said.

'Is tha' wha' it is?' I asked, taking it anyway. 'Any chance of a few biscuits?' I still had had no food since an early hour.

'No,' he said.

'So I suppose tha' runnin' me a bath would be out o' the question?'

'It would.'

'Righ'. So wha's the diddly-dory then?'

'Pardon?'

'Wha's the story? Wha's the plan? Wha' happens next?'

'Oh right. Well when Inspector Deegan concludes his investigations, there'll be a decision on what you're to be charged with. Then you'll be brought before the District Justice, and probably remanded in custody until the trial.'

'Wait. Slow down,' I said. 'Remanded feckin' where?'

'Mountjoy probably.'

'Bloody hell,' I said.

The Joy is a Victorian monument bequeathed to us by the Brits. Although the new Republic had seen fit to rename every street and building after the heroes of the revolution, there were no takers for our premier prison. I had never been inside it but it looked grim enough from the outside. It was modelled on London's Pentonville which is generally regarded as a dismal hole. Mountjoy was originally intended to be only a stopping off place for miscreants on their way to Van Diemen's Land. Its creators would be horrified to know that it's now used to lock people up for years, and that it is permanently overcrowded. In-cell sanitation had been provided by the Victorians but had been removed by an Irish civil servant in 1939 because prisoners were using too much water! Too much water! In Ireland!

I knew several Daymo residents who were then enjoying the Joy's facilities. They were the kind of people who harbour a deep-seated anger towards the world, which manifests itself through regular outbreaks of violence. It also enclosed P. J. O'Connor and his gang of drug dealers. P. J. had not endeared himself much to me by enjoying the comforts of my home and then threatening to shoot me, Peggy and Angela. I don't rush to judge my fellows on a single incident - everyone is entitled to an off-day - but threatening to kill me makes a bad and lasting impression. There may be those who will tell you that P. J. is nothing but a big old softy at heart, fond of kittens and bunnies, but based on my limited experience I preferred to give him a wide berth. Sharing Mountjoy with him did not appeal to me.

The place was also the current residence of Psychy Brennan. Psychy was so named by friends and family who recognised his early interest in cutting people with knives, scissors and other implements. Psychy was doing five years for a one-man assault on a football team which left several of them needing extensive physical and psychological treatment. His defence was that he had been goaded beyond endurance by them beating his team by an unacceptable margin.

The Joy also held Pete Hourican - another man not cut out for civilisation. Known as 'Matches' Pete couldn't resist setting fire to things. If it wasn't for the rainy climate and the diligence of Dublin Fire Brigade, there would be much less of the Daymo still standing today. In a varied career Matches is known to have burned cars, schools, shops, a few houses and a church. His activities were halted when he accidentally soaked himself in barbecue fluid which he was using to set fire to the bins at the back of Magowan's. He self-combusted and was lucky that Betty saw the sudden flash through the kitchen window. When he got out of hospital a wise judge thought that a period behind bars would be good for him and the rest of the community. Miley Magee said that Matches and the Fire Brigade were in it together, as he was all that stood between them and redundancy.

The Joy also housed the Daymo Godfather – the Generalissimo himself, Nosey Dunne. Nosey had interests in all the main spheres of criminal endeavour. All of the Daymo's lowlifes claimed Nosey as their mentor and inspiration. Without him they might have wasted their lives in tedious employment. Instead they were men of affairs, skilled in armed robbery, drug dealing and prostitution. They drove fast cars, squired orange-coloured ladies and sported the latest in designer tattoos. Nosey's usually fastidious attention to detail let him down when a business rival failed to die as Nosey had planned. More than slightly irritated, the fellow decided to turn over a new leaf, and started by appearing as a witness for the prosecution in the case of the DPP v Nosey.

Being remanded to a place where I might rub shoulders with P. J., Psychy, Matches and Nosey held no allure for me. Life with Peggy looked like a lottery win by comparison.

Deegan came bouncing back into the room like a schoolboy on holiday. His features had spread themselves widely to east and west in what I guessed might have been a broad grin.

'Things are looking bad, Frankie boy,' he said. 'Very bad indeed.'

He told me that the Narusian President had had a fit of the vapours, including fainting, talking in tongues and crying for his mammy. He had been carted off to hospital for observations.

'It's been a terrible shock to the poor man,' Deegan said. 'By all accounts, he has a bad heart.'

'Bad heart me arse,' I said sympathetically.

'You'd be better offer saving your breath for your prayers, and hope that nothing happens to him. Because then you really would be for the high jump.'

I mumbled a short prayer that something sudden and fatal might happen to Deegan but I just got an engaged tone.

'It's all very embarrassing for the government. They're putting pressure on the Commissioner and he's putting pressure on me. I'll do what I can for you Frankie. You know that. You know you can trust me. But you have to talk to me boy.'

'I hope ya live long in a place where all the tables have uneven legs, ya bastard,' I said. 'An' will *you* learn to make proper tea,' I said to Uniform A. 'This stuff tastes like it's bin strained through a jockstrap.'

'An' I want a solicitor,' I added.

★★★

The solicitor they found for me was a young lad of about twelve. He said he wasn't long out of law school but he must have meant primary school. His most striking feature was a very large quantity of blond hair. He had used some unguent on it so that it resembled the home of a bird who had missed the course on nest building. He introduced himself as Brendan Kilbride and spoke in that odd Australian / American accent so beloved by young Southsiders. Believing that he was in a room with a dangerous assassin – and a Northsider to boot – he was as skittish as a young horse going into the starting stalls for the first time.

We were in the interview room and he was carefully keeping the heavy table between us.

'Sooo … Mr Flynn. You're in a bit of a pickle. Ha, ha.'

I was glad that he could see the funny side of it.

'The Guards are considering serious charges against you – attempted murder of a foreign head of state, and conspiracy to murder your wife and others.'

'Jaysus!' I said.

'What's that?' He picked up his pen. Everybody in the place wanted to record everything I said.

'J. A. Y. S. U. S,' I spelled out for him, and went on to elaborate. 'It's a load o' bollix. Tha's B. O. L. L. I. X.'

His pen hesitated as he considered whether to write.

'Listen,' I said, trying to maintain the old sang froid. 'I went to the hotel to see someone an' I jus' fell over the President fella. Tha's all. I never met the man before in me life an' I've no wish to meet him again. Now would you an' yer wig go an' tell tha' shower o' half-thicks out there to let me go. Habeus corpus – try tha' one on them - or any bit o' Latin ya like. Bona fide. Dominus vobiscum. Veni vidi vici. They won't have a clue. They hardly speak English, never mind Latin.'

'It won't be as simple as that, Mr Flynn. There are witnesses to the attack.'

'Feck the witnesses. I wouldn't do anythin' like tha'. Ya can ask Betty McGowan,'

He was happy that he had something to write and took to scribbling.

'Betty McGowan?' he asked, trying to strike a knowledgeable 'you interest me strangely' tone, like he was on to something.

'Who is she?'

'She is the licensee o' Magowan's pub in the Daymo.'

I don't like to name-drop but sometimes circumstances demand it.

'And what has she got to do with the incident?'

'Nothin' – but she'll speak up for me.'

'Will she, indeed? Are you on any medications, Mr Flynn?' he asked.

'I had a spoonful o' Syrup o' Figs this mornin',' I explained. 'Jus' to lubricate the system. Things had got a bit bunged up.

It might be the change' in porridge. Ma Larkin makes it outa pebble-dash. Why d'ya ask?'

'In law a man can only be found guilty of acts committed when he is in full control of his faculties.'

'Y'are thinkin' o' claimin' tha' I'm off me trolley? A few shillin's short o' the pound? Away with the fairies? Tha'd never work.'

'You don't think so?'

'No! One look at me an' any judge'd see I'm as sane as ...' I looked around for inspiration but nothing suggested itself. 'As sane as you are,' was the best I could do. 'Ya'll have to come up with somethin' better than tha'.'

He didn't seem convinced.

'Did you have an invitation to the Reception?'

'No.'

'So you were trespassing. You entered a private event without permission?'

I didn't like this.

'Look, I jus' walked in - well, sort o' fell in if ya want to be exact.'

'Are you now or have you ever been a member of a Narusian guerrilla organisation or any group with views on Narusian politics?'

'Wha'!' I said. 'The only group tha' I'm involved wi' is the pub golf society. We haven't sorted out all our policies yet, so I can't tell ya where we stand exactly on Narusia. Neutral, I imagine.'

'Are you or have you been a member of any ther organisation?'

'I was in the FCA in me youth.'

'You were in the FCA? So you have military training?'

'No,' I said. 'It was the FCA. We got free boots, we marched aroun' and we got a fortnight's holiday every year in the Glen of Imaal. I had a football rattle cos we had no blank ammunition. Ya'd get more military training in the Legion o' Mary.'

'Nevertheless I suggest that you don't mention the FCA to Inspector Deegan. He's already building a picture of you as a kind of Irish Rambo.'

It was hardly in my interests but I didn't completely dislike that idea. At that point Deegan and Uniforms A and B came into the room like a delegation.

'Right, Frankie,' Deegan said. 'You can go. Collect your possessions at the front desk and get yourself out of here.'

Rumpole and I looked at Deegan in complete surprise – the first time we had been on the same wavelength since Kilbride had introduced himself.

'Go?' I asked. 'Whadaya mean?' I was miffed that after being shackled to the dungeon wall for hours, I was now being turfed out without ceremony or explanation.

'Is my client not to be charged then?' Kilbride asked.

'Not this time,' said Deegan like a cat watching a mouse disappearing into a hole.

'May I ask what happened?' Kilbride persevered. I could see now that he might have been a terrier if he'd been let loose on cross-examination.

'You can ask all you like but there's nothing I can tell you. We got word from HQ up in the Park – let him go they said. And ours is not to reason why. We follow orders and we take the shilling at the end of the month. Isn't that the way of it lads?'

A and B confirmed that was indeed the way of it.

'This is not the last yis'll hear o' this,' I said. 'I'll be instructin' me solicitor to sue yis for wrongful arrest. An' all me stuff better be there, includin' me umbrella,' I said.

'I know where I'll stick your umbrella for you,' said Deegan, flaring like a tuppenny banger. His fists closed like he was going to belt me, but he overcame his emotions and got the better of himself.

'You will leave with everything you came in with,' he said.

'If there's bin any damage done to me umbrella ...' I said.

I was going to deliver a lecture on my right to life, liberty and free access to my umbrella when I was interrupted by Kilbride.

'Thank you Inspector,' he said. 'Right, Mr Flynn, I think we can be off now.'

Chapter 9

'Frank! Oi! Over here!'

When I emerged from the police station someone was calling me from a taxi. It was double-parked in the middle of the road with its hazard lights flashing. Fearing that it was Joe Horgan I put my head down and steered a course opposite to the way the car was pointed. As it was a one-way street my pursuer would be stymied and unable to follow me. But I overestimated the regard Dublin taxi drivers have for the Highway Code. The car shot into reverse, doing a ninety degree swerve up on to the pavement nearly taking my toes off. The back door opened and Eugene Larkin – for it was he – gave voice.

'Will ya get into the feckin' car?'

A close inspection revealed that the driver was not Joe Horgan. Eugene slid over and I climbed in beside him. Soon we were motoring along at the speed allowed by Dublin evening traffic - about two miles an hour. The stop-start conditions were a concept that the driver had difficulty managing. Every time a gap appeared, he shot off like Stirling Moss only to jam on the brakes after a few feet.

'Wha' are *you* doin' here?' I asked Eugene in one of the intervals when I wasn't being thrown around like a pin-ball.

'It was me tha' got ya out,' Eugene said. 'An' it wasn't easy. It took two Ministerial orders. Two! Agriculture an' Justice.' He looked at me to see how impressed I was, and seeing that I wasn't, he tried harder. 'Have ya any idea wha' it takes to get two Ministers to agree on anythin' in this country?'

I hadn't but I resolved to vote for the governing party for evermore for their public-spiritedness in restoring me to freedom. Why they bothered was the question - especially when the future of Hiberno-Narusian relations seemed to rest on Frankie's head being served up to the Narusians on a platter. I thanked Eugene and asked him for further details. He explained that he was naturally motivated by the ties that bind golf society officers together. But to get ministerial support he needed something more.

'There's a little favour needed, tha's all.'

'Eh?' I asked. 'A favour? Offa me?' I couldn't think what it could be unless the government wanted a loan of my bike.

'All will be revealed when we get to the Unit,' Eugene said.

I didn't much like the sound of that, fearing that the Pearse Street dungeon and the Unit might turn out to be as in frying pan and fire.

'No thanks,' I said. 'Yis can drop me here.'

As we were moving at the pace of an hour hand on a clock, I pulled the door handle to let myself out. It didn't work.

'Relax Mr Flynn an' enjoy the ride,' the driver said.

'Who's yer man?' I asked Eugene.

'Oh yeah, sorry,' Eugene said. 'Frank, this is Malachy Mulligan. Mal – Frank.'

I nodded at Malachy's neck and he nodded back at the mirror.

'So this isn't a real joe maxi?'

'No. Unit staff car. I'm sorry, Frankie,' Eugene said. 'Bu' y'are kinda snookered. Ya have to hear wha' the boss has to say. Then ya can decide yerself whether to play ball or to take up a career sewin' mailbags.'

I slumped back in my seat and contented myself with muttering curses about Narusians, Deegan, traffic and Units.

After jolting along for a while, the car turned up an alleyway and stopped at a security grill. This rolled open, triggered by who knows what, and we proceeded down a ramp into a grubby, badly-lit car park under a nondescript office block. The grill closed behind us. Eugene and Malachy got out. This time my door handle worked fine and I followed them. Malachy led the way to a tiny lift which opened when he pointed something at it. There was not much more space in it than in the average coffin, but somehow we squeezed in.

'This is cosy,' I said. 'Let's not all breathe in together or we're codjoxed.'

'It's a security feature,' Malachy explained. 'A narrow point of entry is easier to defend.'

'As the actress said to the bishop,' I said.

I suspected that the real reason was that small lifts are cheaper than big ones.

'Beam us up Scottie,' I said to Malachy. He found a button to make the thing move, coming close to sexually assaulting me and Eugene in the process. To my surprise, the lift went down rather than up, shuddering like a cheap food mixer as it went. When the door opened, we untangled ourselves and fell out into a brightly lit room. It was nothing more than a windowless concrete rectangle, the size of a tennis court, with about twenty people sitting at desks fiddling with computers. It had all the charm of the inside of a cement mixer. There was a big map of Ireland on one wall next to a menu from Ziggi's Pizzas. Otherwise the place was unadorned. Malachy retreated back into the lift and disappeared behind its sliding door.

'This way,' Eugene said. He steered me to a door in the far wall which led into a reception area occupied by a middle-aged receptionist woman with the sourest expression seen since I bought Peggy a mop for her birthday. If this woman was pleased to see us she hid it well. Her expression said that her day so far had been filled with very stupid people and that our arrival hadn't improved things.

'We're here to see the Eagle,' Eugene told her. I would have laughed but the reception woman's look was daring me to try it and see what would happen. So I didn't.

I fully expected that she would tell Eugene to clear off because he hadn't an appointment. Instead she sighed that standards had hit rock bottom when people could pop in to see the Eagle whenever they bloody-well pleased. A phone on her desk had more buttons on it that the controls of a jumbo jet. She pressed one of them.

'The Falcon is here to see you Sir,' she said.

Sounding more like a duck than an eagle, he quacked something back at her. She waved us towards what looked like a blank wall, but proved to be the inner sanctum. She pressed another button and a piece of the wall clicked open. The Eagle's nest was like a cross between a bank manager's office and J. P. Twomey's shop. There were a few screens on the walls, all turned off. Racing finished for the day, I guessed. The room was dominated by a large grey desk with plastic baskets overflowing with papers. I guessed that he might have liked his glamorous assistant to do some filing for him but he didn't dare ask her. There was also a grey table and four matching chairs. As we came in, the Eagle came to meet us and shepherded us to these chairs. He didn't look much like an eagle. Turkey or dodo maybe, but not eagle. He was short, round and pink, with a mass of grey hair and enough face for two people. The only way this guy was ever going to fly through the air was if he was dropped from a high place. He wore a heavy woollen suit which fit him about as well as a tarpaulin fits a skip. He had extraordinarily big feet for a small man so that turning had to be done in stages.

'How are you Mr Flynn?' he asked.

'Better than I deserve,' I said.

'It's a very great pleasure to meet you. A very great pleasure, indeed. The Falcon has been telling me all about you.'

I couldn't imagine Eugene and this fowl idling the time away discussing F. Flynn, but what did I know? It may be that intelligence experts get an edge on the competition but chatting about random citizens for fun. I suppose that you can only kill so much time on microfilm, invisible ink and untraceable poisons.

'Howya,' I answered, maintaining the Flynn inscrutability.

'I'm delighted that you were able to come,' he said being polite. I assumed he knew that I had been abducted. 'We need your help. In fact, your country needs your help, Mr Flynn.'

I raised an eyebrow to let him know that I was on standby for further information.

'Mr Flynn, what I have to tell you is highly confidential. Highly confidential. Classified information, Mr Flynn. Highly classified.'

I raised a hand to stop him right there.

'Listen, eh …' I hesitated to call him 'Eagle' so I gave it a miss. 'Listen,' I said. 'Ya can tell Frankie Flynn whatever ya like, an' rest aisy tha' it'll go no further. Isn't tha' righ' Eugene … eh, Falcon?'

The Falcon annoyed me by seeming to think about it but nodded his agreement. The Eagle seemed happy that the security vetting process had been satisfactorily completed. He continued.

'Mr Flynn, international relations are very important to a small country like Ireland. Very important. We rely on the support and cooperation of other countries to make our way in the world. Do you follow me, Mr Flynn? We don't want to fall out with anyone, as they could hamster us in the major international organisations in which we work - the EU, the United Nations …'

'F.I.F.A.' I suggested, and he nodded.

'F.I.F.A. indeed,' he said. 'Now, you see your incident with the Narusian President is exactly the sort of thing that we're not keen on.'

'Look,' I said. 'I can explain tha'. Ya see, the problem is wi' Joe Horgan. The Falcon here'll tell ya.'

The Eagle raised a wing to stop me.

'There's no need to explain,' he said. 'We regard all that as water under the bridge. Water under the bridge, Mr Flynn. Mind you for a time it looked as though you would have to be sacrificed on the altar of international relations. Yes indeed, Mr Flynn, on the altar of international relations. But the Falcon had a better idea. You can thank him for your release. You can indeed.'

His habit of echoing his own remarks were beginning to grate on me, but I let it pass, and moved to second the vote of thanks to Eugene.

'Good man,' I said to him. 'I owe ya a pint.'

'We were hoping that you might show your gratitude in a more substantial way, Mr Flynn.'

I wondered if he was angling towards a round of pints and I prepared to disappoint him.

'Mr Flynn, let me be pacific.'

'Sp,' I suggested but it was wasted on him.

'The system of trade between Narusia and Ireland is being disrupted by fraud on an industrial scale. An industrial scale, Mr Flynn. Counterfeit cigarettes, alcohol and electrical equipment are all being sold. Even tea! This means that the tax authorities in both countries are losing out in a very substantial way. We're talking milluns. Milluns, Mr Flynn.'

I assumed that a millun was about a million, and resisted the temptation to suggest that it would buy the lads in the Unit a lot of birdseed. To be honest his story wasn't filling me with horror. One of the key attractions of Magowan's is that it is a thriving marketplace for goods and services at prices which do not include the taxman's mark up. The livelihoods of many of the Daymo's citizens would have been jeopardised by a pettifogging attitude to the laws as they related to patent, copyright and tax. Eugene was well aware of my likely concern and dived in to reassure me.

'We're not worried abou' the odd bottle here or a carton o' fags there,' he said.

'Or a few dodgy DVDs?' I added to help him.

'We leave that kinda thing to the foot soldiers in the Guards,' the Eagle said, keen to get back to the agenda. 'We're talking here about criminality on a very large scale.'

'Ya mean lads completely takin' the piss?' I asked.

'Yes,' he said. 'Exactly. I couldn't have put it better myself, Mr Flynn.'

I began to feel that I could do business with this man. We were singing from the same sheet like the cherubim after months in rehearsal.

'Mr Flynn, we need you to infiltrate the smuggling ring and report back to us.'

This was a jarring note! The Eagle had gone off key. He was squawking some improvisational jazz which was not pleasing my ears. I gave him immediate feedback.

'Ya can feck off,' I said. 'I'm not infiltratin' nothin'.'

'Mr Flynn,' said the Eagle. 'Don't be hasty. You need to think about this. Think, Mr Flynn.'

I thought for an eighth of a second.

'Get stuffed,' I said and any pun was intended.

He sighed and looked at Eugene.

'If Mr Flynn is adamant, then I suppose there's no more to be said. Get Inspector Deegan on the phone and have Mr Flynn picked up.'

'Wow! Hold on,' I said. 'Wait a cotton-pickin' minute.'

I did not like the prospects of going into business with this aviary of eejits, but even less did I want Deegan's fat fingers on my neck.

'Okay, I'll do it,' I heard myself saying before I had worked out whether I would or not.

'Good man, Frank,' Eugene said. 'Welcome on board.'

'Yes, indeed Mr Flynn,' said the Eagle. 'Your support is very much appreciated. We will give you a full briefing and everything you need. And we can't keep calling you Mr Flynn, now can we Mr Flynn? We need a code name. How about 'Robin'?'

I didn't want to be a Robin. Robins are for Christmas cards. I wanted to be a bird with claws and a load of teeth.

'No,' I said.

'Well, if not 'Robin', then how about …'

'I'm not goin' to be a tit or a coot or a cuckoo or a feckin' goose,' I said to help him.

'No, no, of course not,' he said. 'I was thinking of 'Magpie'. That's not taken, is it Falcon.'

'No sir,' said Eugene. I thought about it.

'Very clever birds,' the Eagle said. 'Very clever indeed.'

'An' they can be vicious,' Eugene said, and the Eagle agreed that when riled a Magpie can tear a man limb from limb. We agreed that I would be Agent Magpie and that Eugene would be my handler. I suggested that we could pass information via a secret drop box, but as we were living under the one roof, there seemed no point in going out just for the sake of it.

'The key to the operation is Celestina Gulbis,' the Eagle said. 'That is her full name. She is the person on the ground relaying messages and making arrangements for deliveries. Everything seems to go through her.' He switched on one of his screens and, using a remote, he flicked through pictures of Celestina at various points around the city. She wasn't with anyone else so I couldn't see the significance.

'Surveillance,' the Eagle told me, pleased with himself. 'So far we haven't turned up any useful contacts, but she will have records. Contacts. Transactions. That's what we need.'

'An' wha' am I supposed to do? Ask her for the loan o' them?'

'Wha' we were thinkin' was tha' if ya could get in where she's stayin',' said Eugene, 'ya could have a shifty aroun' an' see wha' ya can find. Ya know yerself.'

'Will I photograph it all on a tiny camera or somethin'? Microfilm like? Maybe disguised as a cigarette lighter.'

'Ya don't smoke, Frankie,' Eugene said. 'So it might be a giveaway. We won't bother with any o' tha'. Jus' find the stuff an' swipe it.'

'The snag is,' I said, feeling bad that I had to piss on their parade, 'tha' she's livin' wi' Joe, an' Joe wants to dance a hornpipe on me head. He's not goin' to sit still while I'm goin' through her drawers. Maybe if yis give me a gun?'

If I was going to play the part of 007 I figured that I should be properly equipped – if not with a little camera, then at least a Walther PPK.

'Yeah righ',' Eugene said, meaning the opposite. 'Ya'll jus' have to stick with wha' ya were goin' to do. Get Celestina to call him off.'

'An' how am I goin' to get at her? We're goin' aroun' in circles here lads.'

'It's alrigh' – we're way ahead o' ya,' Eugene said. 'It wasn't by accident tha' she got invited to the reception at the Four Provinces. We're playin' a game here an' we have most o' the good cards.'

He tapped the side of his nose to indicate where he had the cards hidden.

'Righ' now she's at the Narusian embassy. At a little private get-together for the select. She'll be there for another hour or so. You jus' be passin' when she comes out, an' Bob's yer uncle!'

I looked at Eugene with, if not a new respect, then at least without the usual contempt.

'Perhaps the Magpie might like to change into something a little less conspicuous?' the Eagle asked.

'Eh?' I asked, already having forgotten that I was the Magpie and that I was still dressed like a parakeet.

'Yeah,' Eugene agreed. 'Maybe he's a bit startlin' for Dublin alrigh'! We can kit him out in somethin' more sedate.'

'Oh, righ',' I said. 'A great secret service! Yis have no guns or micro-filmers, but yis have a dressin' up box! I never in all me life!'

★★★

Half an hour later I was leaning on a lamppost on the corner of a street waiting for a certain little lady to pass by. This particular lamppost was just a spit from the Narusian Embassy. This was originally one of the fine south Dublin homes built for Victorian merchant princes. All had long ago been converted into embassies and offices for accountants, consultants and other shysters. In the side streets around were establishments where visiting businessmen could buy a temporary cure for loneliness. The Unit's tailoring department had supplied me with gear from the section marked 'nondescript'. Everything came in quiet shades of mud, mildew and marrowfat peas. I was perfectly camouflaged to hide in a swamp.

Just alongside where I stood was a little boozer, and my plan was to lead Celestina into it as soon as she showed up. My nerves had undergone much jangling during the day, and a pint was calling out to me like a cooling stream to the thirsty hart. I even wondered if I might fit in a sneaky one before she showed up but I didn't dare risk missing her a second time in the same day. My future health, as well as the fate of the nation, rested on me meeting with Celestina. It would have been disastrous if she got past me while I was taking on fluids.

After leaning for about fifteen minutes I saw her emerging from the Embassy. She was dressed demurely in a green floaty thing looking as wholesome as Audrey Hepburn on a bed of lettuce. She trotted down the steps and bounced along the garden path to the front gate. A young Guard in a uniform that he was growing into provided his full and undivided attention. He let her out eyeing like a dog would a lamb chop and watched her all the way to my lamppost.

'There y'are,' I said stepping into her path. She slammed on the brakes, obviously surprised to see me away from my natural habitat.

'Frankee! Why are you doing here?'

'It's not 'why', it's wha',' I told her. 'The question is wha' am I doin' here, an' the answer is tha' I'm allowed out o' the Daymo every once in a while for good behaviour. When I am, I wander here an' there, an' this evenin' I wandered here.'

She laughed, making a gurgling sound not unlike an emptying bath. I guessed that she had been lapping up the Narusian hospitality.

'But, Frankee, at hotel I saw you with police. They said that someone try to kill President. Was it *you*?'

'Noratall,' I said. 'Tha' was jus' a misunderstandin'. I was able to get tha' sorted out no bother. Listen Celestina, have ya got time for a quick drink. I need to talk to ya.' I nodded in the direction of the boozer. She shrugged and in we went. The place was crowded with myriad yahoos, braying at each other like stags in the rutting season. Such creatures need to pose and strut, and are disinclined to sit. Therefore we had little trouble finding a little table and some stools. Leaving Celestina in charge of these furnishings I went to the bar to acquire lubricants. Such was my desperate need, I didn't even remonstrate with the barman when he charged me the price of a Spanish holiday for a badly-pulled pint and a glass of house white which looked like it had been personally passed by the barman. A laboratory analysis would probably have got him a prescription for penicillin. But in fairness, bad pint or not, if I ever more enjoyed the first slug out of one, I can't remember when it was. A balm to my troubled soul, it was like getting into a warm bath after falling into the canal. (And I speak here from experience.)

'Confusion to the enemy,' I said, raising my glass to Celestina.

'What enemy?' she asked. 'For what enemy are you wanting confusion Frankee?'

I resolved to remember how bloody literal this woman could be. There was already a lot of noise and someone had turned up the background music. I shifted my stool closer to her so that she could hear me.

'No enemy,' I said. 'It's a figure o' speech, tha's all. Don't worry abou' it. Listen, I need ya to do me a favour.'

'Yes, Frankee,' she said. 'What is it that I can do for you?'

'It's abou' Joe. He's got a stupid idea into his nut tha' …'

'In his nut?' she asked, confused again.

'His nut. Yeah –his noodle – his head.' I patted my own to indicate the precise body part to which I was referring.

'He's got it into his head tha' I'm finaglin' with his missus.' I could see from her expression that she had lost her place again.

'Tha' me an' Teresa are – ya know – *at it*.' I waved my arms around trying to summon the god of communication out of the air.

'Ya know – the birds an' the bees an' the flowers an' the trees.'

'Flowers?' Celestina clearly wasn't a student of biology but I persevered because I couldn't think of a better way of explaining.

'Yeah. Feckin' flowers,' I said. 'An' bees,' I added for good measure.

'And what do you want me to do with the flowers and bees, Frankee?'

'I want ya to tell Joe tha' it's ridiculous. A load o' cod. Tell him tha' he's after puttin' two an' two together an' come up with forty seven. Have ya me? He's follyin' me aroun' an' he wants to bate the shite out me.'

She was doing her best to keep up but she was already a long way back. God love her but she just couldn't understand plain English.

'Easier you tell him yourself,' she said, and before I could explain the folly of attempting such a thing, there I was doing it. As Celestina was speaking, she looked over my head and gave a little wave. I half-turned and was horrified to see Joe coming across the room towards us.

'I called him when you at bar. He said he come get me.'

I dithered between making a run for it and trying to parley my way out of it. As my legs had turned into boiled spaghetti, the first option disappeared. Anyway I was cornered and there was nowhere to run. Joe's eyes locked on to me like a missile. In three strides he was across the room and had grip on my shoulder.

'Now I have ya, ya sleveen little bollix,' he greeted me. 'D'ya know wha' I'm goin' to do? I'm goin' to break every bone in yer manky festerin' body. I'm goin' to rip yer arm off an' bate ya stupid with it. Then I'm goin' to shove me hand down yer throat an' pull yer lungs inside out. When I'm done with ya, ya'll be atin' yer dinner through a straw.'

The good news was that he hadn't yet embarked on this programme of alterations. Thankfully there a certain decorum bred into Dubliners which frowns upon assault and battery in churches and public houses. Celestina's presence also helped. The code of gallantry requires a chap not to turn a lady's immediate surroundings into an abattoir.

'Joe! What are you saying?' She may have struggled to understand every nuance of ordinary conversation, but she was getting the gist of this one. Something in Joe's tone told her that this was not the usual banter between buddies.

'Why do you speak like this to Frankee?'

Hope fluttered faintly in the Flynn breast. I was like a sparrow in a cat's mouth when the cat's owner tells the beast: 'Naughty Kitty. Let the birdy go.'

'He' a dirty little shit,' Joe explained, still hanging on to me like a lion on to its dinner. 'Him an' Teresa. Behind me back.'

'Joe!' she said. 'But you love me. What do you care about Teresa?'

I silently cheered her on. Joe was caught on what I think are known as the horns of a dilemma. If he persevered with his belligerence towards me, as a competitor for Teresa's hand, he put a question over his credentials as Celestina's paramour. On the other hand, I could feel from his grip that he still had his heart set on beating the crap out of me.

'It's nothin' to do wi' you. It's him … he's a fecker,' he finished, but I thought lamely, like his guaranteed waterproof case had sprung a leak.

'Get stool and sit,' Celestina ordered him. Joe was reluctant to let me go, but after calculating that the odds of me getting away were a hundred to one and drifting, he did as he was told.

'Will ya have a pint?' I asked. I could see that he was about to tell me where to shove it, but he caught Celestina's eye. And anyway the hardwired default answer to that question is always in the affirmative.

'Go on,' he said.

Making my way up to the bar I had a free run at the door but decided against it. For a start, I didn't think that I'd get very far, and in the great outdoors Joe would no longer be constrained by Celestina and pub etiquette. Optimism was also growing that with Celestina's help, I might be able to talk the bugger around. I brought him back a pint and set it before him like a sacred offering.

'There y'are,' I said. 'Get yerself outside o' tha'.'

'Good man,' Joe mumbled the ritual words, and I sat down.

'Bin busy?' I asked him.

'Nah. The town is quiet. Wastin' me time.'

I shook my head in sympathy. Dublin taxi driver are bred to take a bleak view of the world and to share it with anyone who will listen. Show me a Dublin taxi driver, and I will show you a man who believes that new depths have been plumbed in the economy, politics, and the general behaviour of humanity. When on duty, this always trumped Joe's naturally more upbeat disposition.

'It's a hard oul station righ' enough,' I said.

'It's ridiculous,' Joe warmed to his theme. 'I was in the rank at the airport for over an hour, and then I got an oul wan who only wanted to go to Santr!'

'Ya should a told her to take a hike,' I said. 'It prob'ly woulda done her good.'

'Yeah,' he agreed. 'Bu' she was elderly. An' she'd a load o' bags.'

'Yeah, bu',' I said, aggrieved on his behalf.

We shared a companionable slurp of the pints, contemplating the perfidy of taxi users. Observing that hostilities had been cancelled or at least deferred, Celestina excused herself to the powder room.

'Look Joe,' I said. 'Ya really have it all wrong abou' me an' Teresa. I mean ... I wouldn't. Y'know? I mean not tha' I wouldn't. She's a fine woman an' all tha' bu' ... well, I jus' wouldn't. I mean for feck's sake Joe, me an' you go back a long way. Have ya me?'

I thought that I had eloquently stated my case. Joe said nothing and seemed to be thinking. Either that or he was having an attack of wind. I felt that matters were finely balanced and my fate was on a knife edge. As that was uncomfortable I added some further guff for his consideration:

'She was only tryin' to get it up for ya,' I said. 'Tha's all. She was upset.'

'Ya were in the house,' he said. '*My* house.'

'Yeah! I know tha'. Bu' it was only to talk to her. Abou' *you*.'

'Wha' would ya want to talk to her abou' me for?'

'Abou' you an' Celestina … the two o' yis in the fla' together … I mean it's a bit odd… it's not righ' … Yer place is in the Daymo, Joe … in Magowan's. I mean back with yer wife an' kids.'

'I don't see tha' it's anythin' got to do wi' you.'

'Ah Jaysus Joe! O' course it has to do wi' me. I can't stand idly by an' watch ya makin' an eejit outa yerself.' I thought this might not be the right tone, so I quickly added: 'I felt it was me duty – as a close fam'ly friend.'

Joe grunted something which I hoped was a grudging acceptance of my case as outlined, but I wasn't fully out of the woods yet.

'So wha' were ya doin' in me bedroom?' he asked.

'I was hidin' under the bed,' I said. 'Hidin' on Peggy.'

'Ya were hidin' on Peggy?'

'Yeah,' I said. I shuddered as I remembered the terror of being trapped waiting to be jabbed with the brush handle. Joe started to laugh.

'Ya were hidin' under the bed! I woulda paid good money to see tha'.'

He laughed more loudly.

'Jaysus, I can see ya! How did ya get out?'

'Teresa belted Peggy. It caused a kinda diversion an' I was able to scarper.'

'Teresa belted Peggy! Jaysus! Fair fecks to her. Ha! Ha! Ha!'

The more he thought about it, the funnier it seemed to him, so that when Celestina came back he was wiping his eyes with his sleeve.

'Sit down,' he said to her. 'I'll get another drink. Ha! Ha! Ha! Teresa belted Peggy! I've heard it all now! Ha! Ha! Ha!

Joe went up to the bar. Celestina eyed me with wonder and delight.

'So Joe he no longer wants to bate shite out of you, Frankee?'

'No. He's shelved that idea for the moment.'

Chapter 10

A ny military commander worth his epaulettes will tell you that it's asking for trouble to fight on too many fronts at the same time. With détente established with Joe, I was in the slightly better position of being able to concentrate my forces on Peggy, Celestina and the golf.

Back at Larkin's, Ma had been doing her best to annoy me but I was exhausted after a very full day, and she couldn't have gotten a rise out of me with a cattle prod. Eugene was taking his role as my handler seriously and stepped in to protect me.

'Ma, will ya leave the man alone? Have ya no pity on the state tha' he's in?'

'He's in rag order, righ' enough,' she agreed. 'Ya look like shite on a stick,' she said to me.

I wasn't pleased to be thus described. I felt that I had ended the day further ahead of the posse than I had started but I hadn't the energy to debate with her.

'Yeah,' I agreed. 'I'm knackered. So if it's all the one to youse, I'll head for the scratcher.'

Ma looked as disappointed as a cat seeing her prey disappearing down a hole.

I needed the full eight hours as the following evening the Golf Society was meeting to discuss the Kinsella's match. To be on the safe side I had a good thirteen or fourteen hours. I like to do things thoroughly. I was risking life and limb by re-entering Peggy's hunting ground but I went. I knew that the Committee needed me and my motto has always been 'duty above self'. If I'm on a committee, then I'm on it, and I will attend properly convened meetings in spite of dungeon, fire and sword. Besides, I was missing Magowan's. Another few days away and, like an emigrant languishing on distant shores, I'd have started writing ballads about the place.

I had managed to persuade Joe to attend as an observer, hoping to mooch him back into the Committee's fold. If I just sent him along, there was a danger that Paddy would not treat him with the necessary sensitivity and that an even deeper schism would result. I also had to square Joe with Betty, which I did by telling her that his remorse was complete and suggesting that he had served a reasonable part of his sentence. She agreed to allow him in on the strict understanding that even the smallest misdemeanour would see his life-ban restored.

Joe arrived before I had told the others that he was coming. There was a momentary awkwardness.

'Jaysus!' said Paddy. 'Will yis look who's back from the dead? Wha's this his name is again?'

'Casanova,' Miley said.

'Tha's righ'!' Paddy said. 'Come over an' rest yer mickey up on the bar here. Ya mus' be knackered draggin' it around with ya.'

'I'll get it out an' bate yis black an' blue with it,' Joe replied. 'Yis're a desperate bunch o' gobshites an' no mistake.'

I was pleased that the reconciliation was going so well. I relaxed and Betty put away the metaphorical shotgun she had handy.

'Joe, will ya have a pint?' I asked - and without waiting for the obvious answer - 'Betty, will ya put one on for Joe like a good woman?'

As Betty blurred into action, Joe came and sat down. As he was no longer an officer of the Committee he could no longer be on the executive side of the table. He had to sit on the outside with the general membership which consisted solely of Barney Pugh. I detected a glance from him at Miley who was enthroned in the Secretary position, but no more than that.

'I call the meetin' to order,' Paddy declared. 'Can we approve the minutes o' the last meetin'?'

Everyone looked at Miley who looked blank.

'Wha'?' he asked.

'Where's the feckin' minutes?' Paddy asked.

'Wha' are ya talkin' abou'?' Miley asked

'Y'are supposed to write the minutes,' I explained to him. 'Ya have to write down everythin' tha' happens at the meetin'. Tha's wha' the Seckertary is for.'

'Well nobody tol' me tha'. Anyway nothin' happened at the meetin' except Paddy talkin' shite abou' procedures an' protocols.'

Without actually standing, Paddy drew himself up to his full five foot six.

'D'ya mean tha' ya didn't write it down?' he wanted to know. He sounded incredulous that anyone would miss the opportunity to gather his words like gold nuggets.

'I did an' me arse,' Miley said. 'Sure I was bored outa me bleedin' tree.'

'Well, wha' were ya writin' then? Paddy wanted to know. 'Ya were scribblin' away there like nobody's business.'

'Nothin',' Miley said. 'I was jus' scribblin'. There was bugger all else to do.'

'In fairness Paddy, ya *were* talkin' a load o' bollix,' Eugene said, in an effort to pour oil on troubled flames.

'I move tha' the Seckertary be summarily removed from office for gross deleriction o' duty,' Paddy said.

'Hold on Paddy,' I said. Although this was going my way I had to play a shrewd hand. 'Ya can't do tha'.'

Paddy's fuse had nearly burned out and he was ready to blow.

'I mean to say,' I said. 'It's not as though there were important matters bein' discussed. I mean there couldn't a bin. *I* wasn't even here. Were yis even quorate?'

Paddy was now on his feet.

'I can do wha' I like,' he said. 'I'm the President. It's my club. Wha' I says goes.'

'Ah hold on there now a minute Mussolini,' Eugene said. 'I don't remember votin' you supreme powers o' life, death an' the dismissal o' fellow officers.'

'No bag o' wind is goin' to remove me from office,' Miley said. 'Cos I'm resignin'. Ya can take it an' shove it. I've more to be doin' than writin' down shite.'

Paddy clearly wanted to strangle Miley but his position constrained him.

'Righ',' he said. 'Miley Magee has resigned as Seckertary. Take a note o' tha'.'

'Who's goin' to take a note of it when we haven't got a feckin' Seckertary, Paddy?' Eugene wanted to know.

'Joe,' Paddy said. 'Get yerself aroun' here.'

'Proposed,' I said.

'Seconded,' said Eugene.

Joe shrugged and swapped seats with Miley.

Barney Pugh had been sitting quietly during the power play. If Barney ever had a place in the gene pool, it was in the shallow end. His features slowly came to life like a bear waking up after hibernation.

'Ehhh, listen lads,' he said. 'Yis're givin' me a pain in me head. Will one o' yis tell me wha' yis're playin' at? Is it musical chairs or wha'?'

Not for the first time I thought that Barney could use help composing his dialogue.

'Yeah, tha's righ' Barney,' I said. 'Tha's it exactly. Now would ya trot up as far as the bar like a good man an' order a round. I don't know if it's the hot air in here, but the pints are disappearin' like puddles in a desert.'

Barney got to his feet, muttering: 'Smart arse. Everyone aroun' here is a bleedin' smart arse.' But he went and got the pints.

When the meeting settled down again, thoughts turned to the annihilation of Kinsella's. I proposed that losing was not an option and everyone agreed.

'We shall fight them in the bunkers; we shall fight them on the fairways; we shall fight them on the greens and in the rough; we shall fight in the bar afterwards; we shall never surrender,' Paddy said thumping the table and causing a spillage.

'Go aisy, Paddy,' I said rescuing my pint and putting half of it down my throat safe from further earthquakes.

'So wha's the plan, Paddy?' I asked.

'I hand you over to the Treasurer stroke Intelligence Officer, Mr Eugene Larkin,' Paddy said.

'Thank you Mr President. An' it's Hon Treasurer if ya don't mind.'

Paddy grunted a gynaecological expression.

'I've bin makin' a study o' Kinsella's team an' identified the star performers. They've got Gerry Silverman.'

'Gerry the Jew?' Joe asked. 'Are ya serious? I didn't know Jews played golf.'

'Well they do,' said Eugene. 'Maybe it was the forty years in the desert tha' did it. It musta bin great practice for the bunker shots. Anyway, Gerry is their main man.'

'Foreskin!' Joe shouted for reasons which escaped me.

'Steady on lads,' Paddy said. 'Can we have a bit o' decorum an' keep to the agenda, or we'll be here all nigh'. Who else have they got?'

'Brillo Brennan,' Eugene said.

'My Jaysus,' Joe said. 'Brillo Brennan!'

Brillo was the older brother of Psychy Brennan who then resided in Mountjoy Prison. A wise judicial system had placed Psychy there for the safety of the public. Brillo didn't have Psychy's professional commitment to violence, but being from the same bloodline there was always a risk of any routine interaction with him ending with you getting thumped. Brillo had an optical malfunction which made it look like he was always staring at you. This could be misconstrued as aggression but usually there was no misconstruing going on. On one occasion in a pub in Dolphin's Barn his staring led to a fellow drinker taking exception. The man voiced his feelings, asking him what the hell Brillo thought he was staring at, and throwing in some unnecessarily candid remarks about Brillo's appearance. Brillo, probably feeling that mere words could not do justice to the situation, lashed out. He punched the guy a few times and threw a stool at him when the fellow tried to escape. Unfortunately the guy ducked and the stool sailed through a frosted glass window into the street. After being energetically ejected by a posse of bar staff, Brillo sportingly returned the stool through another window.

'Brillo's alrigh',' Paddy said, not sounding like he was altogether convinced. 'He jus' looks a bit mad. Bu' is he and good at the golf, Eugene?

'They say tha' he is. Eyes of a sniper an' the coordination of a ballerina.'

'If ya say so,' said Paddy. 'Who else've they got?'

'Cyril Kavanagh,' Eugene said.

'The Squirrel?' I asked. 'I thought he was dead.'

'He might be but he was in Kinsella's last week,' Miley said. 'Drinkin' a pint an' readin' the Herald. Now tha' ya mention it, he wasn't movin' much.'

'An' he plays golf?' asked Paddy. 'At his age?'

'So sources inform me,' said Eugene. 'By all accounts, he's bin at it man an' boy. He was in the bank back in the day when bank managers did feck all else - before they started meddlin' with things they didn't understan'.'

'Like money,' I said.

'Exacerly!' Eugene said. 'Outa the mouths o' babes an' gobshites!'

'Will ya give over,' I said. 'Gerry, Brillo an' the Squirrel? It doesn't sound like much of an A team to me. They'll be up against the might o' Magowan's. They'll have their work cut out.'

'Yeah,' Joe said. 'I'll bet they're shittin' themselves.'

I looked around our talent pool and it wasn't lapping over the edges.

'So wha's the plan?' Joe asked.

'Tha's wha' we're here to discuss,' Paddy said.

'If we're careful abou' countin' the shots...' Joe said.

'Or not countin' most o' them,' I said. 'Ya might get away wi' tha' with the Squirrel, but Gerry and Brillo are no daws.'

'No, an' if Brillo catches ya cookin' the books, ya'll find yerself up in A and E with a nine iron up yer arse,' Miley said.

'I've bin thinkin',' Eugene said.

'I thought I could smell somethin' burnin' righ' enough,' Joe said.

'Shut up for a minute, will ya, an' give the man a chance,' Paddy said. 'Well, come on Eugene. Stop sittin' there like y'ave a gob full o' sweet tea. Spit it out.'

'Have yis heard o' Sun Tzu?' Eugene asked.

'Yeah,' Miley said. 'He has a takeaway in Dorset Street.'

'God give me patience,' Paddy said. 'Will yis put a sock in it until we hear wha' Eugene has to say? Yeah … thanks Eugene … a pint.'

Eugene signalled Betty for further supplies after he had done an eye-contact census of who wanted one.

'Six pints Betty please when ya get a minute,' he said. Who said that men can't multi-task?

'I've bin askin' meself wha' would Sun Tzu do if he was playin' against Kinsella's.'

'He was big into golf this fella, was he?' Joe asked.

'He was a great military strategist who wrote a book called 'The Art of War'. It's bin a guide not jus' for war but for strategisin' in diplomacy an' in business. I use it all the time in the office,' he said.

'Wha'?' asked Miley. 'To outfox the trees an' fishes? Give us a break.' He laughed as Eugene in the persona of the Falcon gave me, in the persona of the Magpie, a knowing look.

'Yer enemy's weakness is yer strength,' Eugene said. 'We jus' have to focus on our enemy's weakness an' it's game, set an' match.'

'Tha's tennis,' Miley pointed out.

'Feck off Miley,' Paddy said. 'Eugene, will ya talk in words o' one syllable please, for the benefit o' those present who don't have two grey cells to rub together?'

'Gentlemen,' Eugene said. 'Our enemy's weakness is thirst, an' tha's the rock on which they will perish.'

If that was meant to clear things up, it didn't. Eugene was met with a row of faces like bricked up windows. He needed to provide further detail. He collected the pints off Betty as we tried to make sense of it. He seemed pleased that we were still lost when he resumed his lecture.

'When we get to the course, there'll be the usual breakfast laid on – the rashers an' sausages an' tha'.'

We nodded that we were familiar with that concept.

'Makes ya thirsty doesn't it?'

We nodded.

'Well, after they've had it, we make sure tha' there's no water or anythin' to take out with them. Everythin' the place has, we buy it, hide it, rob it … whatever we have to do. The thing is tha' by the time they've done nine holes they'll be gaspin' with the drooth.'

'Yeah, so wha'?' asked Joe.

'So they'll be passin' by the club house an' we'll arrange to have a tray o' pints waitin' for them. Free pints'.

'Free pints?' Barney drifted back into consciousness.

'Except the pints'll be laced with a mickey finn.'

'Mickey Flynn?' asked Barney. 'Any relation, Frank?' Eugene ignored him.

'The particular concoction I have in mind is a laxative which was recommended by a pharmacist buddy o' mine. It comes in a dissolvable powder. He says that half a spoonful in a pint will have a definite effect.'

'How long does it take to work?' I asked.

My man says tha' it's on a fairly short fuse. He recommends standin' clear after the subject has had a good swig. Apparently a full dose is like Krakatoa. The thing is - an' yis need to use yis're imaginations here - a golfer who is concentratin' on keepin' the cheeks of his arse together isn't a golfer at his best.'

Heads nodded in understanding.

'I can see tha' righ' enough,' Joe said. 'But won't they know tha' there's somethin' rotten in the state o' Denmark when their whole team goes down with the trots, and we won't touch the free pints?'

'The thing is tha' there'll be a pint for everyone. The special pints will be jus' for the three star performers. Our lads an' the rest o' Kinsella's muckers won't be affected. We'll have our man on the spot givin' them out so tha' there'll be no mix up.'

'Hold on,' Paddy said, becoming all Presidential. 'There are ethical considerations to consider. Who is goin' to administer what is in effect a poison to fellow golfers in a sportin' competition?'

All hands went up.

'Fair enough,' Paddy said. 'An' ya say tha' ya have the stuff? Have ya tried it?'

'Well, I put a dollop into next door's dog's bowl an' he lapped it up.'

'An' wha' happened?' Joe asked.

'Well he looked a bit stunned before lettin' out a howl like the Hound o' the Baskervilles. Then his arse did a fair impression of a fire hose. I might've overdone it, maybe.'

'Jaysus, we don't want the three lads explodin' all over us, do we?' said Paddy.

'They'll be alrigh',' Eugene said. 'We'll only give them the half dose, enough to keep them anxious but not dissolvin' in a pool o' shite on the fairway.'

'An' how will ya be sure tha' the dose is righ'?' Paddy wanted to know.

'Cos I put it into the pints yis're drinkin',' he said.

There was a stunned silence, broken only by a gurgling sound coming from Barney's alimentary canal.

'Ya did wha'?' Joe asked in a tone I last heard when he was planning to inflict GBH on me.

'It's by way o' bein' a scientific experiment,' Eugene explained, but he was looking worried.

'Have ya taken it yerself?' Joe asked.

'Well no,' Eugene said. 'I'm the scientist. The scientist doesn't be in the experiments.'

'Where's the stuff?' Joe asked. 'Get it out quick. Betty, a pint o' stout please.'

While we were waiting I felt like something had come alive inside me. If a doctor told me that I was expecting triplets and that they were having a kicking competition, I'd have believed him. I could see from the squirming going on around me that the others were similarly afflicted.

Eugene reluctantly produced the powder and Joe poured so much of it into the new pint that it overflowed.

'There y'are now,' he said to Eugene. 'Get tha' down ya. Come on now. Bottoms up.'

'Joe, y'are bein' ridiculous,' Eugene said. He tried to get up but Joe had a paw on his shoulder so he was going nowhere.

'Drink it,' Joe said. 'It's a scientific investigation,' he said, mimicking Eugene.

It being clear to Eugene that he was a dead man walking, he started on the pint with a tentative sip. Then giving himself up to fate he downed half of it in a slug. We sat silently watching him. When I say 'silently' I'm excluding the rumbles and mutters of 'oh my Jaysus / for feck's sake' as our insides took on lives of their own.

Betty was obviously intrigued by the relative quiet.

'Wha's up with yis? Are yis prayin' or wha'?'

Nobody answered her.

'Will I put on another round?' she asked. 'Eh? Have yis lost the power o' speech?'

At that moment Eugene proved that he had not. Making a noise like a cow in the throes of labour, he jumped up and scurried towards the toilet. This wasn't easy as he was trying to move without separating his legs. It seemed vital to keep not just his buttocks clenched, but thighs, knees and ankles too.

'Is he alrigh'?' Betty asked.

'He's grand,' Joe said.

There came from inside the toilet the pitiful howls of a man in distress. If he had been a cow some kind person would have gone in and shot him.

'There's not a bother on him,' Joe said.

Realising that there was only one cubicle in the gents' facilities, and that Eugene would likely be in occupation for some time, Paddy brought the meeting to a rapid close. We all headed home, or in my case to Larkin's. Betty looked as stunned as a parish priest watching her devout congregation leaving halfway through the bidding prayers.

★★★

'Even as a child he was always thick,' Ma was reflecting on her beloved son. 'I mean lots o' young lads are stupid. Ya expect tha'. But Eugene was always a special kind o' stupid. If I told him not to do somethin' cos it'd hurt him, he wouldn't believe me til he tried it. He's bin burnt, electrocuted an' battered so often tha' if he wasn't a card short o' the full deck to start with, he is now.'

After I had attended to urgent business in the Larkin throne room, I reported the main events of the evening to her. I told her of Joe's return to the fold and Eugene's return to a primordial state of liquefaction.

'Maybe Betty Magowan'll send him home in a tin,' she said. 'Tha'd suit him. He was always a bit soupy. Or she could soak wha's left of him up in a bar towel an' send tha'.' She cackled like a football rattle. 'We could wring it out, leave it in the airin' cupboard, an' see wha' there's left of him in the mornin'.'

I marvelled at the depth of a mother's concern for her son.

A car pulled up outside and Ma pulled back the curtain for a look. Eugene emerged from a taxi like toothpaste coming slowly from a tube. After the cab rolled away he moved like a toddler taking its first steps. He put a foot forward a few inches, then another, and slowly built up momentum as he tottered towards the door. His mammy rushed to greet him, flinging open the portal and welcoming him like the long-lost fruit of her loins.

'Look at the state o' ya!' she said. 'Ya look like somethin' fished outa the Liffey. I've seen stale mince with more life in it.'

Eugene didn't seem to have the strength to respond. He got himself into the living room, supporting himself on the wall as he went, and sunk onto a chair.

'Ya stayed on for a bit,' I said, stating the obvious. He nodded. 'We would've waited for ya, bu' we had to run,' I said, again stating the obvious.

'I hope it learnt ya a lesson,' I said. 'My motto has always bin the one abou' doin' unto others. So I don't go aroun' puttin' laxatives into other fellas' pints. Ya have to think these things through Eugene, me oul flower. Ya put somethin' into Joe Horgan's pint an' he'll put somethin' into yours with interest an' bells on. I coulda told ya tha'.'

'A retarded worm coulda told him tha',' Ma said. 'Y'are no ordinary eejit an' tha's a fact. I remember the day ya were born I said to yer father - the Lorda mercy on him – 'there's somethin' missin' in tha' child.' Gormless, I thought. Ya looked lost, like ya'd got off the bus at the wrong stop.'

Having made these supportive remarks she rested her case. It all ran over Eugene like water off a duck. I supposed that he was used to it.

'Bu' Frank,' he said. 'Did the lads think it was a good idea? Ya know – the stuff – to put the mockers on Larkin's?'

'Well, we didn't exactly have enough time to sit around and discuss the pros an' cons of it. Bu' I suppose ya could say tha' the officers were persuaded an' voted wi' their feet.'

'They marched through the 'Aye' lobby?'

'Ran through it more like! In all fairness, ya managed to get the business done withou' the usual messin'. Ya know wha' Paddy'd be like - we coulda bin there til Christmas. No, I'd say ya made their minds up righ' enough.'

'An' we've a fair idea now o' the right dose as well,' he said. 'Ya see the benefits o' scientific experimentation. Wha' I found was …'

He was cut off by some internal flare-up which required a facial contortion and deprived him of speech. He tried to get to his feet, while keeping all systems clenched.

'Give us a hand up outa this quick,' he managed to gasp. 'I need to go again.'

'Get a move on Frank,' Ma said. 'Before me carpets are destroyed.'

Chapter 11

The following day I was catching up on the zzzs, in that state of sleepy wakefulness when reality gets all mixed up with dreams.

In the dream I was having, Peggy was calling my name. It wasn't in the fog-horn fashion she had adopted in recent years, used to command and berate me. This was more in the soft tones of yesteryear when she – and I don't say this lightly – regarded the ground that I walked on as sacred.

'Frank … oh Frank …'

I dreamt that I could feel the light touch of her fingers on my forehead. I sighed and curled up like a cat after its dinner.

'Frank!' The voice shifted a notch or two along the benign to malign scale – representing about ten years' progress in our relationship. Then the caressing fingers became weaponised and poked me in the back.

The contented cat suddenly felt like prey and curled into a tight defensive ball. I dreamt that I suffered a few more pokes, even more vigorous than the first. As this dream was becoming disagreeable I tried to change the channel. My imagination wafted me to Magowan's. I was having a pint and a packet of cheese and onion crisps – always a dream combination. Betty was clucking over me like a hen over her favourite chicken. I reached out for the pint but someone was holding my arm back. I was going to tell the someone to feck off with themselves, when the grip turned into a pull and I was yanked into full wakefulness.

I found myself in Larkin's spare bedroom in accordance with where I had installed myself the night before. My clothes hung over the back of a chair as per where I had left them. Ditto my shoes were where I had shuffled out of them. The two large items now unexpectedly present were Ma Larkin, smiling like the bad guy in a Bond movie just before he says 'Goodbye Mr Bond', and Peggy who seemed to be busying herself trying to pull my arm off.

'Waaah!' I said or something similar, as I couldn't conjure up a better bon mot to suit the occasion.

Peggy growled like a sheep shearer struggling with an uncooperative sheep – irritation mixed with a firm resolve to get the job done.

'Ah,' Ma said. 'Tha's lovely. The two love birds reunited!'

I had managed to squirm up the bed, over the pillows and a bit up the wall so that I was now almost fifty per cent vertical. From this vantage point I was better able to survey the lay of the land and give thought to my defence. Peggy also seemed happier with my changed position like it was where she had been intending to drag me. She let go of my arm and stood back.

'So this's where y'ave bin?' she asked. 'I might've guessed. I knew it'd be with some useless waster outa Magowan's.'

Ma cackled in agreement: 'Yep – tha's where he was alrigh'!'

Happy that she had me surrounded, Peggy planted her arse on top of my clothes on the chair. This squashed my shirt and any option I had of grabbing my gear and legging it. I was confused by the fact that she wasn't already busying herself scattering my limbs and organs like leaves in the autumn. In fact, a close reading of that body language that I know so well, suggested that my mutilation was not on schedule immediately. I didn't quite relax, but of the six hundred muscle groups in my body, five or six eased back on the vice-like grip.

'It was very hurtful, ya know,' Peggy said, 'jus' leavin' like tha' … withou' sayin' a word.'

I struggled to reconcile my flight to safety with Peggy's characterisation of me casually strolling off like Rhett Butler taking his leave of Scarlett O'Hara. Peggy sniffed and flapped her hand in front of her face to fan back an imaginary tide of tears. She turned to Ma to solicit a sympathetic vote.

'Men,' she said. 'They're all the same, aren't they?'

Ma Larkin agreed that indeed they were.

'Gobshites,' she said.

'Bastards,' Peggy said.

'Tha' an' all,' Ma affirmed.

'Mrs Larkin came around to see me this mornin',' Peggy said. This stirred my interest - not just in what they might have been chatting about – but because I had been labouring under the understanding that the old bat couldn't get farther than a few feet without assistance. She caught my eye and cackled.

'She told me wha' y'ave bin goin' through,' Peggy said.

I was mystified, and Ma was giving me no clues regarding what line of bull she had been feeding Peggy. Depending on her caprice I was either in clover or in shit. Like a gladiator my fate rested on the whim of a mad emperor's thumb. She cackled a bit more.

'Ya coulda come home ya know,' Peggy said. 'Any time. The door was always open to ya.'

I vaguely nodded that I did indeed know that, although I was pretty sure that I did not. It made as much sense to me as dousing myself in petrol, applying a match and being confident that I would find it a pleasant and warming experience.

'Mrs Larkin says tha' ya haven't bin well,' Peggy said. 'An' tha' ya find it hard to talk abou' yer problems. 'Bu' ya were always like tha'.'

'An emotional spastic,' Ma said. 'God love him.'

'There's no need to worry abou' it,' Peggy said. 'Lots o' people have breakdowns. Half o' the actors in Hollywood have had them. Ya'll be grand. Remember wha' Eileen Quigley went through? An' there's not a bother on her now.'

She was referring to a member of her extended family of lunatics. Even amongst that star troupe of fruit bats, Eileen stood out. She had very strong religious convictions. Once she slipped into a confession box in Gardiner Street, emerging stark naked during mass and asked the priest to baptise her. Peggy thought that the odd thing about that was that Eileen was already baptised! On another occasion Eileen handed herself in to the Guards, confessing to being an accessory in the murder of Jesus. They said they'd let her off with a caution if she promised not to do it again. She was a vegetarian and she was adamant that animals and even plants have souls and guardian angels. If so, Bertie's has been asleep on the job for a long time.

I couldn't imagine what standard Peggy was using in deciding that there wasn't a bother on Eileen now. In my considered view – and I am a connoisseur in the field of loonies – Eileen was nowhere near being able to sign anything containing the phrase 'I, Eileen Quigley, being of sound mind ...'

'Thanks,' I said, feeling that I needed to say something, but still not sure whether the conversation was developing in my interests.

Peggy stood up and lunged towards me. I shrank back like a snail before an avalanche of salt. I feared that all the guff up to then was some dirty trick to get my guard down. Peggy put her hand on my shoulder – not in the style of sheep shearer, but gently.

'Between us, we'll get through it so we will,' she said. 'Now tha' y'ave given up the drink, ya'll be alrigh'.'

Ma put her hand over her mouth to choke off a cackle and managed to turn it into a coughing fit.

'I told Peggy tha' y'are a changed man, Frankie,' Ma said. 'Tha' y'ave realised tha' the drink is the source o' all yer troubles. Bu' now tha' y'ave taken the pledge, y'are a new man.'

'It'll do ya good,' Peggy said. 'Sure yer insides mus' be like a distillery barrel - pickled wi' wha's bin sloshin' around in there all these years.'

'Sure the poor man can hardly be blamed for half his actions,' Ma said. 'Sure he's bin demented wi' drink.'

'I might've known,' Peggy said. 'When I think abou' you an' the Horgan one! I mean to say – Teresa Horgan - sure ya'd want to have somethin' gone loose in yer head! Mind you, I won't forgive her for takin' advantage of ya.'

'Bu' I didn't … I never …' I said.

'He doesn't remember,' Ma told Peggy. 'Tha's one o' the effects.'

'Do ya remember hidin' under her bed?' Peggy asked me like she was talking to a slow child or a pet.

I weighed which answer might do me least harm. While I was weighing, she moved on.

'Under her feckin' bed, he was!'

Ma looked mightily impressed by this snippet.

'Jaysus!' she said.

'Yeah - it was gas! I've never laughed so much in me life.'

I couldn't remember Peggy laughing then, or at many other times. Maybe I really was losing my grip.

'Wha' ya need is a good tonic,' Peggy said. 'I'll talk to the chemist an' see wha' they have. Maybe cod liver oil or Parrishs Food.'

'Or a good dose o' syrup o' figs,' Ma threw in, pawing the ground with a cloven hoof. 'Sure he's all bunged up. He's like a concertina with a strap tied around it. Loosen him up an' he'll be grand.'

My system was still getting itself back together from Eugene's poison. Any further loosening and limbs would start to fall off. I gave Ma one of my looks that turns normal people into granite, but it didn't work on her.

'Yeah bu' ...' I attempted to intervene before the pair of witches got around to eye of newt and toe of frog, but it was useless.

'Maybe best to go for the lot,' Peggy mused. 'To be on the safe side.'

'I would,' Ma agreed. 'A cocktail o' goodness. In for a penny; in for a pound – tha's your motto, isn't it Frankie? We'll soon have a bit o' colour back in yer cheeks - all four o' them! Anyway, get yerself up out o' tha' bed an' go home with this good wife o' yours. I'll bet ya can't wait to rip the knickers off her.'

To her credit, Peggy went red as I went green.

★★★

On reflection I was pleased that my deft management and understanding of the human psyche had got me back into Flynn HQ and the bosom of my telly. I had subtly manoeuvred Ma Larkin into doing my bidding. If I had asked the old gargoyle to go to Peggy and spin her some yarn about me turning into Matt Talbot, she would have told me to get lost. Knowing this I had used psychology like a judo expert. And here I was, once again lord of the Flynn manor and estate.

When I arrived back, like Caesar after knocking hell out of the Gauls, I found Bertie curled up on my chair. I suspected that the bugger had made it his own during my absence. Instead of leaping up to greet the old master in a display of loyalty that makes dog ownership such a joy, Bertie scowled and growled at me. I read the bared teeth not as a doggy smile of welcome but that the mutt regarded himself as the new pack leader.

The gauntlet he was throwing down said that if I had thoughts of regaining supremacy I would have to fight for it.

Needless to say up with this I was unwilling to put. We Flynns are a proud people and we do not kow-tow to bow-wows. I tipped the chair forward so that he was turfed onto the floor. This did not please him. He issued a war cry and made a charge at my ankles with sabre (i.e. teeth) drawn. Finely judging his advance, I stood aside like a matador at the last second and gave him a good kick up the arse as he shot past. I may even have cried: 'Olé!' If I didn't, I should have. Anyway the kick seemed to settle the matter. Bertie is not as stupid as most humans I know. I could see him weighing up the wisdom of continuing the joust, and after only a moment he decided that it would not be in his interests to persevere. He gave a few yaps which I interpreted as: 'Sir, I yield to your authority and superiority. The chair is yours.' He went and sat in his old place and I took up position in mine. If he had been wearing a cap I think he would have doffed it.

In my first couple of days back, Peggy constantly rattled around me with hoovers, mops and brushes, complaining that I was getting in her way and was generally a waste of space. 'Y'are neither tool nor ornament,' she told me more than once. Clearly she was delighted to have me back. She was also pleased that she thought she was purging me with her patent medications, but with some sleight of hand I managed to share it between the kitchen sink and Bertie's drinking bowl. I reckoned that if it didn't kill him it might give his coat a nice shine.

But if you are thinking that all was now rosy in Frankie's garden, you are mistaken. The honour of Magowan's and of the golf society still rested on my shoulders. Technically Paddy Mulhall was President, but he was only the puppet head of a regime that was really all mine. Paddy had some things in abundance - like his belly and his big mouth - but he couldn't outsmart a sheep. As the society's creator and driving intelligence I felt the burden of leadership weighing heavily. Even with Joe back in full training, and armed with a fool-proof plan to nobble the opposition, I fretted. The other matter scrummaging for my brain space was the business of getting Joe back to Teresa - but only after I could get the information for the bloody Unit from Celestina. Napoleon will have gone through something similar the evening before Waterloo, and I didn't want to make a hames of it like he did. Therefore I was not relaxed and at my ease. I would have paced up and down except that I am more of a sitter than a pacer. Whoever it was that said 'uneasy lies the head that wears the crown' had it bang on.

There was also the supreme irritation that Ma Larkin had told Peggy that I had forsworn the drink. Orange juice was uncharted territory for me. I have heard of people who swear by the stuff and who claim that it does wonders in fighting germs and restoring hair loss, but two nights in Magowan's lapping it up had not convinced me. I can drink nine of ten pints of stout and there wouldn't be a bother on me. The quality of conversation and debate is not affected. I might just become slightly more comfortable and relaxed. But after two glasses of juice I am bloated and farting like a trooper, and becoming irritable. It was also alarming and dismaying for those who knew and loved me. They found it unsettling as it challenged everything they knew to be pure and right and true. It was like Gandhi telling his followers that the only way to get ahead in life was with a gun. But Peggy was convinced that my mental health depended on me steering clear of anything distilled or fermented. She had even hidden the few bottles of firewater that I keep at home for medicinal purposes. A forensic search of the premises had failed to find any trace.

To make matters worse Peggy read in one of her magazines that Henry the Eighth's tetchy moods were brought on by a surfeit of meat. Therefore, possibly fearing for her neck Peggy had embarked on a root and branch review of the Flynn menu. The effect of this was that it now consisted mostly of roots and branches, and very little of anything that had ever drawn breath. The day I came back from Larkin's she went to the shops, or to the woods, and filled the cupboards with stuff that would have had me drooling if I was a budgie. In fact I was staring at a packet of chia seeds and thinking that my cup couldn't run over with much more effluent, when Eugene rang.

'Hello, Magpie, is tha' you?' he asked.

I chirped that I was that very bird and enquired what the hell he wanted.

'The Eagle wants to know how y'are gettin' on,' he said.

'Jaysus, Eugene,' I said. 'Will yis give me a chance to catch me breath?! If you an' Peggy would give over poisonin' me wi' laxatives an' chia seeds, I might have the energy …'

'Wha's chia seeds?' Eugene asked.

'They're like magic beans,' I said. 'Ya stick them up yer arse an' gobshites stop askin' ya stupid questions.'

'Okay, there's no need for tha',' Eugene said. 'This is official business. I need to make me report.'

'Look,' I said. 'I told Joe tha' I wanted to meet him over in his place to go over the golf thing, an' I'm doin' tha' this evenin'. I don't know whether Celestina will be there or not. Either way I'll see if I can have a deco aroun' an' see wha's wha'. Will tha' do ya?'

'I suppose it'll have to,' he said.

'It will,' I said. 'I'm not a bleedin' miracle worker.'

'Yeah,' Eugene said. 'Bu' don't forget tha' the Eagle is holdin' Jim Deegan on a short leash. Ya wouldn't want to risk tryin' the man's patience.'

'Feck off,' I said. Perhaps not the most professional way to end a business call, but I was like a camel finding that the final straw was attached to a brick.

That evening, after dining on a collation of unidentified root vegetables, I headed for the centre of the metropolis. It was a typical Dublin summer evening with a brisk gale and rain coming down as thick as soup. Thankfully the Lord in His wisdom had put a chipper beside the bus stop. I fell on it like a wolf on a sick lamb and acquired a take-away order of cod and chips. As I was waiting for the bus and lining my inner cavities, an oul wan turned to a black guy in the queue and said: 'Shockin' weather isn't it? I bet ya wish ya were back in Africa.' In as fine a Dublin accent as I've heard in years, he answered: 'Only when I meet the likes o' you.'

There was a pub across the street and I could smell and taste the stout from where I was standing. It was only the willpower of the Flynns that kept me at my station - well, willpower and fear of Peggy's formidable breathalyser skills. That woman could detect a molecule of alcohol through a concrete wall. She is forever accusing me of having drink taken, and to the best of my memory she has never been wrong.

I found Celestina alone at the flat. She said that Joe had a fare to some rural wasteland, but by then was expected to be speeding back to civilisation. I declined her offer of tea. As a man of the world I know that foreigners have the reverse Midas touch when it comes to tea. Let them touch a tea bag with boiling water and the result is lukewarm piss. How they do it is a mystery. I've stood and watched them go through the correct procedure, but the result is always the same.

Celestina was in the state of semi-nudity that she regarded as appropriate for entertaining guests. God knows what she would wear if she was having a quiet evening relaxing on her own. Arms, shoulders, and legs wafted from a black chiffony thing, like they were under the influence of a gentle breeze. I thought to myself that if she was planning on living long-term in Ireland, early death from hypothermia was a certainty.

'So, Frankee,' she said. 'You and Joe are friends again?'

'Ah yeah,' I said. 'Sure there was never any problem really. Me an' Joe are cast from the same whatyamaycallit.'

'The same …?' Celestina was unfamiliar with the term.

'Mould. Pod. Hewn from the same rock. Y'know wha' I mean.'

She didn't.

'Dojamaflip,' I said and left it at that. If her command of English was limited to 'hat', 'mat' and 'cat', she was beyond my help.

'I think that Joe was not happy before, but now he is happy again,' she said. 'Last night he was very good in our lovemaking. I think a man can only do it when he is happy. Is it not so, Frankee?'

I had no wish to discuss or even think about that class of thing. I would sooner have shared Bertie's dinner as chat about Joe's carnal manoeuvrings. This woman was capable of sharing intimate details in the way that ordinary people swap recipes. I am an Irishman, not a Frenchman or an Italian. Given the climate, the church and the nature of Irish women, it's a wonder that we do sex at all. But we certainly don't talk about it. So I needed to change the subject. I feared that she might ask me what my own favourite position was, and 'the bar stool' would only have confused her.

'Yeah, maybe,' I said. 'How are ya gettin' on at work?'

'Oh, I do not work at golf club any more. I have new job. With Narusian colleagues in Dublin. Is business – I help with papers and translations.'

I thought that the translations would have been fun to see and hoped that they didn't include instructions for operating machinery.

'Congratulations,' I said. 'All the best wi' tha'. Where is it? An office somewhere?'

'Not office – only here,' she said waving a vague arm. I looked around and could no turning wheels of industry. She followed my gaze and said:

'Is in other room – in box.'

'Tha's handy,' I said. Ya keep it all in a box. Is it a big box?'

She thought this was very funny and laughed.

'No, not big box – come see.'

I was reluctant to follow her, fearing that the little reserve she had might be lost altogether in the boudoir. The room had very little in it other than a bed, covered by a red duvet thing that looked like it had been pumped full of air, and about a hundred pillows. Not a sign of a good Catholic blanket or a candlewick bedspread anywhere. The place smelled like Arnott's perfume department. I gagged and it was only the Flynn breeding that stopped me from spitting.

'Here is box,' she said, pointing to the holy-grail. In a previous career it had served as the residence of twelve bottles of wine. It matched the surroundings in a way that a banana box never could. With the overpowering smell, my mind wandered off to where I didn't want it to go. I imagined Joe as Nero slurping wine from a slipper with Celestina draped around him like an octopus. I shook my head to clear the image.

'A career in a box,' I said. 'Tha's great.'

'Is very important papers,' she told me.

From where I was standing I could only see documents standing on their ends with a few yellow labels poking out at intervals. It was obviously the stuff the Unit was excited about. If I could get my hands on it they would get off my back, and I could retire to civilian life. But I couldn't just ask her for it – 'any chance of a loan o' yer box' didn't seem like a winning proposition. And I couldn't just grab it and run. What was required was guile and subtlety. Aladdin's missus parted with the magic lamp for a shiny new one so I thought I'd give that a go.

'Ya'll need somethin' better than tha',' I said. I had seen our Marian with fancy box files where papers could be filed alphabetically. 'In business,' I said, 'ya have to invest in plant an' equipment. Infrastructure. When Arthur Guinness started he only had a sheaf o' barley an' a bucket o' water. He realised tha' he couldn't quench the thirst o' the nation with tha'. He needed a factory, workers, filin' cabinets, tea-breaks … the whole shemozzle.'

Celestina had lost me again.

'I need shemozzle?'

'Not immediately,' I said. 'Righ' now, ya jus' need a new box. One wi' sections for puttin' different things in. If y'are goin' to be in business, ya have to do it righ'.'

'So I need other box?'

'Ya do. Don't worry abou' it. I'll get ya one outa Eason's.'

'I can get more box from shop on corner,' she said. 'Is no problem. Shop has plenty boxes.'

I shook my head sadly.

'No,' I said. 'Ya don't understan'. It's the way ya have to do things. It's like the law.'

'There is law for boxes?' she asked.

'There is,' I said. 'The Storage o' Papers an' Miscellaneous Articles Act. Ya have to have a proper box. Tha's all there is to it.'

This seemed to push the right button. Narusian children are obviously brought up with a respect for the law and the need to obey every nuance. In Ireland laws are regarded as guidelines. They are discretionary, advisory things. The legislature is made up of a bunch of yahoos with nothing better to do than dream up ridiculous rules that are best ignored. It is understood that even their best efforts couldn't be expected to foresee all the circumstances that might apply. Hence the need for discretion. The average Irishman only feels that laws should be interpreted rigidly to other people, and where failure to do so would adversely affect his own interests.

'Look, don't you worry abou' it. Jus' give me the stuff an' I'll nip into Eason's tomorra an' sort it out for ya. I'll see wha' they have an' get one tha' fits. It'll all be grand … legal an' above-board.'

She was looking undecided so I went past her and took up the box. She didn't object.

'I'll have it back to ya tomorra. How's tha'?'

'That is good,' she said accepting it. 'You are kind.'

Now that I had the stuff in my mitts, I wasn't letting go.

'Righ',' I said. 'I'll be off so.'

'But, you want to see Joe,' she said. 'About golf?'

'Oh tha',' I said. 'That'll be alrigh'. Joe'll be tired. Tell him to leave it to Frankie. It's all in safe hands.'

'Not in box?' she asked.

Only I knew better, I thought that she might have been attempting a joke.

Chapter 12

'This is fantastic work, Frank,' Eugene said. 'The Eagle will be delighted.'

I didn't care how delighted the Eagle might be. My limited aim was to keep the Eagle and Deegan at the indifferent end of the indifferent-to-pissed-off-with-Frankie scale. Anything more was a waste of effort. As soon as I got back home I had called Eugene with the news that I was in possession of the goods. He was all for coming around immediately and taking the box to the Unit but I told him to feck off as I needed my rest. Not that I got much! My burden of care was enough to keep a rock awake and I was trying to lose consciousness on nothing more than a swig of Listerine.

I had just drifted off when Eugene was hammering on the door like the Israelites at the gates of Jericho. Even Peggy was still in bed and she is normally up and creating havoc before dawn. Bertie was barking his nut off, pretending to be a guard dog. He is unused to receiving callers at such an hour and felt some doggie obligation to raise the alarm. Realising that it was bloody Eugene, I despatched Peggy downstairs to tell him and Bertie to desist from the racket-making, and for Eugene to come back at a more civilised hour, like maybe tea time. Two minutes later Eugene and Malachy had invaded my private chamber and were making serious nuisances of themselves.

'Tea Mrs,' Malachy shouted down the stairs to Peggy like a surgeon instructing his assistant. Even in my semi-comatose state I thought he was pushing his luck addressing Mrs F in such a cavalier manner.

'Where's the box?' Eugene wanted to know.

From the depths of stupor I told him where the box was resting and may have added a suggestion regarding where he might stick it.

'Come on Frank,' he said. 'Chop, chop. We have the car outside and we want to get outa here before it's up on blocks.'

'It'll be alrigh',' I said. 'The scangers don't get up before noon. Wha' time is it anyway?'

'Quarter past seven,' he said. I opened an eye to check the bedside clock for verification of this incredible information. It was true.

'Ah Eugene, would ya ever …'

Peggy arrived with a tray bearing tea and toast. She didn't seem to be bearing Malachy any ill will. 'Get tha' down yis,' she said. She sat down on a chair and the lads lined up beside her shoving their snouts into the trough. I sat up and joined in before all the toast was gone.

'This is grea',' I said in what I hoped was a sarcastic tone. 'We mus' do it more often. Feel free to drop in any time.'

'Are yis goin' into town?' Peggy asked. 'Ya could give me a lift. Drop me outside Clery's if it isn't outa yer way.'

'No can do, Peggy,' Eugene said. 'We're on official business. Against regulations.'

'Regulations me arse,' I said. I wasn't keen on having Peggy along, but I wasn't going to have any wife of mine oppressed by the State in my own bedroom.

'Yis can give her a lift, or yis can feck off,' I said.

Unfortunately the mention of official business had stimulated Peggy's interest. Until now she had assumed that this early morning raid must was something to do with the strange rituals of golfers. She may have been aware that dedicated members of the golf cult like to be on the first tee to witness the sun rising and hear the sparrows gargling and cleaning their teeth.

'Official business?' she wanted to know. 'Wha' are yis talkin' abou' – official business?'

I drew breath in preparation to issuing some line of bullshit. I don't know exactly what it would have been – just that when Peggy has me in a spot I open my mouth and stuff comes out - and it usually does the trick. It's a kind of Darwinian auto-response that's been bred into husbands down the ages. Every man I know has a strong bullshit gene, those that don't having long ago gone the way of the dodo. But before I could let loose Malachy was in the hole, digging like a Kerry man who has lost a euro.

'I'm afraid that we are not at liberty to reveal that information, Mrs Flynn. It's subject to the Official Secrets Act and only available to authorised officials.'

It was still early and Peggy wasn't properly warmed up yet. A few hours later she would have taken Malachy's Official Secrets Act, buttered it and shoved it down his throat. Instead, strangely, she seemed to be thinking before she spoke. The pause was enough for Eugene to save the day by blowing smoke across the battle field.

'Tha's righ',' he said. 'If we told ya, we'd have to kill ya. Strict rules o' the Society. Isn't tha' righ' Frank?'

'Spot on,' I said.

Peggy had long ago concluded that I and anyone who associated with me were morons of the first water, and she regarded time spent thinking about our concerns as time wasted. She shook her head in irritation and finished her tea.

'Golf society!' she said. 'Bunch o' eejits! Come on then if yis're comin'.'

She gathered up the crockery even though we weren't finished with it.

'Come on you. Get yerself outa tha' bed. Y'are like King Tut lyin' there, surrounded by yer stalactites.'

'Ya mean 'acolytes',' Eugene said and his whole life passed before my eyes.

'Don't you get smart wi' me, Eugene Larkin,' Peggy said. 'I know wha' I mean, an' if I call ya a stalactite, then y'are a feckin' stalactite. Yer mother told me all abou' ya, so ya needn't be comin' in here givin' me elomocution lessons. Come outa here now the pair o' yis an' let tha' gobdaw get himself up.'

They withdrew and I prepared myself to meet my public.

★★★

On the way into town, Malachy hit the kerb twice and came within a Rizla of hitting a bus.

'For God's sake,' I said to him. 'Ya nearly hit tha'.'

'I nearly hit wha'?'

'The bus,' I said. 'Tell me this - when was the las' time ya had yer eyes tested?'

He didn't answer as he spotted a red light just as he was passing it and had to suddenly drop anchor. We were nearly dissected by the seatbelts.

We dropped Peggy off beside Clery's as instructed, and Eugene crossed over to Eason's to get a folder for Celestina. Weaving around Trinity College towards the Unit Eugene told me again of the Eagle's delight.

'It's a great day for the Unit. Tha's a fact.'

'Yis're marvellous,' I said. 'Bu' don't forget who it was tha' went into the valley o' death to get it for yis. Me!' A thought occurred to me. 'I don't suppose the Eagle'll be so pleased tha' he'll lay a little golden egg for Frankie?'

'Ah no,' Eugene said. 'The Unit doesn't have a budget for tha' class o' thing. Other than yer properly incurred expenses. An' ya'll have to be charged for the clothes we gave ya. Government property, y'know.'

'So all I can get is a refund for me bus fares, an' I'll have to pay for the rubbish tha' yis got from the charity shop? Thanks for nothin'!'

The car had by now bounced its way into the underground car park.

'Thanks Malachy,' I said. 'Y'are a great driver.'

'Ah I dunno,' he said modestly. 'I'm no Jackie Stewart, but I reckon I'd be on the podium righ' enough.'

We got out, Eugene carrying the box like a new born babby, and headed for the lift. A sign said that it was out of order.

'We'll have to go down the secret stairway,' Malachy said.

'Yeah, I suppose,' Eugene said. 'Where is it?'

'I dunno. I'll ring an' ask.'

Malachy pressed a couple of buttons on his mobile.

'Howya Eileen? Howsitgoin?' he said, launching into the essential small-talk precursor to any serious conversation between Irish people.

'I didn't think ya were in today,' he said. 'I thought ya said ya were goin' down to yer sister in Wexford.'

There was a pause while Eileen updated him on the reasons for the changes to her plans. I discerned that Eileen's cat had succumbed to a feline ailment and she felt that it would be unreasonable to ask her neighbour – who was happy to undertake routine cat-feeding duties – to sit at the cat's bedside, holding its paw and giving it warm drinks. She went on to say that the visit was not cancelled, merely deferred. Malachy seemed relieved.

'Ah good,' he said. 'Ya'll prob'ly enjoy it more then. Withou' the worry like. Listen, will ya do us a favour Eileen. Me an' the Falcon are above in the car park ... an' the lift ... ah ya know about it bein' broke ... o' course ya would ... anyway ... where's the feckin' secret stairs? ... Yeah ... Righ'... Grand ... Ah, yeah, I thought they might be there right enough ...

- 186 -

What is it? … Four, five, seven, nine. Gotcha …thanks … see ya in a minute … yeah, bye … thanks.'

He ended the call and led us towards a corner of the car park.

'It's over here behind the bins,' he said.

We found a steel door with a sign cunningly misinforming the world that this was a store room containing cleaning materials, and furthermore that they were hazardous. That would have slowed down the enemies of the state as they would have had to pause to do a health and safety assessment before progressing. Inside there was a key pad on the wall.

'Four, five, seven, nine,' I reminded Malachy when he looked doubtful.

'Thanks,' he said, and pressed the buttons. The back of the store clicked open and we descended a flight of concrete steps, went through another door, and once again we entered into the throbbing heart of the Unit. As at my last visit this was the limit of Malachy's jurisdiction. He turned and left us. A woman, whom I assumed to be Eileen, looked up and, demonstrating her talent for intelligence, said: 'Ye got in alright?'

Eugene confirmed that we had indeed got in, and Eileen directed us to a room she referred to as 'Briefing One'. Eugene explained to me that this featureless box was used for ultra-confidential briefings. He said that the walls were made of concrete or lard or something impenetrable. He said that it was bug-proof, sound-proof and bomb-proof. Unfortunately it wasn't idiot-proof. As the Eagle approached, Eugene stood in the open doorway and said at the top of his voice: 'Isn't it great, sir? The Magpie is only after gettin' the whole kit and caboodle for us.'

The Eagle came in and closed the door behind him. The room was about ten foot by six. A nine by five steel table filled it so that we just about managed to squeeze ourselves onto three chairs around it. The Eagle and Eugene sat down opposite me like in an interview. On the wall over their heads a white plastic thing blinked a red light. I nodded at it and said: 'Camera, I suppose? Yis're recordin' every word are yis?' They glanced around at it and seemed surprised to see it.

'No,' Eugene said. 'I think it's a burglar alarm.'

'Ya think!' I echoed, tempted to add some sarcastic flavouring to the remark, but I stayed strong.

'Have you looked at the documents?' the Eagle wanted to know.

'No, I haven't,' I said. 'Wha' would I be lookin' at them for?'

Eugene and the Eagle dived into the box like two kids opening their Christmas presents. When Eugene seemed to be leading the extraction, the Eagle glared at him so that Eugene backed off leaving his boss at it.

'It looks like the business alrigh', doesn't it?' Eugene asked.

'It does,' the Eagle confirmed. 'Dates. Manifests. Suppliers. Distributors. Bank details. Let's give it to Eileen and get the lot copied.' Eugene gathered the papers up and flew off like a falcon going to build its nest.

'We'll organise the originals into your new folder and you can be on your way,' the Eagle said to me. 'Do you know Mr Flynn, you're a natural at this type of work. A natural!' I was not surprised that he recognised talent when he saw it.

'The Flynns always had a bit o' tha' in them,' I told him. 'Subterfuge. Smoke an' mirrors. The oul sleight o' hand. I don't need to tell *you*.' He nodded that indeed I did not. 'I'll give ya an example,' I said. 'Every year me an' the missus used to have a chalet in Butlin's. It was supposed to take four. D'ya know how many we used to get into it?' He didn't even try to guess. 'Twelve,' I said. 'In fairness, tha' was the record. It was usually only eight or nine. The kids an' their pals an' a few cousins. Still, it needed guile to pull it off. The security was deadly. Even the chamber maids would've bin at home in a POW camp. They did their rounds with mops an' sniffer dogs. Bu' I laughed at their best efforts. They were suspicious but we were never caught.'

I could see that he was impressed.

'Well you certainly have a talent, and you can be proud that you've used it in the service of your country. The Minister would like you to know that he is very appreciative. Of course there can be no official recognition. We are all unsung heroes here.'

'I don't suppose the Minister'd be appreciative enough to slip me somethin' unofficial for me trouble?' I asked, chancing my arm.

The Eagle looked as sad as a wet hen.

'Not possible I'm afraid,' he said. 'In the old days we could do things, but now it's all signed requisitions and auditors.'

He shook his head remembering the halcyon days of his youth when envelopes stuffed with cash were part of a day's work. We silently agreed that political correctness and an unhealthy public interest in the affairs of men like the Minister, the Eagle and me had brought the country to a sad state.

'A coupla tickets for the All Ireland maybe?' I asked, giving it a last go.

He winced sadly. 'But if there's ever anything we can do, anything at all … a word in the right ear would be no problem, if you know what I mean?' He tapped his nose which confused me. He may have been aiming at his ear and missed.

At that point Eugene returned with Eileen. He carried the boxes and she had two heaps of papers.

'Here we are now,' she said like a kindergarten teacher. 'We'll get the originals into your nice new file for you, and you'll be all set.'

She commenced sorting the papers with the practiced hand of a Mississippi card player.

'It's important that there should be no suspicion,' the Eagle said to me. 'Just behave naturally.'

'Naturally?' I asked, not sure what that might look like. I act naturally all the time until someone tells me to do it, and then I don't know how.

'Jus' be yerself Frank,' Eugene said. 'An eejit.'

'Feck off,' I replied. It may have been undiplomatic language but I meant every word.

'Now,' Eileen said, slipping the last paper into the file. She gave it a little pat and pushed it across the table to me. She smiled encouragingly like I needed to be coaxed into taking it. I put it under my oxster and stood up.

'Righ',' I said. 'I'm outa here, an' with a bit o' luck I won't be back.'

'Your help is much appreciated,' the Eagle said. 'Much appreciated.'

'I'd love to tell yis tha' it's bin a pleasure, but it hasn't, so I won't.'

The Eagle gave me an understanding handshake and Eileen smiled at me sympathetically like I was a toddler who had had a trouser incident. 'I hope yer pussycat gets better soon,' I said to her, wriggling free of Briefing One's furniture and heading for the secret staircase.

'Malachy's outside,' Eugene said. 'He'll give ya a lift.' But I was keen to sever all contact with the Unit at the earliest opportunity so I just got Malachy to point me in the direction of the street, and I was gone.

★★★

Celestina was thrilled with the new box file. It was divided into concertina slots – one for each letter of the alphabet - other than X Y and Z which shared a slot. This may have been unfortunate as I suspect that most words in Narusian start with one of those letters.

'Frankee,' she said. 'You are very good. Is very good file.'

She beamed at me in the manner Eileen would use on a kid who had done well in a colouring competition. I waved her thanks away and asked her where Joe was.

'He is doing deliveries for me. He collects from airport and delivers. In taxi,' she added in case I was picturing him going around Dublin with a hand cart.

I wasn't happy that Joe was getting into this, especially as he wasn't clued in to the fact that there was shady work afoot - and certainly not that the forces of law and order were massing with bloodhounds, court orders and manacles. It would have been a disaster if Joe was caught with a Toyota full of contraband – especially if it was before we won the golf match. I resolved that I would have to tip him the wink.

'Wha' time is he due back?' I asked.

She shrugged.

'He said he go to meeting later,' she said. 'For golf.'

It had slipped my mind that the golf committee was meeting in Magowan's that evening to fine tune the match strategy.

'Righ',' I said. 'I'll see him then. An' c'mere, do me a favour will ya? Don't give Joe any more delivery jobs for a while. I need him to be in trainin' for the golf. D'ya see?'

She didn't.

'Trainin',' I repeated while I mimed a bit of weight-lifting. It didn't help.

'Look, jus' don't give him any more jobs for a few days. No more. Nix. Nada. Feck all.'

I hoped that the general gist had percolated but I wasn't confident.

★★★

Later that day I was back in the happy home, pleased to have rid myself of Celestina's file and not to have the sword of Deegan and the Unit hanging over my head. Bertie gave the outward impression of being reconciled to my return from exile. But deep down I knew that the little bastard was as pissed off with me as the goody-goody brother was with the Prodigal Son. I patted him on the head, not out of any affection but in a proprietorial way, just to show him who was boss. He pulled a face and tried to shrink away so I ruffled his fur to annoy him. Knowing what a perfidious hound he is, I stayed on guard. Bertie has a set of gnashers on him that could shred steel, and he is not beyond using them.

'Will ya leave tha' poor animal alone,' said the love of my life. 'It'd learn ya if he took a lump outa ya.'

Peggy wandered off to the kitchen to do something with meat or veg.

'Fleabag,' I said and Bertie growled. I thought of taking a swipe at him, but he was half-expecting it so it would have risked a finger. I decided to wait until he was having his dinner when he would be fully concentrated on the job in hand. Then I'd give him such a boot up the hole that his testicles would make his eyes light up like pinballs. Our eyes locked and I think he was reading my mind. He showed me a line of teeth which I don't think was an attempt at a smile.

'Angela is comin' aroun' in a minute,' Peggy said.

'Is she?' I asked. Just when I think all is rosy in the garden another hurricane is forecast.

'She is,' Peggy said. 'She wants to eat the head off ya - after wha' ya done.'

'If it makes her feel better,' I said.

'It won't make *you* feel better anyway - I can tell ya tha'. She'll go through ya for a shortcut.'

This was not much of a surprise to me. Protocol demanded that Angela would have to come round and give me a Bertie-style welcome home. In the strange fiction of the Irish household the woman is always the wronged party in any matrimonial disagreement. It was the man's lot to take all the vilification that the females could conjure, and shut up about it. I am well used to the 'bad cop / worse cop' routine which Peggy and her eldest daughter have worked on me over the years. If one of them accuses me of the slightest misdemeanour, the other is on hand to support the charge with half-baked or even no evidence. If either feels miffed by my acts or omissions, the other magnifies and exaggerates the alleged effect. My tiniest whimsical remark is blown out of proportion, and I get accused of bullying, mental cruelty and ruining lives. Defending myself is like wielding a parasol against a fire hose.

Peggy saw Angela at the garden gate and went to meet her. I heard her giving Angela a briefing by the door before she led her in like a trainer steering a boxer into the ring. Peggy looked confident that the bout would end in the first round with me lying in a bloody heap. All the Flynn females were built on thoroughbred lines but Angela took after her mother, who was bred for plough-pulling and heavy lifting.

'Well, look wha' the cat's dragged in,' Angela said, referring of course to yours truly. I passed up the opportunity of pointing out that we did not have a cat, due to Bertie's cat-intolerance. Instead I conceded the floor and allowed her to make her opening statement.

'I hope y'are ashamed o' yerself - after wha' y'are after puttin' me Ma through?'

This was a trick question based on a debatable premise. There was no way to respond that would leave me anywhere other than up to my neck in it. I resolved on silence as the best policy, so it was to my great surprise that I heard myself speaking.

'Look, Angela,' I said - immediately regretting these words as being construable as heartless and unfeeling. Peggy would have been a mere amused spectator until I opened my big mouth. Now that I had foolishly indicated - even in this tiny way - that I might plead anything other than 'guilty as charged' I was in big trouble. Peggy started to screech like Angela's theoretical cat caught in a vice.

'Did ya hear tha'? Tryin' to wiggle his way outa it. Tha's typical! Typical! Tha's wha' I've had to put up with for years. Since you an' Marian were little, he's bin the same. Takes responsibility for nothin'. Nothin's ever his fault. A proper man'd apologise.'

'Tommy would,' Angela agreed.

Tommy was Angela's hypochondriac husband. He hadn't had a drink since their youngest was born when my encouragement for him to join the celebrations hadn't ended well for him. I couldn't imagine him needing to apologise for anything, other than maybe his existence.

'Look,' I said. 'The whole thing was jus' a misunderstandin', tha's all. Yer mother got the wrong end o' the stick...'

Peggy jumped to her feet, so that she and Angela had me surrounded on four sides. I was like a canoe on rough seas being run down by oil tankers.

'Wrong end o' the stick!' Peggy shouted into my face. 'If I had a stick now I'd bate ya goodlookin'.'

'Y'are too soft on him, Ma,' Angela said, showing a deplorable lack of filial loyalty to the man who had dangled her on his knee, and let her ride on his back until her broadening dimensions made this dangerous. 'Ya let him get away with murder. If Tommy did the half of wha' he does, I'd swing for him I would.'

'Ah, y'are blessed wi' poor Tommy, God love him,' Peggy said. 'Not a useless soak like yer father, spendin' mornin', noon an' nigh' up in Magowan's.

'Hold on a minute,' I said coming up for air. 'I'm not goin' to sit here in me own home, listenin' to this tripe. Angela, I'll ask you to mind yer own feckin' business...'

'I won't…' she said.

I cut her off by holding up my hand like Canute, but with more effect.

'Wait,' I said. 'Stop gabbin' an' ya might learn somethin'. Yer mother an' me are well capable o' sortin' out our own differences. If she has somethin' in her craw she's well capable o' spittin' it out, without you stickin' yer oar in. Am I right or am I right?'

I looked to Peggy for verification. She seemed to be struggling with the pros and cons of Angela's oar being shoved into her craw. While she did so Angela had another go:

'I was jus'…'

But I felt that I had momentum on my side.

'Well jus' don't bother,' I said. 'There's no market for it here. Now if there's nothin' else, I'm goin' down to Magowan's for a sarsaparilla.'

Peggy seemed to be still considering oars and craws, and Angela's wind had left her sails, leaving her momentarily becalmed. Knowing that this state of affairs would not last long, I gathered up my outdoor raiment and exited without further comment. As I passed Bertie on my way to the door I thought that he looked up at me with a new respect.

Chapter 13

I tried to make a virtue of my soft drink misery by suggesting that the lads join me on the wagon. 'Ya don't get Seve an' Tiger goin' on the lash when they're in trainin',' I told them.

Barney Magee looked as disgusted as if I had proposed some communal lewd act while the rest just laughed as they would at the nonsense of a child. Betty glared at me like I was trying to steal the bread from the mouths of her starving children – if she had any children and they were starving, only she hasn't and they're not.

'It's your round Frank,' Joe said, 'so pay up and shut up.'

'Yeah righ', hold on,' I said. 'Betty, give us five pints an' another one o' them orangey things.'

The orangey thing was a chemical compound made of salt, dye, corn syrup and monosomething glue. No orange that ever hung from a tree had been harmed in its creation. I tried dropping a vodka into one, to add a natural ingredient, but it only made it worse. It was like cough medicine laced with battery acid. When I was passing the pints to the lads, some creamy head spilled onto my hand. I licked it off and nearly cried. It was like nectar, although to tell the truth I've never tasted nectar but from the excellent reviews it gets, it must taste like a good pint. I would have given unto the half my kingdom for a pint. My hi-viz poison had the taste sensation of something infected.

'Tha' stuff is agreein' with ya, Frankie,' Miley said. 'Y'are lookin' well on it.'

'Yeah,' Paddy agreed. 'Y'are gettin' a lovely tan. Like yer man on the telly – whassisname?'

'Yeah,' Miley said. 'The gay fella.'

'Wha?' Paddy said. 'I didn't know he was gay. Where did ya hear tha'?'

'Are ya jokin' me or wha'?' Miley asked. 'O' course he's gay - ya jus' have to look at him. No man has skin tha' colour unless he's gay.'

'Well Frankie has,' Joe contributed.

'Well, maybe Frank is after goin' over to the other side. Have yis seen his new golf outfit? He looks like a bleedin' rainbow.'

'Feck off,' I said.

'Frank, there's nothin' to be ashamed of,' Paddy said. 'Y'are among friends here. If y'are explorin' yer sexuality, tha's yer own business. We'll understan' if y'ave decided to give it a go. C'mere, tell us this - I saw ya were walkin' funny comin' back from the bar. I suppose it mus' be sore at first, is it?'

I wasn't amused.

'Wha's wrong with ya Frank?' Joe asked. 'Ya've a puss on ya like a buckled wheel.'

It was true that my disposition was far from sunny. I was in 'deep depression, sudden squalls may be expected' territory. I was pining for a pint, anxious about the golf, and having the piss extracted from me through every orifice. I looked at the orange gloop in my glass and gave serious thought to upending it over my tormentors. My hand was stalled only by Betty's code of behaviour which takes a dim view of people throwing drink around.

'Feck off,' I said, and lest there should be confusion as to who exactly should feck off, I added: 'Feck off the lot o' yis.'

Of course they were delighted to have irritated me to this extent. That part of the meeting having been concluded to their satisfaction, they settled down to business. Paddy remembered his position of authority and called the rabble to order.

'Settle down lads,' he said. 'Item one. How are we fixed for Saturday?

'Everythin' is sorted,' Eugene said. 'I've got the stuff an' Ginger has volunteered to come an' look after the half-way refreshments.'

'No better man for the job,' I said.

Ginger made a living providing the Daymo with satellite TV services without anyone being bothered by monthly payments. A few quid into his fist and you could have every channel known to man with no further strain on the bank balance. So as our need was for a man with a flexible moral code, we had the right candidate in Ginger.

'He's happy to put the stuff into the Kinsella lads' pints?' Paddy asked.

'No bother to him,' Eugene confirmed. 'Didn't bat an eyelid. It was like tellin' him that they'd want sugar in their tea. He's such a natural born chancer he'll look them in the eye an' tell them to enjoy.'

'I was thinkin',' Paddy said.

'Tha' musta hurt,' Joe said.

Paddy looked dignified, or maybe constipated, and continued: 'We'll have to make out tha' we're sufferin' too – so tha' they don't cop on tha' it's only them. D'yis folley me?'

We all nodded at the wisdom of this - well, all except Barney, who was having his usual difficulty keeping up.

'Wha' d'ya mean?' he asked. 'We won't be drinkin' the quare pints. We'll be grand.'

Paddy put his hands to his head in frustration.

'God help us!' he said. 'We'll jus' be lettin' on. Actin'. Ya can act can't ya? Y'ave bin actin' the eejit for years. All ya have to do is rub yer belly. Moan. Push yer dinner away.'

Barney was struggling with the idea of pushing his dinner anywhere other than into his gob.

'Don't worry,' Joe said. 'If he's lookin' too healthy, I'll give him a good kick in the knackers that'll put him in the righ' frame o' mind.'

'Thanks Joe,' Paddy said. Barney looked confused as to whether he should also thank Joe.

The talk then turned technical and I will not detain you here with the details. For example opinion was divided on the best approach to the tricky fifth green which is surrounded by bunkers. There was also heated discussion on the best club to use on the exposed twelfth tee in the event of a strong crosswind. This stuff is meat and drink to golfers but is of no interest to the general sane reader. Therefore rather than risk numbing your brain I will move on.

★★★

The competition fell on a typical Irish mid-summer's day. Rain was driving in from several directions at once. It was that special Irish stuff that is wetter than elsewhere in the world – a mush of liquid and vapour that gets into places that would be proof against liquid alone.

We met at Magowan's and Paddy had organised a minibus to get us out to Dunsheelin. In the clubhouse there was a spread of sausage and rasher sandwiches. The staff were under strict instructions to dodge requests for tea. Darren, the catering manager, was by now well used to our little eccentricities so the request didn't faze him. As long as we weren't ordering up baskets of fruit, he was happy.

As I watched the rain lashing down outside I would have been happy to scratch the whole thing. Then the Kinsellites started slagging us off, so there could be no retreat. Their golf society was going for years so the members had built up a fair amount of kit. This included rainwear that would have kept them dry in a car wash. By contrast, what we had was only designed to keep the worst of the weather off while running from the pub to the bookies.

'I hope yis get the weather yis're hopin' for,' Squirrel Kavanagh said, enjoying the spectacle of us in our anoraks. He was wearing something designed for a helicopter rescue crew.

'They're hardy bucks – the men from Magowan's!' Brillo Brennan said in mock homage.

'We'll be alrigh',' I said. 'Ya can't swing a club properly if y'are dressed like a feckin' astronaut.'

'Where did ya get them clubs, Frankie?' Squirrel wanted to know. 'I've never seen tha' make before.'

'Well ya wouldn't, would ya,' Brillo said helpfully. 'They're bespoke. Isn't tha' righ' Frank? Didn't ya have them specially made to suit ya – with you havin' yer arms longer than yer legs?'

This got a great laugh and I was irritated to see Barney joining in.

'It's wha' ya do with them tha' matters,' I said. 'It's all very well goin' out on the course lookin' like mannequins, but can yis play? Tha's the question.'

I felt that that was indeed the question. And based on our plans for nobbling the enemy I was fairly sure of the answer. I looked forward to seeing the Squirrel trying to find his arse in his huge romper suit.

'Tha' thing y'are wearin' looks fairly waterproof righ' enough,' I said to him.

'Ya could go scuba divin' in it, and' ya'd stay as dry as a camel's mickey,' he assured me.

His outfit had elasticated neck, cuffs and ankles and I had pleasant thoughts of the pressure building up inside until his vital juices exploded out through those very portals. I hoped to be present at the time – but not too close obviously!

'Come on lads,' I said. 'Get them rasher sandwiches into yis. It'll keep yer strength up.'

When I saw Barney heading for the buffet, I grabbed a hold of his collar.

'Not you, y'eejit,' I hissed. 'Let the lads have them. Build up their thirst like.'

A light flickered on in the cavern between his two ears. 'Oh, righ',' he said winking at me broadly like Buttons in Cinderella. 'I'm with ya. Say no more.'

I felt like saying that he had a brain like a brick but he was diverting away from the food table, so I didn't want to burden him with more information than he could handle. I joined Joe who was outside on the porch admiring the rain.

'It's down for the day,' he said. 'Look at tha'.' He indicated ponds and lakes forming on a fairway down below the clubhouse.

'Jaysus,' I said. 'Feck the golf. We could have a boat race instead. Ah well, I suppose we'd better get the show on the road. Once more unto the breach, dear friends!'

Wha'?' Joe asked.

'Never mind,' I said. 'It was somethin' I saw in a fillum. I hope Ginger'll be here when he's needed.'

'I spoke to him las' nigh'. He has to do an installation in Finglas. Then he's comin' on here.'

'Do they have tellies in Finglas?' I asked.

'Apparently so.'

'I didn't even know they had electricity.'

'Tha's the march o' progress for ya. Toilets. Baths. The lot. Even in Finglas where ya'd think there'd be no call for them.'

'I suppose the EEC insisted? Harmonisation - isn't tha' wha' they call it? If the Germans have baths, eventually they find their way to Finglas. But y'are sure Ginger knows where he's comin' an' wha' he's to do?'

'Yeah – don't worry about it. Ginger has it all sorted.'

Like a fool, I accepted this assurance. I should have demanded oversight of Ginger, even though this would have been difficult. As a man who operates on the wrong side of the law, Ginger is suspicious of scrutiny. And discussing it reasonably with him would have been tricky as his vocabulary is limited to 'yeah', 'no' and a few swear words. Where these are insufficient to do justice to his strong opinions he expresses himself through violence, where his eloquence knows no bounds.

As it happened Ginger was delayed at his Finglas appointment. After he had concluded the installation, the householder foolishly tried to renegotiate the agreed price. He might have felt that Ginger's position was compromised and that Ginger would have nowhere to go to enforce the original contract. Such duplicity was not new to Ginger. He may have been disappointed at his client's stance but he would not have been surprised. As a man of the world, or at least of the Daymo and Finglas, he had met such double-crossing before, and had a well-rehearsed response. He held the householder by the throat and threatened to drill a hole in his head. When the man understood that the balance of negotiating power had tipped against him, he agreed to reinstate the initial agreement. Ginger would not have taken any personal offence and with the business satisfactorily concluded, they parted amicably.

However the delay had disrupted Ginger's schedule, so that he had to step on the gas as he exited Finglas (an excellent idea at any time). Unfortunately, in the driving rain he didn't notice that the vehicle he overtook at sixty miles an hour in an area where the authorities have expressed a preference for thirty, was a police car. Normally you can rely on the lazy bastards to do nothing in such conditions, as climbing out of the warm into the elements is hardly in the best interests of health. But these were enthusiastic rookies, and they pulled Ginger over. At least the bad weather discouraged them from examining the contents of his van, as they would have found telecommunications equipment that had been removed from a warehouse during a recent break-in. They satisfied themselves with the light banter which policemen employ on these occasions.

'Good morning sir. Is there a fire somewhere?'

'No' tha' I'm aware of.'

'And are you aware of the speed limit on this road, sir?'

'I dunno. Thirty or forty?'

'And what speed were you doing, sir?'

Ginger would have been aching to employ a crude response, but he wished to terminate the interview as soon as possible. Some residue of sense, buried within him and almost forgotten, kept his mouth shut. He pulled a face that he hoped would serve as a submissive smile and muttered an apology. The cops issued him with paperwork and a lecture on the importance of obeying speed limits. He thanked them and apologised again. As soon as he was out of sight, he put his boot back on the accelerator and flung the paperwork out the window.

In spite of his efforts, when he bounced into the club car park, the leading group was tacking up the ninth fairway. Ginger raced into the bar and set the staff to pulling pints. He hadn't time to carefully apply the correct laxative dosage to the three pints set aside for the Kinsella A-team. Flustered as a canary in a cattery, and fearing observation of the staff, he scattered the powder more widely than intended, and in varying measures. As he met us at the tenth tee with a tray of pints he wasn't very sure which ones were safe for consumption and which were not. One pint of stout looks pretty much like another and our plan depended on there being no discernible difference. What was he to do? He thought of having a spillage and starting the process all over, but he had neither the time nor enough of the stuff remaining. So he guessed, said nothing, and left the rest in the hands of the Lord.

In fact, after nine holes, things were going reasonably well for us and we were leading by a short head. The first group was made up of me, Joe and Paddy against Gerry Silverman, Brillo and the Squirrel. The monsoon was not favouring the skilful, and they were having a tough time of it aided by some razamazoo from us. They had lost an extraordinary number of balls in the poor visibility. Basically, if we got there first, their balls had often disappeared. The murk also facilitated strategic rearrangements so that our balls always seemed to land on more favourable lies. You might also regard our scorecards as favourable lies, as we didn't bother recording every unsatisfactory shot. Brillo Brennan lost his temper on the fifth when he badly sliced his tee shot. The ball shot off into a fairy glen from where it would never be recovered.

'A bloodhound couldn't find tha' if it was wrapped in a rasher,' I told him.

He fixed me with his famous stare and in a rage threw his offending three-iron into the undergrowth after the ball. Gerry Silverman tried to give him some coaching on the correct way to hold the club when taking such shots. It was kindly meant but unwelcome. Brillo told Gerry to stick his advice in a dark place, and added some uncalled for and unflattering comments about Gerry's skill, parentage and looks. Gerry took umbrage at being compared to an epileptic gorilla and grabbed Brillo by the collar. Brillo said that was typically Jewish as it was just what they had done to Jesus. I didn't know that Jesus played golf but the discord amongst the enemy was pleasing to see.

When we spotted Ginger with the pints, it was like the scene in the cowboy pictures when the herd smells water and stampedes. In the melee Ginger struggled to steer each of us towards the correct pint, but I was pleased to see the pains he took to do it. The Squirrel almost had his top lip fastened onto a glass when Ginger unceremoniously wrestled the pint off him and handed him another. Cyril accepted this as one of Ginger's little foibles and said nothing. The three Kinsellites were particularly keen to take on fluids after their earlier salt intake. We were relatively restrained and, as I was still on the wagon, I sipped on a luminous mouth wash. I quietly thanked Ginger for his services as we pointed ourselves at the back nine.

'Yeah, well,' he replied, seeming more reticent to accept my gratitude.

We continued hacking and slashing until we got to the fourteenth tee. I noticed a new sound had been added to the raging tempest around us. The whooshing and gurgling definitely hadn't been there before. Joe stepped up to the driving position and rested his ball on a plastic peg. His bending action was cautious, and his stance was a clear amendment to what he had used on earlier holes. We golfers adjust all the time as we strive for golfing nirvana, so I didn't read too much into it at first. Joe's head was down, and his feet were planted in the regulation position, but there was something else. There was a new tension in the buttocks like they were clinging onto an icy ledge. Joe's expression had also changed from purposeful golfer to a man trying to crack a walnut using facial muscles alone. I had not yet put two and two together, but mentally I was reaching for a calculator.

After we had all teed off, Joe said: 'Youse lads fire on ahead - I need to see a man about a dog. I'll catch yis up in a minute. No cheatin' now!' he had the cheek to add. After Gerry, Brillo, the Squirrel and Paddy had moved off, he whispered to me: 'Jaysus Frank, I think tha' gobshite is after mixin' up the pints. Me insides feel like the dam at Ardnacrusha after a month o' pissin' rain. Oh feck!'

Without further chat he disappeared into the nearby foliage. Although out of sight, I could hear him making the sounds of a man giving birth to a broken bottle.

'Frank', he called weakly after a while, 'are ya still there?'

'Yeah,' I confirmed. 'Upwind, thanks be to God!'

'Have ya any paper?'

'Ah come on, Joe! We haven't time for ya to be sittin' readin' the Irish Independent.'

'Ya know bloody well wha' I'm talkin' abou'. Have ya got paper or not?'

'No,' I said. 'The only paper I have is Gerry Silverman's score card. I'm not an expert on the rules, but I suspect tha' wipin' yer arse on a competitor's score card might get ya disqualified.'

'Ah for feck's sake!' I sensed exasperation. 'Wha' abou' a rag or a bit o' cloth?'

'I've only got me golf towel, but I need it for dryin' me balls, so y'are not havin' tha' either.'

After thinking for a bit he asked: 'I don't suppose ya have four fives for a twenty?'

We laughed so much that Joe tripped over his trousers and fell into a bush. Somehow he managed to restore himself to a semi-civilised state using dock leaves and whatever other vegetation there was to hand. He emerged looking like he'd been gang-raped by a herd of bulls. He was soaking wet and covered in mud and his face bore the marks of his dive into the bush. We looked down the fairway and found it looking like the Marie Celeste. Six golf balls lay scattered where they had dropped, and sets of clubs were abandoned like orphans. Of the lads there were no signs.

'Leave them in peace for a minute,' Joe said. 'I know wha' it's like. The poor divils' world'll be fallin' out o' their arses.'

'They'll have lovely undergrowth here next year. People'll be askin' the gardener wha' his secret is, an' he won't have a clue!'

As we waited, we stood on our opponents' balls to push them into the soft muck.

'They'll need a JCB to get them out,' I said.

A moment later Brillo tottered out of the woods looking like he had lost weight since we had last seen him. His face, normally the colour of raspberry jam, had dropped to a healthier candy pink. I showed him that his ball seemed to have landed on a soft area and sunk a bit but he didn't seem to care. There was still no sign of the others.

'Gerry!' I called. 'Gerry! Paddy! Cyril! Where are yis?'

There was a rustling away to my right. The leaves parted like the Red Sea and Moses stepped out. Gerry looked like a Moses who hadn't got his timing right and the Red Sea had dumped on top of him. Even in the pissing rain, he looked especially damp and wrung out. If he said he'd been to the blood bank and donated half of all he had, I'd have believed him.

'Are ya alrigh' Gerry?' Joe asked him. 'Ya look a bit shook.'

'I don't feel well,' he said. 'I'm givin' up. I'm goin' home.'

'Ya can't do tha',' I said. 'Ya'll lose the competition. What about the honour o' Kinsella's?'

Gerry spoke movingly on a range of topics including the honour of Kinsella's, golf and Irish weather. As he was doing so, the Squirrel, Brillo and Paddy crawled out of the ooze like early forms of lizards. For the first time in his life Paddy had lost the power of speech. The Squirrel and Brillo said that they were retiring from the field with Gerry, and the three of them tottered away looking like infantrymen at the end of Passchendaele.

★★★

The post-match meal was a lacklustre affair. All of the Kinsella's team and half of ours went home early. Amongst those remaining there was little interest in a session. Joe was drinking sweet tea, I was on the fruit juice and Paddy was toying with a hot whiskey. Ginger was sticking to soda water as he was still feeling hounded by the gendarmerie. Only Barney and Eugene were on pints as they had been lucky in the laxative roulette, but they were going easy in deference to the prevailing mood.

Our host, Darren, looked confused and unsure whether he should be pleased or not. As a professional who prided himself on knowing his customers, he had his bar staff primed for a severe test of their mettle. He will have slept badly the night before agonising over whether he had enough barrels of stout and security staff. And here they were, looking like a bunch of bored teenagers at a high mass.

'Well, we won anyway,' Paddy said.

'Well yeah,' I said. 'With a little bit o' shenanigans.'

'It's all part o' the modern game,' Paddy said. 'Professionalism. The will to win. Givin' yer team the edge.'

'Although Ginger kept it even enough,' Eugene said.

Both teams had been equally affected by the dodgy pints but our lads had the advantage of knowing what was going on. Eugene's experiment had the positive effect of letting us know that there was light at the end of the tunnel. The Kinsella men thought they were being liquidised from within and would die a lonely death out on the fairways as they turned into puddles of shite to be washed away by the rain.

'It wasn't my fault,' Ginger said. 'I've been tellin' yis wha' happened til I'm blue in the face. Between tha' thievin' louser in Finglas an' dem blue bastards harassin' tradesmen goin' abou' their lawful business ...'

'Their lawful business!' Eugene echoed.

'Yeah,' Ginger said, glaring at Eugene.

I wanted to capture Paddy's post-match analysis for the nation. I held my juice bottle up like a microphone.

'This is Frankie Flynn reporting from the course where I'm joined by the winning President, Mr Paddy Mulhall. Paddy ya must feel very proud?'

I held the bottle over for Paddy to speak.

'Pride is not the word I'd use,' he started.

'I didn't,' I said, but the point was too subtle for him and he continued.

'Satisfaction at a job well done – tha's the word I'd use. I took these lads from nothin', an' I moulded them into the team tha' we see here today. They showed great character. They kep' their focus in spite o' the meedya speckalation abou' Joe Horgan's private life …'

'Steady on now Paddy,' I said as Joe looked like he mightn't be amused. 'An' ya continue to deny the stories abou' the drugs in the dressin' room?' I asked.

'Completely,' Paddy said. 'We have a strict code. Drugs're not allowed in the dressin' room. We're not feckin' savages.'

'Could I ask a question?' Eugene piped up.

'We have a question from the studio panel. Go ahead Eugene Larkin.'

'Hello Paddy.'

'Hello Eugene.'

'Your team obviously wanted it more today than Kinsella's. There was a real hunger for it. Is it true tha' ya have a no-sex rule on the nights before big matches?'

'Ah listen Eugene. Most o' the lads haven't had a ride in years. It'd be cruel to deprive them if they managed to get lucky the nigh' before a game.'

'So wha's next for the team, Paddy?' I asked.

'Well, they're drained emotionally - an' in every other way - so they'll need a wash, a dose o' Imodium an' a night's sleep. Bu' we migh' go out on the lash tomorra.'

'The open top bus maybe?' I asked.

'In this weather? Would ya ever … !'

'Well thank you, Paddy Mulhall. An' congratulations once again on this magnificent victory. Now it's back to the studio.'

I looked to my invisible producer for the signal that the broadcast had ended, and when it had, I said: 'It's a wrap. Thank you, Paddy.'

'Was tha' live?' Barney asked.

'Yeah,' I said. 'Well, after a ten second lag in case Paddy said somethin' stupid.'

Barney nodded that he could see the sense in that.

'Let's drink up an' get outa here,' Paddy said. 'I want to get me arse within twenty paces o' me home facilities an' keep it there until it stops holdin' me hostage.'

Ginger gave Paddy and Barney a lift, and Joe took me and Eugene. As we dropped Eugene off, he invited us in to say hello to his mother. I told him that I'd rather fondue my privates. He said that in our line of work that could be all part of the day's work.

'Wha' did he mean abou' 'our line o' work'?' Joe wanted to know when we were alone.

'Who knows?' I said. 'Who ever knows wha' Eugene is talkin' abou'? How's Celestina?'

'Fecked if I know,' he said. 'She's chargin' aroun' the town like a bluebottle in Clery's lighting department.'

'Her business is keepin' her busy, is it?'

'Yeah. I was givin' her a hand doin' deliveries, but I haven't done any for a few days.'

'Good,' I said.

'Eh?'

'I mean y'ave enough to be doin'. Ya don't want to be deliverin' stuff on top of everythin' else.'

'Do I not? Tha's me job! Do ya think I drive this thing aroun' cos I like motorin'. I'm not Mister Toad, y'know!'

Although I was sworn to secrecy, Joe was my oldest pal. I felt compelled to nudge him around imminent danger. I needed a subtle hint, but he was pulling up at my front gate and I hadn't time to polish the hint as I would have liked.

'Celestina is mixed up with a crowd o' Narusian gangsters - smugglin' counterfeit stuff. She's the bookkeeper or somethin'. They're so thick tha' the cops are all over them. They could be grabbed any minute.'

Joe had stopped the car and was staring at me.

'Is there somethin' on me face?' I asked.

'Tell me all tha' again,' he said. 'Only this time take a breath or two in the middle in case ya pass out.'

I repeated the gist of it and he asked me the question I hoped he wouldn't.

'An' how do you know all this?'

The Flynn brain whirred into action and within a second had produced a range of possible lies. Unfortunately all were too implausible to get me out of the car without a fat lip. I decided on the truth – or on a slightly edited version of it.

'I'm workin' for the Unit,' I told Joe. 'Wi' Eugene. It's all top secret. I have a code name an' all - Magpie.'

'Magpie!' he said. 'So bein' a layabout an' a drunk is jus' a front? Really y'are a spy? An' yer code name is Magpie?'

On reflection I thought that some of the lies I had rejected might have worked better.

'Look Joe, my mission was to get Celestina's papers.'

'Like any magpie would…'

'They were copied. The Unit's people are goin' through them. They'll be figurin' out wha's wha'. There could be a raid any minute.'

'Yeah – I can see you an' Eugene burstin' through the winda in yer wet suits. Frank, ya need to go back on the drink fast. Y'are losin' yer grip.'

'I'm serious, Joe,' I said. 'Her nibs'll be in the wimmin's section o' the Joy an' if you're implicated, you'll be in the men's, sewin' mailbags.'

Joe had shut up talking. The penny was dropping, although it was taking its time.

'Y'are not pullin' me leg then?'

'No, I'm not. Bu' look, I'm jus' tellin' *you*. Y'are to say nothin' to Celestina, or ya'll drop me in it. Then it'll be me tha's in choky for breachin' state security or somethin'.'

That prospect didn't seem to be worrying him too much.

'I'll have to tell her.'

'Bu' she'll tip the gang off.'

'No she won't. I'll tell her not to. An' ya can tell Eugene to feck off an' leave her alone.'

'I can't do it,' I said. I was going to add that it was above my pay grade except that I didn't have one.

'Frank, y'are tryin' me patience. If it helps to keep ya focused I could thump ya in the head a few times.'

In the circumstances I assured him that would not be necessary. I said that he could leave it to me and that all would be well. Precisely how I was going to conjure up that happy state of affairs, I didn't know. As is too often the case I felt like a mere prawn in the great game of life. Self-sacrifice is my motto and it is never in my nature to put myself first.

When you are one of life's givers it's hard to turn off the tap. But the burden of looking after Joe, Teresa, Celestina, Peggy, Ma Larkin and the whole apparatus of the state was wearing me out.

Chapter 14

The following afternoon, tired of endlessly juggling my problems, I was taking time out watching one of those reality TV shows. I would have changed the channel but the remote was too remote from where I was sitting.

These reality shows have no relationship to any reality I've ever known. This one was about a gang of Californian youths who were long on white teeth, blond hair and orange skin, and short on brains. It was hard to believe that someone in tellyland had said: 'Hey guys, I've got a great idea. I know where there's a bunch of morons talking drivel. Let's get a camera down there and grab it while it's hot.' Instead of telling him to clear his desk and pursue a career in sanitation, those in authority hailed him a genius and made him a senior vice president. Even after the show had been recorded, sense might have prevailed and the tape burned. But no, without even rudimentary editing, it was served up in all its undiluted glory, like a turd on a plate.

The level of conversation reprised that of our distant ancestors when they still resided in trees. Every inane utterance was greeted with an 'Oh my god! That is so cool!' as these simple people were impressed by every little thing.

I would have stirred myself to switch it off except that it was annoying Peggy even more than it was annoying me. In fact she had instructed me to change the channel. Instructed me! Obviously that had tied my hands completely. A channel change now and my life wouldn't be worth living. The precedent would be established and I would be her plaything forever.

'I'm watchin' it,' I told her. 'It's interestin'.'

I could see her low opinion of my intellectual abilities dropping another notch, but I stuck to my principles.

'Is tha' Joe Horgan's car pullin' up outside?' she asked.

I stretched my neck to look out the window. As I explained before, it is not customary for the Daymo's leading citizens to make social calls on each other. The neck stretching didn't work, and I had to stand up to check the evidence. Joe was getting out of his car and proceeding to our front door in a purposeful manner.

'It's Joe alrigh',' I said, giving Peggy full credit for her lookout skills.

I muted the Californians as I went to meet him, whipping the door open so that he almost fell through it. Observed at close quarters, Joe appeared distraught. At least he was distraught if the relevant symptoms are hand-wringing, head-shaking and making noises like a cat with a fur ball.

'Whassup with ya?' I asked, in my most concerned manner.

'She's ...,' he said. 'Airport. Gone.'

He was looking like one of those wan and pale ladies in period dramas who swoon a lot. I decided that if he did any swooning I was getting out of his way. He might have been wan and pale but he was still built like a bomb shelter. If he did swoon, there were no smelling salts in the house, but a blast of Bertie's breath could revive the dead.

The words he spoke had given me only the slightest of clues, but I had sifted them, selected what was relevant, and surmised that Celestina had fecked off.

'Are ya alrigh'?' I asked, as he swayed in front of me like a tree in a gale. 'Here, come in outa tha',' I said pulling him through the door behind me. He limped in and dropped into my chair. Bertie raised his head and watched me with a keen interest, but in the circumstances I decided to allow Joe to stay there.

Peggy's normal rule would be to deal decisively with any pal of mine coming uninvited into her living room, they normally being as welcome as banjo players in an orchestra. She wasn't exactly strewing rose petals in Joe's path. She was wearing the expression of a house-proud woman who has had a load of dung dumped on her Axminster. But oddly she was doing nothing about it. Joe's distressed state was apparent and some dreg of the milk of human kindness was overcoming her normal instincts. She even offered him a cup of tea.

'Thanks Peggy – thanks, thanks very much,' he said with more gratitude than was warranted. Tea is after all just tea. This was more like Peggy had promised to pay off his mortgage and shoot Teresa.

'Jaysus, it's as well ya didn't offer him a biscuit as well,' I said, but the joke sailed into the ether, unappreciated.

'So, wha's the story, Joe?' I asked. 'Ya look like yer numbers came up in the lottery, an' y'ave lost the ticket.'

'I told her wha' ya told me,' he said.

Peggy gave me a glance which said: 'I want to know exactly what Joe Horgan is talking about. I want all the details and if you lie, I will know and I will make the remainder of your life hell.' I shrugged to indicate that I would reveal all to her later, if she would just wait until I had dealt with Joe. When you're married as long as we are, glances and shrugs can convey all that, and much more.

'Did ya?' I asked him. 'An' she's after leggin' it?'

'I told her tha' it'd be alrigh',' he said. 'Tha' she was jus' an innocent party. Tha' she'd nothin' to worry abou'. I said tha' you were sortin' it out. She was very upset bu' she seemed okay with it - until I tol' her abou' you copyin' all them papers an' givin' them in. Then she did her bleedin' nut. I've never seen anythin' like it! The things she said abou' ya, Frank!' He looked at Peggy. 'I wouldn't repeat them in front of you, Peggy. All I'll say is that she swore she was goin' to tell some people an' tha' they'd do ya.'

A shiver started near the back of my neck and went in a sort of tidal wave down to my feet, upscuttling everything as it went. I glanced through the window in case large bald men in leather jackets were approaching. They weren't.

'Wha' do ya mean 'do me'?' I asked. 'It's nothin' to do with *me*.'

It was one of those rhetorical questions. I realised that a disgruntled criminal with anger management issues and a baseball bat might not think logically. Even to an internal optimist like me, my prospects looked bleak.

'Wha' did she tell them?' I wanted to know immediately whether I needed to apply to the Unit for a safe house and plastic surgery.

Peggy couldn't manage to keep quiet any longer.

'Wha' are yis talkin' abou'? Who's goin' to do him?' she asked Joe. 'An' for wha'? If there's anyone goin' to do it, they'll have to get in a queue behind me.'

'It's nothin',' I said. 'Don't worry about it.'

'Joe Horgan,' she said. 'You'd better tell me wha' in hell is goin' on or I won't be responsible for me actions.'

Joe looked uncomfortable and he may have still felt under some obligation for the tea.

'It's a kind of a long story,' he said. If he thought that that pathetic response was going to loosen her grip on him, he was mistaken.

'I'm in no rush,' she said. 'Jus' spit it out.'

'Go on an' tell her,' I said. 'So much for state secrets! If the Narusians don't get me I'll be hung for sedition or somethin'! Fire ahead - ya might as well put an announcement in the Herald, cos if ya tell *her*, it'll be all over Dublin in an hour.'

Peggy gave me one of those looks much favoured by Medusa. I shrank back and shut up. Joe cleared his throat in an 'if you're all sitting comfortably, I'll begin' kind of way. He proceeded to give Peggy a full warts-and-all report on Celestina's criminality and my role in gathering essential evidence for the state.

'Did ya ever, in yer wildest dreams, imagine tha' I'd be workin' for the government?' I asked her.

'Y'are not *in* me wildest dreams, so shut up an' let him finish,' she said. 'This is better than a fillum.'

I didn't appreciate Peggy being entertained by the prospects of her imminent widowhood. She seemed untroubled by the danger I was in. Joe wasn't worried about me either, consumed as he was by the pain of his lost love.

'I told her she'd nothin' to worry abou',' he said. 'I told her tha' I'd look after her. No one was goin' to harm a hair of her head.' He became animated. 'Only over my dead body!'

This drivel was getting us nowhere. I wasn't interested in Joe's dead body. I was interested in the chances of mine getting that way. I wanted to hear only the facts as they affected the life expectancy of F. Flynn. Joe's expressions of devotion to Celestina were commendable but of no interest to the current audience. As Joe wasn't getting the reaction he wanted, he looked to Bertie for support and reached out to pat the beast's head - always a mistake. But Bertie was feeling magnanimous. He has occasionally shown romantic leanings when I've brought him on walks to Magowan's. He issued a yellow card in the form of a growl, rather than the straight red of a bite. Joe got the message and withdrew his hand from Bertie's personal space.

'She wouldn't talk to me. When I came in earlier she had her bags packed. She wasn't even goin' to wait to see me, only I came back early. Out to the airport. Tha's where she wanted to go.'

'To get on a plane somewhere?' I asked.

'No,' he said. 'She heard tha' ya can get on a ship from there but she was misinformed. O' course she was gettin' on a plane!'

I didn't like his tone, especially as he was still in my chair, but I wanted to hear the story so I let him continue.

'So I dropped her off. She wouldn't even let me come in.'

'Jus' as well,' Peggy said. 'Their car parkin' charges are ridiculous. Mary O'Connell's son left his car there when they went to Majorca, an' the car park cost more than the holiday.'

'Peggy will ya hold the travel advice for a minute!' I said, and if I was showing exasperation, I didn't care. 'Joe, please, in words o' one syllable, will ya tell me where she's gone an' who she tol' abou' me an' them bits o' paper?'

'No,' he said.

'Wha' d'ya mean 'no'?'

'Ya wanted words o' one syllable,' he said. 'Look Frank, I don't know where she's gone. She got outa the car an' went into the airport. After tha' I don't know. She coulda gone to Narusia. She coulda gone to China. I don't feckin' know. All I know is tha' she's gone. An' I don't know who she talked to. She didn't say. So stop askin' me stupid questions.'

'I wonder would the Unit give me a gun?' I asked aloud.

'Wha' good would a gun do ya? These people are professionals,' Joe said.

'Yeah, but *you're* not,' I said.

'Ya can shoot me if ya like,' he said. 'I don't care.'

Then Joe did something I hope never to see again. It was as surprising and horrible as that scene in Alien when the creature burst out of someone's chest. Joe convulsed like he was having electric shock treatment. He twisted his face like he was wringing out a wet cloth. It turned the colour of blackcurrant jam and water started running out of it. After a few seconds of incomprehension I realised that the bugger was crying. Peggy tried to hand him his tea but he waved it away. Then, to my utter horror, he stood up, lumbered over to me like Frankenstein's monster and put his arms around me. Joe is bigger than me and soon I was suffocating under hot, wet Irishman. I knew how Captain Ahab must have felt, lashed onto the side of the whale. I patted his back and may even had said 'there, there' hoping this might be enough to get me released. It wasn't. It just encouraged him. He was juddering like a locomotive trying to get away from a platform. I pulled my head back to gasp in some air. This put his big, red, wet face in front of and above mine. He leaned down and I feared that he was going to kiss me. He put his forehead on mine and said: 'Yermebesfren,'

'Grand,' I said hoping that would call the meeting to a close. 'Tha's great.'

He leaned down and wiped his nose on my shoulder.

'I don't know wha' I'd do withou' ya,' he said. 'You an' Peggy. Yis're both great.'

He somehow managed to hold on to me with one arm while he lassoed Peggy with the other one and dragged her into the scrum. We lurched up and down the room for a bit, Joe making wailing and slurping noises, and Peggy telling him that everything would be grand. I stood on Bertie during one pass and the little shit bit me.

Eventually we managed to get Joe disentangled. Peggy produced my whiskey bottle from wherever she had it hidden, and poured him a glass. I was in such a state of pain and confusion that I forgot I was on the dry, and took a swig out of the bottle right in front of her.

'Wha' am I goin' to do?' Joe asked. 'I've made a righ' hames o' things. I've lost me home, me wife, me children…'

'Maybe a few pints in Magowan's,' I suggested, as the whiskey reminded me of simpler, happier days.

'Go aroun' an' get Teresa Horgan, this minute,' Peggy commanded me. 'We'll get this sorted out once an' for all.'

'Ya mus' be jokin',' I said. 'I'm not goin' anywhere next nor near her.'

'Frank!' Peggy barked at me in her gruppenfuhrer voice which discouraged debate.

Two minutes later I was on Teresa's doorstep, and somehow or other she got the impression that Joe wasn't well. In fact she seemed to think that he was close to death, and that there was no time to lose if she was to see him again this side of eternity. Although I had a head start on her and she was still in her slippers, she beat me by half furlong back to Flynn HQ.

When we arrived, Joe wasn't exactly composed, but he wasn't as decomposed as when last seen. The wailing and gnashing of teeth had been replaced with snorting and snivelling. He looked like a huge strawberry ice cream that was melting. He was not a pretty sight but beauty is in the eye of the beholder, and Teresa seemed to think that he was just the thing. As she came through the door, she gave him the quick once-over and ceased to function as a normal human. Her face became a pixelated version of itself, and her arms waved around like she was treading water. She took to caterwauling at volumes recently heard from Joe. This reminded him of the fun to be had from wailing and he joined in. She was doing the soprano line while Joe gave us a passable baritone. Bertie joined in every time they got to the chorus. I could have cried myself but I didn't. Instead, I stared hard at Peggy and - not giving a shite - took another good inch out of the whiskey bottle.

Teresa had joined Joe on my chair and they were all mixed up together like steak and kidney in a pie. Conversation between them was limited and interrupted by regular slobbering. From what I could gather from my position in the stands, they seemed pleased to see each other. Joe was blaming himself for everything from the fall of Adam to the price of the pint, and Teresa was telling him that it was all her fault for not dusting properly under the bed. I can't remember the exact details.

My thoughts were focused on my chair, in case it decided that Teresa's arrival was the final straw, and it collapsed. Its arms were breathing in and out as the pair of them went about the messy business of restoring harmony. I looked to Peggy for help.

'A cup o' tea?' she asked, employing her standard resolution to every crisis.

The magic phrase did remind the pair that there are certain social niceties to be observed in other people's chairs. Teresa jumped up but kept a firm hold of one of Joe's soggy paws. Joe started rubbing his face with his other hand like a cat having a wash.

'Thanks Peggy,' Teresa said. 'A cuppa tea'd be lovely. God! Wha' are we like?!'

I could think of various suggestion but kept them to myself.

'Tea for me an' you Teresa, but not for them two. Yis don't want tea,' Peggy instructed us. 'Frank, get Joe up outa tha' chair an' bring him down for a pint.'

I felt that I had entered some strange new topsy-turvy world. Peggy has been complaining about my occasional visits to Magowan's since before I can remember. Now this! It was even more momentous than when I had changed from Y fronts which had completely changed my outlook on life.

'An' ya'd better have one yerself when y'are there,' she said. 'I can't bear the puss on ya any more. The sooner we get life back to normal aroun' here the better.'

Even though a fugitive from Narusian hit-men I boldly went out with Joe. I thought to myself: 'My name is Francis Joseph Flynn. Captain of the Golf Society. Ex shop steward of the Irish Painters and Decorators Union. Loyal customer of Magowan's pub. Father to a pair of daughters, husband to a fearsome wife – and I would have my pint.'